FIRST SKIRMISH

The young mountain man, Art, didn't feel panic or fear. He knew what had to be done. He didn't shout, just carefully aimed his rifle at another of the Indian riders and slowly squeezed the trigger. The weapon kicked him back and black smoke exploded from the barrel. The attacker, about the sixth along the line, fell from his horse. There were two down.

The Indians kept coming, and now they had their own rifles and bows at the ready. Arrows thunked into the earth by Caviness, Matthews, and Hoffman. McDill frantically reloaded and lifted his gun, just in time for a ball from one of the Indians to whiz past his head, missing him by just a few inches.

In a huge explosion of gunpowder and shot, the island defenders fired almost simultaneously, causing the Indians' horses to rear and wheel madly, splashing and snorting. The trappers were cutting down the odds with each passing minute.

In the melee, a couple of the Blackfeet had managed to pull the bodies of the fallen braves from the river and put them on the riverbank, so they wouldn't be trampled by the repeated charge against the island. All the whites could see was the splashing and the oncoming arrows as the Indians kept up the attack, even in the face of strong gunfire.

It was a miracle that Art had not lost a single man yet. He looked around and saw that his men were fiercely concentrated on doing their best to fire, reload, fire, and reload—again and again, almost like machines. He was proud of them, but there was no time for sentiment. He focused on his own job, and was able to get off another shot. This time he hit one of the horses, which went down in a violent, trumpeting death.

PREACHER'S PEACE

William W. Johnstone

PINNACLE BOOKS
Kensington Publishing Corp.
http://www.kensingtonbooks.com

One

Under a bright blue sky, white snow was still glistening in the mountains, but new-growth green signaled the welcome arrival of spring in the lower elevations. A tall horseman rode through a narrow valley where the river meandered along a rocky bench, wooded by pines, willow, and aspen. The rider, dressed in buckskin, appeared and disappeared effortlessly as he blended in with nature.

The river splashed and babbled over rocks worn smooth by centuries of flowing water. From its depths, trout leaped into the air to snare flying insects that hovered over the sparkling surface. In the sunlit glades nearby, wildflowers bloomed in a profusion of color, scenting the air with their sweet fragrance.

The rider who came onto this scene was an impressive man, with a full mustache, square jaw, straight nose, and steel-gray eyes staring out from under a wide-brimmed hat. He sat his horse easily and was leading two mules, both packed to their maximum carrying capacity with beaver pelts. In a country where a man's deeds and character counted for more than his family name, this man who would someday be known as Preacher, was still known only by a single name, Art.

Art took a long pull from his canteen, corked it, and

hooked it back on the pommel of his saddle, then shifted around to look at the two mules plodding along behind him. For some time now, he had been aware that two Indians were dogging him, riding parallel with him and, for the most part, staying out of sight. They were good, but Art was better. He was on to them as soon as they started shadowing his trail.

Art knew that the Blackfeet were denying white trappers access to the rivers and streams in the upper Yellowstone, but he was well out of their territory now. If these were Blackfeet, what were they doing this far down the Missouri River?

As soon as the stream rounded a bend, Art slipped his Hawken rifle from its saddle sheath, dismounted from his horse, and gave it a slap on the rump to keep it moving along. He wasn't concerned about the horse and mules getting away—they had been following the stream so rigidly that he was sure they would keep going in that direction, moving slowly and deliberately enough that he would be able to catch up with them again. Using the sharp bend in the stream as concealment, he quickly primed his weapons, cocked the hammers on his rifle and his pistol, and waited.

Art didn't want to kill them, whoever they were. He knew there were times when one had to kill and when those times came, there was no place for hesitancy. He had killed more times than he wanted to recall, starting with river pirates back on the Ohio River, English soldiers during the Battle of New Orleans, and Indians in various battles in between. And he knew he would kill again, but to the degree that he could, he made a compromise with grim reality. He would kill only when he had no other choice. It was the kind of man he was.

The Indians on his trail approached his position so skillfully that he could barely hear them. Not one word was spoken, and the rocks that were disturbed by the horses' hooves moved lightly, as if they were dislodged by some wild creature.

Art watched; then as they came around the bend, he stood up suddenly, his Hawken pointed menacingly toward them.

"Ayiee!" one of the Indians exclaimed in a startled shout. His horse reared, and he had to fight to bring it under control. The other Indian raised his bow. The arrow was already fitted. He aimed without hesitation.

"No, don't!" Art shouted, but his shout had no effect. The Indian released the arrow and it whizzed by Art, coming so close that he could feel the air of its passing. Art pulled the trigger on his rifle; it roared and bucked and poured forth a cloud of smoke. The Indian who had shot at him tumbled from his saddle.

The other Indian, his horse now under control, knew that Art could fire the rifle only once. Realizing that he now had an advantage, he released an arrow toward Art, but missed. Dropping his rifle, Art raised his pistol and fired. The charge in the pistol exploded, sending a shudder through the shooter's powerful arm. The Indian's face disintegrated in a bloody red pulp as the ball struck him right between the eyes.

As the powerful echo of the last shot was still reverberating through the canyon, Art went over for a closer examination of the two Indians he had shot. As he suspected, both were dead, but something he didn't expect was to see that they were Arikara.

Why were the Arikara trailing him? As far as he knew, the Arikara were not causing any problems. Of course it might have nothing at all to do with any problems between the Arikara and the white trappers. These two could well be a couple of renegades just after his pelts. He knew that the load on his pack animals would tempt any thief, red or white.

Art recharged and reloaded both his weapons, then mounting one of the Indian ponies, galloped down the stream until he caught up with his animals. Letting the Indian pony go, he remounted his own horse and continued his journey.

Rendezvous at Clarks Fork

The smoke from hundreds of campfires could be seen from miles away. And if the smoke wasn't enough, there were also the smells, some pleasant, like the aromas of cooking meat, and others not quite so pleasant, such as the stench of hundreds of mountain men who had neither bathed nor changed their clothes for the entire winter. This was an important gathering place for trappers from the mountains, fur traders from the East, Indians of many tribes, explorers, mapmakers, merchants, whiskey drummers, card-sharks, whores, Indian squaws and their children by various fathers—some of whom might even be here.

For the trappers, this would be their first brush with civilization after a long winter of self-imposed exile in the mountains. It was the only encounter most would have, because they would sell their pelts to a furrier, trade for the few things needed to outfit them for the next year, then spend the rest of their money on whatever items the enterprising merchants would bring with them. Once their money was gone, they would disappear back into the mountains for another long year of solitude.

Though much younger than most of the other trappers, Art had grown to manhood in the mountains and knew the mountains and streams as well as the oldest and most experienced trapper present. He rode into the camp, sloping down a ridgeline leading his two mules.

"Art!" someone called. "Art, how are you, boy?"

The man who hailed Art was Clyde Barnes, a longtime friend. Art waved at him, then, using his knees and a tug on the reins, headed his animals over toward him. Dismounting, he tied his horse to a sapling before looking around the sprawling, crowded encampment. The camp was alive with activity, like a giant beehive or anthill.

"Looks like quite a few of the men have made it down already," Art said.

"Yep, reckon you're one of the last ones to come in," Clyde said. He cut a chew off his plug of black tobacco and stuck it in his mouth. "But from the looks of your load there, I'd say you had reason to be late. Looks to me like you had a helluva good year, friend."

"It was a tolerable year," Art replied evenly. He was not given to overexaggeration, or much talk at all. He stared across his mule at Clyde as he busied himself unloading the furs.

"Uh-huh," Clyde said, smiling. "More'n tolerable, I'd say."

"I was sorry to hear about Pierre Garneau."

"Yeah," Clyde said. "I told him he had no damn business goin' back to New Orleans. He was a mountain man, through and through, not some New Orleans citified dandy-man. But he said that's where he come from, and that's where he wanted to die. Pretty definite about it. And that's what he done, by gar. He died of the swamp fever."

Art credited Clyde and Pierre Garneau with saving his life. Nearly ten years earlier, Art had been found in the mountains, more dead than alive, by the two men who were then trapping partners. They nursed Art back to health that year, and shared their take with him. They didn't have cause to help him, could have left him to die all alone out there. Although Art had long ago gone his own way, and sometimes even went for an entire year without seeing either one of them, he had always counted Pierre and Clyde as close friends.

Then, two years ago, Pierre had decided he was too old to spend another bitter winter in the mountains. They threw a memorable going-away party for him at Rendezvous that year.

"You sold your plews yet?" Art asked. "Plew" was another word for *pelt*.

"Yeah," Clyde answered. He spat out a dark, evil stream of tobacco juice. "Got me a dollar and a half a pelt for 'em, I'll tell you."

Art looked up in surprise. "A dollar and a half apiece? We got two and half last year. Did the market drop on furs?"

"Not as much competition this year," Clyde replied. "Ashley ain't sent anyone out."

William Ashley, who had his office in St. Louis, was the leading furrier, the best known and most respected, and his presence always ensured a fair price.

"He get out of the business?"

"Not from what I've heard. He's still buying furs back in St. Louie. But like the man says, we ain't in St. Louie." Clyde gestured around the encampment and wrinkled his nose.

"I reckon not," Art said. He ground-staked his animals, free of their burden after their long journey, and found a seat on a fallen tree trunk. The weight and tension of hundreds of hard miles melted from his shoulders. Rendezvous was like home to him, maybe the best home he'd had since he was a boy. God, that seemed so long ago, when he had left his ma and paw and the other kids to seek adventure . . .

"Say, did you hear about the big battle last summer?" Clyde asked, working another chew in his mouth.

"What battle was that?"

"Twixt the soldiers and the Indians. The soldiers belonged to an outfit called the Missouri Legion."

Art shook his head and shrugged his wide shoulders. "Didn't hear anything about it."

"Well, wasn't that much of a battle the way I he'ered it told," Clyde said. "More shoutin' than shootin'. Couple of white men killed, maybe as many as fifteen or twenty Arikaras. Then the Arikaras run away and that was the end of it."

"The Arikaras? Not the Blackfeet?"

"Arikaras," Clyde said.

"Well, then, that might explain it."

"Explain what?"

Art told Clyde of his encounter with the two Indians on the way down to Rendezvous. He was still bothered by the fact that he'd had to kill them both.

"I thought maybe they were just a couple of renegades," Art said. "Never thought we'd have any trouble with the Arikara."

"Yeah, that's what I thought too. I mean, the Arikaras can be dealt with. It's the Blackfeet that would as soon scalp you as look at you."

"What do you reckon got into their craw?" Art asked.

"From what I he'ered, a couple of Ashley's men traded them some bad whiskey for good plews. Once the Indians sobered up, they realized they had gotten the raw end of the deal. They got even by stealing nearly all of Ashley's supplies. One thing led to another; next thing you know, there was an army of soldiers and trappers here to teach the Indians a lesson."

"Doesn't sound to me like that was any too smart." In fact, it sounded downright stupid and wrong to Art. "The Blackfeet already keep us out of their country. Sounds like the Arikara are going to be doin' the same thing. So, with Ashley not here, who's doin' the tradin'?"

"Fitzhugh from Cincinnati and Peabody from Philadelphia."

"Neither one of them's paying more'n a dollar and a half?" Art asked.

Clyde shook his head. "No. The bastards got together on it, I'm sure of it. Mr. Ashley never would do that. He knows that without us, he's got no trade. And if we can't make a decent livin', then he won't have us."

"That's the long and short of it," Art agreed. It was the way of trapping and trading, the way he had learned over the years of back-breaking, dangerous life in the mountains.

"You know what they say he's payin', back in St. Louie?" Clyde asked.

"What?"

"Five dollars apiece."

"Five dollars?"

"Yep," Clyde said. He glanced at the two carrying racks Art had unloaded. "If you could get those plews to him back in St. Louie, why, you'd make yourself a fortune."

Art examined his pelts for a moment, absorbing the idea of a better, fairer payment. Made sense to him. "Yeah," he finally said. "Yeah, I would, wouldn't I?"

"Course, to get that kind of money, you got to take 'em to Ashley. Might as well have to take 'em to China, far as I'm concerned."

"Five dollars?" Art scratched at his jawline, feeling the need for a bath and a bedroll, but adding up the dollars in his mind.

Clyde stared at his young friend. "Art, don't tell me you're really thinkin' 'bout doin' that." He brought another foul chew up to the front of his mouth, ready to fire it like a minié ball.

"Five dollars apiece is a lot of money," Art said emphatically.

"So it is, but what do you need all that money for anyway? What you going to spend it on out here?"

Art smiled. "There's always things to spend your money on," he said. "And five dollars is a lot of money."

"Yeah, you keep sayin' that. And I keep hearin' you say it. But Ashley is in St. Louie and you are here. Like as not, if you started out today, you'd be two, maybe three months getting there, and that's only if everything went like it's supposed to. You could lose all your pelts along the way. Fact is, you could lose your scalp along the way."

"Maybe," Art said. He knew the risks, but was calculating the return in his mind.

"I'll be damned. You're going to try it, aren't you?"

After only the slightest hesitation, Art nodded. "You want to come along?"

Clyde shook his head. "I done sold my catch."

"Buy 'em back."

"I done spent all my money."

"I'll tell you what. If you'll come with me, help me get my plews back to St. Louis, I'll give you a quarter of them."

"A quarter of them? How many is that?"

"Forty-five," Art answered. "At five dollars apiece, that would be two hundred and twenty-five dollars."

"Two hundred twenty-five dollars?" Clyde gasped, almost choking on his own saliva and 'bacca juices. "That's more'n I made here for a whole winter's trapping."

"What do you say? Want to come with me?"

"Hell, yes, I'll come," Clyde said, smiling broadly, exposing a jagged row of black and yellow teeth. He ran his hand across the top of his head and spat violently. "I may wind up losin' my scalp over it, but I reckon it's a chance worth takin'. Anyhow, it's been quite a while since I seen me a real town. I might just enjoy that."

"First thing we've got to do is sell off our animals and get us a boat," Art proposed.

"A boat? Wait a minute, you plannin' on goin' all the way to St. Louie by boat?"

"Sure, why not?"

"Why not? 'Cause I don't feel like paddling all the way to St. Louie, that's why."

"You don't have to worry about that, Clyde. It's purely downstream all the way, which means the river will take us. All we have to do is put the boat in and keep it in the center of the river. Like slicing a pie."

"There's another thing," Clyde said sheepishly, his eyes squinting. "I can't swim. Besides which, maybe you don't have to paddle, but I can't believe you can just put a boat in the water and expect it to float you there. You gotta know what you're doin' and where you're goin'."

"I do know what I'm doing," Art said. "I've been on flatboats before. I know the river."

Clyde stroked his chin as he examined his young friend. "You're crazy, you know that."

"You still going with me?"

Clyde laughed. "Yeah," he said. "I'm still going with you. I reckon I'm crazy too."

Arikara Village, Sunday, May 23, 1824

In a place not too far from where the two Indians had attacked Art, several Indian warriors were sitting in a large council circle engaged in the ritual smoking of an ornately carved and feathered ceremonial pipe. The council had been called when the bodies of two of their warriors were brought back to the village. Now the women were weeping, while the men of the village were trying to decide what should be done to answer this outrage. Their honor and the honor of the dead were at stake.

"They were killed by a white man who takes beaver," one of the council elders said.

The leader of the council, whose name was Buffalo Robe but was called The Peacemaker, held out his hand, and the others looked at him, awaiting his words.

"I know that the blood runs hot in our young men," he began. "And there are those who would seek revenge." He put his hand over his heart. "My heart demands revenge as well"—he moved his hand to his head—"but my head tells me this would not be a wise thing."

"No, no, we must have revenge!" one of the younger warriors declared.

Again, The Peacemaker held out his hand. "I have listened to the words of your heart. But those are words of passion, not words of wisdom. Here is what my head says. Have you forgotten that the white man sent an army against us? Have you forgotten that they had many guns and we had few, and they killed many of our brothers, while we killed but few of them? If we go to war, we will have more weeping among our women, and more of our tepees will be empty."

"What of Red Hawk and Mean to His Horses?"

"Does the sign not show that Red Hawk and Mean to His Horses attacked the white man? If this is so, they wanted to do battle, and they lost. I say no more war."

One of the men sitting in the circle was Standing Bear. Standing Bear's Indian name was Wak Tha Go, and that was the name he used. At six feet six inches, Wak Tha Go towered over every other man in the village, in fact over most men throughout the country. He got his height, unusual for an Indian, from the very tall French trapper who had raped his mother. Now, as the pipe was passed to him, he took a puff into his lungs, then fanned the smoke from the bowl into his face. A medicine man of the Arikara, Wak Tha Go belonged to the Bear Society, and was now wearing a bearskin robe as a symbol of his station. When he stood, wearing his robe, he could frighten those who didn't know him, for with the robe and his size, he was very much like the bear he emulated. He was a strong, courageous warrior who had proved himself in many battles.

"What does the medicine man-warrior Wak Tha Go say?" the warrior who had been speaking with The Peacemaker asked. He turned to Wak Tha Go. "Do you who stand as tall as the tallest bear counsel peace as well?"

"If you kill the cub of a rabbit, the rabbit's mother will turn and run. If you kill the cub of a bear, the bear's mother will turn and fight." Wak Tha Go looked at The Peacemaker. "The Peacemaker would have us be rabbits." He fingered the bearskin robe he was wearing, then lifted it with one hand high above his shoulder. "I belong to the Bear Society. I am not a rabbit!" he said resolutely.

"Aiii yi, yi, yi!" the others in the council shouted, for they realized that Wak Tha Go had just made his decision to take revenge.

"Wak Tha Go! Will you lead us?"

"Yes."

"The trappers are gathering for their Rendezvous," The Peacemaker said quietly, and the others were silent and listened. "There are more trappers there than there are arrows in all our quivers. Would you lead our men to slaughter?"

"We will fight like a bear," Wak Tha Go said in reply, looking at each man in turn around the council circle. "But we will be smart like a fox. We will not attack them in Rendezvous."

* * *

Upper Missouri River, Wednesday, May 26, 1824

Johnny Swale, Billy Harper, and Eddie Meeks had left Rendezvous two days earlier and were now headed back into the mountains. They had enjoyed a successful trapping season, and the same pack animals that had taken their furs down to be sold were now loaded with supplies they had bought to see them through until next season. Included in the packs was an especially precious cargo: several jugs of whiskey.

Although the whiskey was meant to be a year's supply, the men had broken out one jug already, and were passing it back and forth even in the first miles of their journey.

"Hey, Billy, you know that little ol' Indian gal of Dempsey's?" Johnny shouted. Johnny was riding in front, Billy all the way to the rear.

"Yeah, I know her. What about her?" Billy called back.

"You think she's worth a hundred plews?"

"What do you mean, is she worth a hundred plews?"

"I mean a hundred beaver pelts. You think she's worth that?"

"I don't know," Billy answered blankly. "Why do you ask?"

"'Cause Dempsey lost all his trappin' money in a poker game and he was lookin' to sell her. Quiet Stream, he said her name was. She was some good-lookin' for an Indian. Fact is, if I hadn't already sold my furs, I mighta took him up on it."

"What would you do with some Indian girl?"

"Ha! I'd keep her to warm my bed on those cold winter nights," Johnny said. "That's what I'd do with her."

"You're full of it, Johnny. You . . ." That was as far as he got before there was a too-close whooshing sound, then a thump. "Ughhh!" Billy grunted. It was the last sound that ever came from his mouth.

Hearing the unusual sound behind him, Eddie turned, just in time to see Billy tumble from his horse, an arrow sticking out from between his shoulder blades.

"Indians!" Billy shouted, before he himself was cut down by three arrows.

Johnny didn't wait to check on the fate of his friends. Instead, he slapped his legs against the side of his horse and urged it into a gallop.

"Ayiee!" Wak Tha Go shouted, urging his own horse into a gallop after the white trapper.

If Johnny had released the rope leading to his pack mule, he might have gotten away. But that mule was carrying nearly everything he owned. He thought, once, about dropping the line, but couldn't make himself do it.

Because Johnny was slowed by his burden, Wak Tha Go was able to come right up on him. When he looked over toward his attacker, poor Johnny couldn't believe his eyes. It looked as if a bear was riding a horse! He pointed his pistol and pulled the trigger, but the gun wasn't primed so it didn't fire. He cursed and began to weep. The last thing he saw on earth was the hideous grin on the giant bear-man's face as he brought his war club down on Johnny's head.

St. Louis, Wednesday, May 26, 1864

W.C. Philbin nodded his rather large, baldish head and made a few appropriate comments in order to prove to Mrs. Abernathy that he was listening to her. In fact, he was having a hard time paying attention because he knew she would only be repeating the same thing she had been harping on for the last two years.

Philbin was the director of the St. Louis Home for Orphaned Boys and Girls. The orphanage was located in a large two-story building that had been left to the city in the will of Mason Pierpont, Mrs. Abernathy's father. It was left with the stipulation that it would be used to provide a "safe, clean, and moral home for the unfortunate children of the city."

W.C. Philbin believed he was doing that, exactly as dictated by the will. But Mrs. Abernathy had recently learned that a rather significant portion of the money that was needed to run the home was being donated on a monthly basis by a woman known only as Jennie.

"I cannot bring myself to believe that you accept her money," Mrs. Abernathy said.

"Why shouldn't I accept it? Her money spends as well as anyone else's money."

"I shouldn't have to explain the why of it to you, Mr. Philbin. My dear, late father specifically stated in his will that this fine old home would go to the city, provided it is used to house our poor, unfortunate orphan children in a place that is safe, clean, and moral." Mrs. Abernathy sternly held up her finger. "Morals, Mr. Philbin, morals. *Her* house, the so-called House of Flowers? It is nothing but a whorehouse. I need hardly explain to you that the conduct of that woman is anything but normal, let alone clean or moral. She is a common prostitute. Filthy, filthy!"

"She may be a prostitute, Mrs. Abernathy, but I assure you, she does not ply her trade in the St. Louis orphanage. And there is nothing common about her. Her monthly contribution makes up almost fifty percent of the operating budget. Why, without her, I don't think we would even be able to keep the doors open."

"Nevertheless, I want you to stop accepting donations from that woman," Mrs. Abernathy insisted. She sniffed as if to acknowledge a foul odor in the air.

"If we do that, Mrs. Abernathy, we will have to start looking for emergency homes for all our children."

"Are you telling me you won't turn her away?"

"I'm telling you I can't," Philbin said. "Not turn her money away and survive. You seem not to understand. . . ."

"Very well. I can see right now that I will have to find some other way to keep that woman from polluting the morals of our dear, precious children." Mrs. Abernathy stood up then to her full majestic height and matronly girth, and started toward the door. Before she reached the door, she turned back toward the upset orphanage director.

"I never thought I would see the day when I would go to court to try and overturn the will of my father, but I'm convinced that had he known a low-life prostitute would be frequenting this place, giving you her filthy sin money, he would never have left our home to your care."

"And I am equally convinced he intended this home to be used for the good of the children," Philbin said. "And to that end, I will accept money from whatever source I can, as long as it is not illegal."

"Good day to you, Mr. Philbin," Mrs. Abernathy said haughtily. She slammed the door behind her as she left.

As Mrs. Abernathy was leaving, Jennie was just arriving, having been brought to the orphanage by carriage, driven by an old, white-haired black man who wore a beaver hat. The contrast between the two women was quite pronounced. Jennie was young, slender, and very pretty. Mrs. Abernathy was in her late forties to early fifties, very stout, and plain-looking, to put it kindly. When she saw Jennie, a scowl crossed the society lady's face, making her even less attractive.

"Wait here, Ben," Jennie said to her driver.

"Yes'm," Sam said.

"Hello, Mrs. Abernathy," Jennie said, smiling broadly. "Isn't this a lovely day?"

"Hrumph," Mrs. Abernathy grunted, pointedly turning away from the young woman.

Jennie was still looking back over her shoulder when she stepped into the orphanage.

"Good morning, Mr. Philbin," she said when Philbin came to meet her. "I've brought my contribution."

Philbin held up his hands, as if about to refuse the money. "Miss Jennie, I . . ." he started, then paused.

"Yes?"

Philbin let out a big sigh, then reached for the money. "I thank you," he said.

Two

Missouri River, Monday, May 31, 1824

Art and his friend Clyde Barnes experienced a few anxious moments when they first saw the Indians, but realized quickly that the handful of men and women who had come down to the bank to wave them ashore were Mandans who wanted only to trade.

"Do you think we should put in?" Clyde asked.

"No point in being unfriendly," Art replied, turning the tiller to land the boat. When they got close enough, Art tossed a rope to the Indians and, by sign, indicated they should make the boat fast by looping the rope around a tree. The Indians complied easily, and in so doing, pulled the boat ashore.

There were a total of eight Mandan Indians in the party, six men and two women. Two of the men were old and gray, while one of the others looked to be still in his teens. The remaining men and women were probably of middle-adult years. One of the older men pointed to his chest.

"I am Tetonka," he said.

"I am Artoor," Art said, using the pronunciation of his name that the Shawnee had used when he lived with them, seemingly many years ago. From them he had learned many of the ways of the Indian peoples.

"Do you want to trade, Artoor?" Tetonka asked.

"What do you have to trade?"

Tetonka spoke to the others, and they began to display their wares, from rawhide shirts to moccasins, pipes, and rattles. One of the items was a very pretty dress of white doeskin, finely worked with red, green, and blue dyed quills. Clyde pointed to the dress.

"I'd like that," he said.

"What do you want with that?" Art asked.

"Who knows?" Clyde said. "When we get to St. Louie, I might just give it to a pretty girl."

Art laughed, and Clyde began bargaining with the Indians. One of them pointed to a frying pan.

"Art, you have a frying pan, don't you?" Clyde asked.

"Yes."

"I thought so. We don't need two, and I can always get myself another one with all the money I'm goin' to make." He handed the frying pan over, then took the dress.

During the course of the trading Art got three rabbits, three combs of honey, and some wild greens. The trading ended to the mutual satisfaction of all. As Art was untying the boat, Tetonka came over to speak to him.

"You are good men," the old Indian said. "My heart will be sad when you are killed."

"What are you talking about? We aren't going to be killed," Art said.

Tetonka nodded his head sadly. "Yes, you will be killed soon." He signed as he spoke, making a slashing motion across his throat when he said *killed*. "There are many Arikara who want to kill all white men. Yes. When they see you, they will kill you."

Art knew that Tetonka wasn't lauding the fact, but was giving Art a warning of the danger ahead. Art's only question now was if this was a warning against the Arikara tribe in general, or a specific warning.

"Have you seen the Arikara?" Art asked.

Tetonka nodded again, and held up seven fingers. Seven was a very precise number, which had to mean that this was a specific warning about a particular war party.

"Where are they?" Art asked.

Tetonka pointed downriver. "Where river does this," he said, signing a curving motion with his hand. "There is big rock over the river. They wait on rock."

Art put his hand on Tetonka's shoulder. "Thank you, my friend," he said. Neither he nor the Indian smiled, but both felt the friendship between them.

"What was the big parlay with the old chief about?" Clyde asked as he finished carefully packing his loot.

"We've got trouble ahead," Art said.

"What kind of trouble?"

"Arikara."

"Damn," Clyde said, understanding the severity of the warning. "So what do we do now?"

"We'll position the load so that we're in between the bundles," Art suggested. "That should be good enough to stop any arrows they might shoot at us from ashore."

It was about another mile downstream before the river curved again. At the bend in the river Art saw a large rock, part of which hung out over the water. "There it is," he said.

"Yeah," Clyde replied nervously. "I see it."

Between them they had two rifles and two pistols, all charged, loaded, and primed. In addition they took their powder horns and lead-shot with them as they squeezed in between the two rows of bundles. They were ready when the boat drew even with the rock.

"There's one," Clyde said, drawing a bead on an Indian ashore.

Art stuck his hand out to keep Clyde from shooting. "No," he said. "Let's not shoot unless they shoot first."

Clyde eased the hammer back down. "If you say so," he said.

When Two Ponies saw the boat coming downriver, he signaled Wak Tha Go. Wak Tha Go then passed the signal on to the warriors who waited in canoes. This would be the third time Wak Tha Go and his war party had encountered white trappers since leaving the village. On the two previous encounters, they had killed the trappers, but gotten little for their efforts. But this boat was laden with pelts and supplies, and would be a great coup, one that the village would sing about around the campfires. The women and the elders, as well as the warriors, would be pleased.

Armed with one of the rifles they took from the trappers they had attacked earlier, Wak Tha Go ran across the cape to be on the other side of the river bend. From there he would have an excellent, unobscured view of the boat as it approached, and of the attack of his warriors.

On board the boat Art watched the Indian closely until they slipped by, unchallenged. He was about to breathe a sigh of relief when, ahead, he saw two canoes coming swiftly toward them.

"Art!" Clyde called.

"Yes, I see them," Art replied evenly, betraying no emotion, no fear. "Get ready."

There were at least four men in each canoe, and they were paddling hard to close the distance. One man in each canoe launched an arrow toward the boat. Because Art had been expecting an attack from the riverbank, he and Clyde had moved everything to provide protection from the sides. While that protected them from any attack from the riverbank, it left them exposed to a frontal attack. As a result, both arrows came dangerously close: The first stuck in one of the bundles; another stuck in the deck of the boat.

"Take the one on the right!" Art shouted.

The canoe on the right was the closest. Art shot at the canoe on the left, and had the satisfaction of seeing the Indian in front tumble out, along with his oar. And as the Indian fell, he also upset the canoe, which was exactly what Art had hoped would happen.

"Damn!" Clyde shouted in disgust when the bullet he fired missed its mark and made a splash in the water near the pursuing canoe.

Clyde then pulled his pistol and started to shoot it.

"No!" Art shouted. "You reload! I'll do the shooting for both of us!"

"Good idea," Clyde agreed, handing his loaded pistol to Art.

Art held his shot, waiting for the canoe to come much closer. During that brief period, the Indians shot several more arrows, many of them coming uncomfortably close. Finally, the canoe drew within pistol range. Art aimed and fired. He hit the lead paddler, but unlike the man in the first canoe, this one fell back, and the canoe did not swamp.

In the meantime, the other canoe had been righted, and the Indians had climbed back aboard and resumed the chase.

Art killed a second man in the canoe on the right, and because two of their number had now been killed, they started paddling back down the river in order to join up with the other canoe. Doing so put them out of pistol range.

Clyde handed Art a loaded rifle. "Here," he said. "And the other one is loaded too."

"Thanks," Art said. One of the Indians seemed to be giving instructions to the others, so he was the one Art

selected as his target. Raising the rifle to his shoulder, he
took careful aim, then pulled the trigger. The talkative Indian fell into the river and began to float away, face down
in the water.

That left only two Indians in each canoe. When the Indians saw that the odds were now much less favorable to
them, they turned and began paddling hard for the bank.

"Ha, ha, ha!" Clyde shouted, standing up and moving to
the edge of the boat. "Run, you cowardly bastards, run!"
he shouted.

On shore, Wak Tha Go watched with disbelief as his
men were shot down, one by one. What he had thought
would be an easy killing raid had turned into a disaster.
Who was this trapper who killed almost every time he
fired his rifle?

Wak Tha Go raised his own rifle. He wanted to kill the
white man who was so deadly with his own shooting, but he
could not get a good shot at him. The other man, though, the
one who had been loading the rifles, was within easy range.

"If I cannot kill you, white man, I will kill your friend,"
Wak Tha Go said under his breath.

Just as Wak Tha Go was about to pull the trigger, Art
happened to catch him out of the corner of his eye.

"Clyde! Get down!" Art shouted.

"What for?" Clyde asked, turning toward Art with a
big grin on his face. "They're skedaddling like pups.
Why, I . . ."

That was as far as Clyde got. There was an angry buzz
in the air, followed by a distant explosion, then a thump as
the bullet plowed into Clyde's back and exited through his
chest.

"What?" he asked in surprise as he tumbled back against the plew bales, then slid to the deck in a seated position. He put his hand on his chest, then pulled it away to examine the blood that had pooled in his cupped palm. "I'll be damned," he said, more out of almost childish curiosity than anything else.

Art grabbed the rifle that Clyde had just loaded. He looked toward the riverbank, hoping to get a bead on the Indian who had shot Clyde, but the Indian was nowhere in sight.

"Damn!" Art said in frustration.

"Did he skedaddle?" Clyde asked with a strained, lopsided grin on his stupid face.

"Yes," Art said, squatting beside his friend.

"That means we run them all off, didn't we?"

"Yes," Art said.

"Ha! I reckon we showed them not to tangle with the likes of us," Clyde said. Clyde coughed, and as he did so, flecks of blood came from his mouth. "Oh," Clyde said. "Oh, that's bad, ain't it?"

"I won't lie to you, Clyde," Art said. "You're not goin' to make it."

"I'm not? You want know a funny thing? It ain't hurtin' all that much," Clyde said.

"Can I get you something? A chew of tobacco? A drink of whiskey?"

"Some whiskey maybe," Clyde said.

Art pulled the cork on a whiskey jug, poured some into a cup, then held the cup up to Clyde's mouth. Clyde took a couple of deep swallows, then chuckled.

"What is it?" Art asked.

"I was just wonderin' what ol' St. Peter is goin' to say when I show up at them pearly gates with liquor on my breath."

"I don't reckon he'll say much of anything, given the

way things are," Art said. He wanted to strangle his friend for his stupidity. He wanted to save his life, but knew it was finished.

"Wonder if ol' Pierre is there . . ."

"Sure, he is. I expect he'll be standing there to meet you himself," Art said. "He'll probably fix you some of that crawfish pie he was always talking about."

"I'd rather have some beaver tail. Never knew anyone who could cook beaver tail like Pierre."

"It was good," Art said, remembering it from the many times Pierre had cooked it for him as well.

"Art?"

"Yes?"

"I want you to do somethin' for me."

"What's that?"

"You know that purty dress I bought? Well, once you get to St. Louie, I want you to give it to a purty girl."

"Do you have someone in mind?"

"No," Clyde answered. He coughed again, struggling to smile as the color drained from his hard-weathered face. "You pick one out for me. I was just goin' to give it to the first purty girl I seen who would take it."

"I'll find someone," Art promised.

"You know, it's beginnin' to hurt now. Fact is, it's hurtin' somethin' fierce."

"Want some more whiskey?"

"I don't reckon," Clyde replied. "Ol' St. Peter might close an eye to me havin' whiskey on my breath, but don't know how he'd take to me bein' drunk."

Clyde closed his eyes and was silent for a long time. Art bent over to see if he could hear his friend breathing, but he couldn't. He was going to have to put ashore in order to bury him, but he didn't want to do it yet. He needed to make certain he was far enough downriver to be away from the Indians who had attacked them.

Then Clyde surprised Art by speaking one more time. "Lord, I sure would've loved to see me a purty girl in that purty dress," he rasped. Those were his last words.

Art didn't come ashore until after dark. By that time he had drifted far enough downriver that he was sure there were no more Arikara bucks around. He also figured that the darkness would offer some protection and allow him to bury his friend safely and in peace.

Art dug a grave about one hundred feet from the river's edge, then lowered Clyde into the hole and covered him up. He gathered stones to cover the grave in a primitive sort of cairn, a sort of civilized gesture that would have been unfamiliar to the man buried beneath the cold earth. Afterward, he stood alongside the freshly dug grave, took off his own hat, and held it across his heart.

"Lord, this fella's name I'm sendin' to you is Clyde Barnes. He probably drank too much, cussed too much, and gambled too much. That's the way it is with mountain men, but you, knowin' everything like you do, probably already know that. But that means you also know what was in his heart, and Lord, when you look into his heart you'll see Clyde was about as fine a man as there could be.

"Clyde has some friends up there, and I'd like for you to arrange to have them come meet him, take him under their wing, and show him around. I've got a special reason for asking this, Lord, because truth to tell, it was Clyde and Pierre who took me in when I first come to the mountains. They were good men, both of 'em, and once you get 'em up there and give 'em a chance, why, I think you'll see that too.

"I know there's probably some proper way to end prayers, but I can't think of any way of endin' this one except to just end it. Amen."

St. Louis, Wednesday, June 2, 1824

When Theodore Epson, the chief of tellers of the River Bank of St. Louis, passed by the boardroom of the bank, he saw that it was filled with women, all of whom seemed to be talking at once. Smiling, he shook his head and walked on by. Women . . . strange creatures all.

Making such a meeting room available to the public had been Epson's idea, and he'd convinced the board of directors that it would be very good business for the bank. The board had accepted his proposal, and today was a good example of how it was being put to use. The ladies all belonged to the Women's Auxiliary of the St. Louis Betterment League, and its president was Sybil Abernathy, wife of Duane Abernathy, the chairman of the bank's board of directors.

As he closed the door between the front and back of the bank, Theodore Epson heard Mrs. Abernathy banging her gavel to call for quiet.

"Ladies, ladies, may I have your attention please?" Mrs. Abernathy said.

Most of the conversation halted, though there was one woman in the back who continued to hold court with the three or four who were gathered around her.

"Mrs. Peabody!" Mrs. Abernathy called. "Would you please take your seat now?" When she got no response, she shouted. "Mrs. Peabody, would you *please* take your seat now?"

"All right, all right," Mrs. Peabody answered. "You don't have to shout. I'm not deaf, you know."

In fact, Mrs. Peabody was quite deaf, so deaf that she didn't even hear the other ladies laugh at her patently absurd declaration.

When all were quiet and seated, Mrs. Abernathy began the meeting.

"Ladies, I called this special meeting today because I am deeply concerned about the state of morals of our city, more specifically the lack of morals in our fair metropolis. I have heard it said that the people back East sometimes refer to St. Louis as Sodom and Gomorrah on the Mississippi. If we are to build a decent society here, if we are to be recognized by our Eastern cousins as a civilized city, then we must take action immediately to stop this moral decay."

"What moral decay are you talking about, Sybil?" one of the ladies asked.

"What moral decay? Well, I'm talking about this . . . this Jennie woman, who doesn't even have a last name, and the house of prostitution she operates right under our very noses."

"Has she done something?" another asked.

"Of course she has done something. She is operating a house of prostitution," Sybil Abernathy said in exasperation. "Didn't you hear what I just said?"

"Well, yes, but there have always been houses of prostitution, and there always will be. You know how the men are, or at least some of them, none of *our* husbands or brothers, I'm sure. The way I look at it, better to have someplace like that where you know where it is, than to have women of the evening roaming our streets."

"And we don't have that, Sybil," another pointed out.

Mrs. Abernathy was obviously surprised by the reaction she was getting. She had expected overwhelming support for her campaign to rid St. Louis of Jennie and the ones who worked for her in the House of Flowers. Instead, she was getting resistance.

"Sin is sin, and immorality is immorality, no matter where it occurs," Mrs. Abernathy said.

"Of course it is, and I'm not justifying what she does," one of the women said. "It's just that she is discreet and she does stay out of everyone's way. I guess I never considered it as much of a problem."

"What about the orphanage?" Mrs. Abernathy asked.

"What about it?"

"Perhaps you didn't know that she donates a rather healthy sum of money to the orphanage every week."

"Why, I would think that to be a good civic-minded thing to do," one of the women said.

"Would you think it to be a good thing if you knew that she recruits her prostitutes from among the children of that orphanage?"

"What?" several of the ladies shouted.

"You don't mean that she actually uses the children?"

Mrs. Abernathy smiled with sly satisfaction. Now, at last, she had gotten them into the proper frame of mind to consider this grave matter that was affecting the city they claimed to care about so deeply.

"As far as I know, she doesn't use the very young children," Mrs. Abernathy said. "But two of her prostitutes are former residents of the orphanage home."

"Oh, my, but that is terrible!" someone said.

"We must do something about this!" another added.

Mrs. Abernathy nodded in triumph. "And do something we shall," she said.

Arikara Village, Wednesday, June 2, 1824

When Wak Tha Go returned to the village, it wasn't in the triumphant manner that he had envisioned, but rather in disfavor. His adventure had cost the lives of four of his eager young warriors, and the widows and families of the slain wept bitter tears of grief. All turned their back on him, blaming him for the deaths.

Wak Tha Go went from tepee to tepee to plead his case, but none would hear him. When council met that evening, Wak Tha Go was not invited to sit in the first circle. Angry at being ostracized, he hung back in the darkness, watching the others as they sat around the fire, mourning and listening to ageless stories and songs.

Wak Tha Go felt they should be telling stories and singing songs of his great deeds. After all, he had personally killed one of the white men who had killed the three warriors. And before this, there had been other encounters with the white trappers in which the Indians emerged victorious, killing the trappers while not losing even one of their own. They had taken booty and scalps, counted many coups. In any war, there was bound to be loss. Why could the others in the village not see this?

The Peacemaker was a chief, but not an all-powerful, autocratic chief. He ruled by persuasion and counsel, and always with advice and assistance from the other elders in the tribe. There was a difference between leading during peacetime and leading during battle, however. War chiefs were neither appointed nor elected. A war chief assumed a position of authority, and if others chose to follow him his authority was validated. Peace chiefs and war chiefs usually coexisted and supported each other—but these were extraordinary times.

In the case of Wak Tha Go, his authority as a warrior chief had lasted only as long as he was successful. Now his rank within the tribe was no higher than anyone else's.

"Grandfather, tell us a story," one young boy asked of The Peacemaker.

"Yes, Grandfather, tell us of Buffalo Cow Woman," another said.

The Peacemaker was not their blood grandfather, but

was addressed as such by many of the young. Not only was this a token of respect for The Peacemaker; it also, by implication, included the young person in The Peacemaker's family. Elders, whether they held the status of chief or not, were automatically respected by younger people.

"Buffalo Cow Woman?" The Peacemaker said. "You want to hear of the mother of us all?"

"Yes! Yes!"

"Then gather close so that your ears do not fail to hear the words I speak, for I must speak them quietly." He held his finger to his lips in a shushing motion. "If Buffalo Cow Woman hears us speaking of her, she may get very angry. And if she gets very angry, she will gallop through the village, trampling every tepee, and putting out all the fires. She will cause the meat to go bad and hide the honey and take away the rain. If she does that, we will all . . ." He paused for a long moment, looking directly into the faces of all the children who were now hanging on every word. "Die!" he barked.

The younger children began to whimper in fear. Even the older children shivered, but they were older and braver, and did not cry.

Wak Tha Go had been just on the periphery of the council circle, listening to everything that was being said. When he saw the council circle dissolve and saw the children move toward the center, and heard The Peacemaker start his story about Buffalo Cow Woman, he snorted and walked away.

"Buffalo Cow Woman," he said under his breath, scoffing at the name. Everyone in the village was listening to children's stories when they should be listening to stories about his great exploits and even greater plans for the fu-

Three

After Art put into shore and secured the boat, he carved a mark in the railing. He had no idea what the date was, though he figured it to be sometime in mid-June or later. If he had remembered to find out the date before he left Rendezvous, he would know now, because he had carved a notch for every day since he left. He had been on the river now for thirty days. The days had been long and lonely since Clyde's death.

Once he made camp, Art took his rifle out into the woods, and less than half an hour later was back with a rabbit. He skinned the rabbit, salted it well, skewered it on a green willow branch, then put it over a fire, suspended between two Y-shaped sticks. Within minutes the rich aroma of roasted rabbit filled the air.

Art had never gone down the Missouri, so he really had no idea how far it was to St. Louis, nor how long it would take him to get there. He was sure that the river didn't go in a straight line. In fact, what with all the twists and turns, he would be surprised if the river route didn't double the distance a crow flies. But he had neither horses nor mules, and floating down the river—even if it was longer—was certainly superior to walking.

Shortly after nightfall, as Art was laying out his bedroll,

he became aware of eyes staring at him from the dark. With the hair on the back of his neck standing up, he slipped his pistol from his belt and stared into the black maw that surrounded his camp.

"Who's there?" he called.

There was no response.

"Who's there?" he called again, and this time he augmented his call with the deadly click of his pistol being cocked.

A low, frightening growl came from the darkness.

"Are you a wolf?" Art called. Thinking to lure the animal from the darkness, he took a piece of rabbit and held it up. "Come on in, boy. Come get this meat."

Tossing the meat about ten feet in front of him, he raised his pistol, ready to shoot the moment the wolf showed itself.

It wasn't a wolf, at least not a full-blooded wolf, though the dog clearly had many of the markings and features of a wolf. The animal walked into pistol range, growling, its eyes locked on the mountain man while it was moving toward the proffered morsel.

Art lowered his pistol and watched the big dog use its powerful jaws to pull the meat away from the bone. The dog fascinated him, not only by its size and power, but also by the way it carried itself. It clearly showed no fear of him.

When the dog finished the first piece of meat, Art threw another piece out—this one closer than the first. The dog came for it. By the time he threw the last piece of meat, the dog was quite close—close enough for Art to touch, and he did so, rubbing the dog behind its ears.

"How'd you get way out here in the middle of nowhere?" Art asked.

Though the dog didn't snuggle against Art's hand, it was

friendly enough to be nonthreatening; the growling had ceased.

The dog slept near Art that night. When Art got ready to leave the next day, the dog jumped onto the boat with him.

"Shoo," Art said, waving his hand. "Get off."

The dog walked to the front of the boat and sat there, staring at Art with penetrating eyes.

"What are you doing? You can't go with me."

The dog made no effort to leave.

As a young boy, Art had once owned a dog. He remembered that Rover would go fishing and hunting with him, and he smiled.

"I guess you would be good company at that. All right, you can stay," Art said.

The dog came much closer.

"So, what shall I call you? How about Rover? I used to have a dog named Rover."

The dog growled.

"You don't like Rover? How about Skip? That's a good dog name."

The dog growled again.

"All right, suppose I just call you Dog and be done with it. If you even are a dog . . ."

The dog made a few circles on the deck of the boat, lay down with his nose between his paws, and closed his eyes. Art laughed. "All right, you seem to like that name, so Dog it is."

Over the next several days, Dog proved to be more than just good company. One night, as Art was making camp, Dog disappeared. Art thought that he had run away, but a short while later Dog returned to camp, carrying a rabbit in his mouth. He dropped it at Art's feet, providing them with their dinner for the night.

* * *

House of Flowers, St. Louis, Tuesday, June 22, 1824

Jennie was in the kitchen, taking inventory of her food items. She had to keep a well-stocked kitchen because most of her girls not only worked there, they slept and ate there as well. She was measuring the flour, trying to determine how much she would need, when a girl came in.

"Miss Jennie?"

Turning, Jennie saw Carla. Though Carla lived there, she wasn't really one of Jennie's girls, in that she wasn't a prostitute. She worked as a waitress at LaBarge's Tavern, and paid for her room and board at the house, though Jennie charged her far less than the going rate.

"Yes, Carla?"

"Deputy Constable Gordon is here to see you."

"Thank you, Carla. Would you tell him I'll be just a minute?"

"Yes, ma'am. Or if you want to, you can go talk to him and I'll put things away in here."

"Would you, Carla? That's sweet of you," Jennie said. Taking off her apron and making a quick adjustment to her hair, Jennie went into the parlor. Deputy Constable John Gordon was standing in the foyer, rolling his hat in his hands. Jennie smiled broadly as she approached him.

"Why, John, I didn't expect to see you here this time of day," she said. "You don't usually come until it's quite late."

"Uh, sorry, Miss Jennie, but this ain't exactly a business call."

"John, you know I don't like to treat my callers as customers. I would hope that all of your calls are more social than business."

"Yes, ma'am, but, well, this ain't social either."

"Oh?" Jennie replied, her face registering her curiosity. "If it isn't business nor social, what is it?"

"Sort of duty, you might say," Deputy Constable Gordon

said. "The chief constable would like to see you down at
his office. He asked me to come get you."

"All right, John. Just let me get my portmanteau and I'll
be right with you."

Because he had ridden a horse down to Jennie's, Deputy
Constable Gordon waited for Jennie's driver, Ben, to bring
her carriage around. He rode alongside the carriage as Ben
drove Jennie to the chief constable's office.

"Shall I wait here, Miss Jennie?" Ben asked.

"Yes, Ben, if you would, please," Jennie said.

Jennie had no idea what the visit was about until she
stepped into the office. There, she saw Mrs. Abernathy and
two other women, all of whom greeted her with sour expressions.

"Miss Jennie," the chief constable started.

"Do you feel it is necessary to address a colored woman
as *Miss?*" Sybil Abernathy said. "Because I certainly
don't."

In surprise, Jennie jerked her head toward Mrs. Abernathy.

"Don't look at me, girl, like you don't know what I'm
talking about," Mrs. Abernathy said. "Are you going to
deny that you are a colored slave girl?"

"Now, Mrs. Abernathy, if that is true, who does she belong to?"

"She belonged to a man named Bruce Eby," Mrs. Abernathy said.

Surprised to hear the name of the man who had once
owned her, Jennie looked down toward the floor.

"Is that true, Miss, uh, Jennie?"

"I used to belong to him. I'm a free woman now," Jennie said.

The constable stroked his chin. "Then, you *are* colored?"
He shook his head. "You sure don't look colored to me."

"I'm Creole," Jennie said.

"Creole, colored, it's all the same," Mrs. Abernathy insisted. "The point is, she was the legal property of one Bruce Eby."

"Was?" the constable said, looking at Mrs. Abernathy. "Even you are saying she was, and not is, the property of this man, Eby. Where is he anyway? Why isn't he making a claim?"

"He can't claim her because he is dead," Mrs. Abernathy said. She pointed to Jennie. "And she killed him."

"What?" the constable replied. He looked sharply at Jennie. "Is she telling the truth? Did you kill your master?"

"No, sir, I did not kill him," Jennie said.

"If she didn't kill him, she was the cause of his being killed," Mrs. Abernathy said.

"Is that right? Was he killed because of you?"

"In a way, I suppose that's right."

"When did this happen? And where?"

"It happened several years ago," Jennie said. "At Rendezvous on the Missouri River."

"And you were his slave?"

"Not when he was killed. Another man won me, just before the killing. And he's the one that set me free."

"Can you prove that you were set free, and don't belong to the estate of the man you say was killed?"

"I can," Jennie said. "I have a letter of manumission, given to me by the man who had just won me, fair and square, and signed by two witnesses."

"Where is this letter of manumission?" the constable asked.

"I keep it . . ." Jennie started, then she glanced over toward Mrs. Abernathy. "I'd rather not tell you where I keep it."

"Ha!" Mrs. Abernathy said. "You won't tell us where you keep it, because it doesn't exist. You don't have a letter of manumission. You are a runaway slave."

"I am not a runaway slave! I am a free woman!" Jennie insisted.

"Can you get that letter, Miss Jennie, and show it to me?"

"Yes, I can do that."

"Please do so."

"Arrest her, Constable. Arrest her and put her in jail," Mrs. Abernathy demanded.

"I can't do that, Mrs. Abernathy."

"What do you mean you can't do that? You heard her confess that her master was killed because of her."

"Maybe he was killed because of her, and maybe he wasn't. But that doesn't give me any cause to arrest her. In fact, even if she killed him and it happened at Rendezvous on the Missouri, I still couldn't arrest her, because that would put it way out of my jurisdiction."

"Am I free to go?" Jennie asked.

"Yes, I can think of no reason to hold you."

"Wait!" Mrs. Abernathy said. "What about the fact that she is using girls from the orphanage in the House of Flowers?"

"What?" Jennie and the constable asked in unison.

"You heard me. Some of the girls who work for her now came from the orphanage house. Isn't there some law that would deal with that? Because if there isn't, there should be."

"Some girls? What girls?" the constable asked.

"Carla Thomas is one," Mrs. Abernathy said. To Mrs. Abernathy's surprise, both the constable and the deputy constable laughed.

"What is it? What's wrong?" Mrs. Abernathy asked. "Do you find that funny?"

"Yes," the constable said. "Mrs. Abernathy, everyone knows that Carla Thomas just lives in the House of Flowers. She's not a prostitute."

"Nevertheless, to even have a young girl living there is wrong."

"She's nineteen years old," the constable said. "And I reckon she's old enough to live anywhere she wants. I don't see as I have any right to tell her she can't stay there."

Mrs. Abernathy glared at the constable, deputy constable, and Jennie for a long moment before she spoke.

"I can see now that you aren't going to do anything to rid us of this . . . this blight on our city, are you? You are going to allow this whore, and the whores who work with her, to continue to corrupt the morals of our young men."

"We have no laws on the books against keeping a bawdy house, Mrs. Abernathy," the constable explained. "The only law we have is one that prohibits women from plying their trade on the street. And as far as I know, neither Miss Jennie—"

"Miss Jennie? Why are you calling a colored woman Miss? Even if she was freed, she is still colored, and certainly doesn't deserve being addressed as Miss."

Constable Billings sighed. "As I was about to say, neither *Miss* Jennie"—he came down hard on the word *Miss*—"nor any of her girls have ever violated that particular law. So, to answer your question, Mrs. Abernathy, no, I don't intend to put her in jail, run her out of town, or even close her establishment. Now, if you ladies will excuse me, I have work to do."

Mrs. Abernathy pulled herself up to her full height, then looked at the two women she had brought along for moral support.

"Come, ladies," she said. "It is clear that we can expect no support from Constable Billings." She stared at Billings. "Don't forget, Constable, we have a federal marshal in St. Louis. Since you refuse to do your duty, I will go to him."

The constable looked back at Jennie. "Miss Jennie,

you're sure you can find the paper that proves you're free?"

"Yes, sir, I'm sure."

"You'd better go get it and bring it to me as quickly as you can."

"Yes, sir."

"I assure you, this isn't over," Mrs. Abernathy hissed. "I am a determined woman and I will find a way to rid our city of this filth."

The House of Flowers

Back in her room, Jennie opened the chest that sat at the foot of her bed. In the bottom of the chest, under a quilt, there was a locked tin box. Opening the box, she removed a little packet, bound by a red ribbon. When she untied the ribbon, she saw what she was looking for: the all-important letter of manumission.

Holding the letter in her hand, she let her mind drift back to the day it was signed, some six years earlier.

Bighorn Mountains, Spring of 1814

Jennie was tired. It was more than the bone-weary, back-sore tired that comes from working; it was the kind of deep-down tired that begins to tell on a person who has been through several years of "being on the line," selling her body to trappers and tradesmen, soldiers, scouts, and anyone else Bruce Eby offered her services to. Furthermore, it was a tired that wasn't ameliorated by any money she might earn. For Jennie was not only a prostitute, she was property—a slave owned body and soul by Bruce Eby.

Eby had brought Jenny to Rendezvous, a seasonal gathering of fur trappers, mountain men, and traders, because he could sell her services for three times what the market would bear in a city. But even with the increased cost, Jennie—an exceptionally pretty young woman of nineteen—had been doing a brisk business. For three days and nights, the line outside her tent was unabated, interrupted only when Eby reluctantly gave her a couple of hours to sleep.

Now, however, because of the excitement of an upcoming shooting match, Jennie was able to find a respite from her activities. Taking advantage of the break, she stood just in front of her tent, looking toward the gathering crowd of shooters who were preparing for the upcoming match.

Some of the shooters were cleaning their guns, others were sighting down the barrels of their rifles at the targets they would be using. Some shooters just stood by calmly. In that group of quietly confident men, she saw and recognized a young man she had known from before—when he was a boy and she was still a young girl. No, she reminded herself. Art may have been a boy then, but she hadn't been a young girl. She had never been a young girl.

"Art?" she called. "Art, do you remember me?"

Startled to hear his name spoken by a woman, Art turned to see who had called him. He saw a young woman between eighteen and twenty, with coal-black hair, dark eyes, and olive skin. For a moment Jennie could see the confusion in his eyes; then she saw that he recognized her.

"Jennie? Jennie, is that you?" he asked.

She smiled at him. "You remembered," she said.

"Yes, of course I remember."

Spontaneously, Jennie hugged him. He hugged her back.

"Here, now, that's goin' to cost you, mister," a gruff voice said. "I ain't in the habit of lettin' my girls give away anything for free."

Quickly, Jennie pulled away from Art, an expression of fear and resignation in her face.

"If'n you want to spend a little time with her, all you got to do is pay me five dollars," the man said.

"You are Bruce Eby," Art said.

Eby screwed his face up in confusion. "Do I know you, mister?"

"No," Art answered. "But I know you. What have you got to do with Jennie?"

"Ahh, you know Jennie, do you? Then you know she's the kind that can please any man."

Art looked at Jennie, who glanced toward the ground. "He owns me," she said.

"What about it, mister?" Eby said. "Do you want her, or not?"

"Yeah," Art said. "I want her."

Eby smiled. "That'll be five dollars."

"No," Art said. "I don't want her five dollars worth. I want to buy her from you."

Jennie's heart skipped a beat. Art wanted to buy her? Could he? Oh, please, Lord, that it be so, she prayed quickly.

Eby took in a deep breath, then let it out in a long sigh. "Well, now, I don't know nothin' 'bout that. She's made me a lot of money. I don't know if I could sell her or not."

"You bought her, didn't you?"

"Yes, I bought her."

"Then you can sell her. How much?"

"One thousand dollars," Eby said without blinking an eye.

"One thousand dollars?" Art gasped.

Eby chuckled. "Well, if you can't afford her, maybe you'd better just take five dollars worth."

"No," Art said. "I reckon not."

"On the other hand, you could come back next year. I

'spec she'll be a lot older and a lot uglier then. You might be able to afford her next year."

Jennie looked at Art. For just a moment there had been a look of anticipation and joy in her face. Then, when she realized that her salvation was not to be, the joy had left.

"I'm sorry, Jennie," he said.

"I am too," Jennie replied. She fought hard to hold back the tears.

"Shooters, to your marks!" someone called.

Looking away from Jennie, Art picked up his rifle and walked over to the line behind which the shooters were told to stand. Jennie went over as well.

Jennie stood in the crowd with those who weren't in the shooting contest to watch. There were a few favorites, men who had participated in previous shooting contests, and the onlookers began placing bets on them.

The first three rounds eliminated all but the more serious of the shooters. Now there were only ten participants left, and many were surprised to see the new young man still there. Even Jennie was pleasantly surprised to see that Art was still in contention, and privately she began pulling for him, hoping and praying that he would do well.

"All right, boys, from now on it gets serious," the organizer said. "I'm putting a row of bottles on that cart there, then moving it down another one hundred yards. The bottles will be your target, but you got to call the one you're a-shootin' at before you make your shot."

As Jennie looked up and down the line of competitors remaining, she saw that one of them was her master, Bruce Eby. Eby had the first shot. "Third from the right," he said. He aimed, fired, and the third bottle from the right exploded in a shower of glass.

This round of shouting eliminated four competitors; the following round eliminated two, and the round after that eliminated two more. Now only Art and Eby remained. A series of shots left them tied.

"Move the targets back another one hundred yards," the organizer ordered, and two men repositioned the cart.

By now all other activity in Rendezvous had come to a complete halt. Everyone had come to see the shooting demonstration. Only two bottles were put up, and Eby had the first shot.

"The one on the left," Eby said quietly. He lifted the rifle to his shoulder, aimed, and fired. The bottle was cut in two by the bullet, the neck of it collapsing onto the rubble.

"All right, boy, it's your turn," the organizer said.

Art raised his rifle and aimed.

"Boy, before you shoot, how 'bout a little bet?" Eby said.

Art lowered his rifle. "What sort of bet?"

"I'll bet you five hundred dollars you miss."

Jennie saw Art contemplating the offer. She didn't know if he had that much money or not. And if he did, she didn't know if he was confident enough in his shooting to take Eby up on his offer.

"Ahh, go ahead and shoot," Eby said. "I'll be content with just beating you."

"I'll take the bet," Art said.

"Let's see the color of your money."

Art took the money from his pocket, then held it until Eby also took out a sum of money. Both men handed their money over to the organizer, who counted and verified that both had put in the requisite amount.

"It's all here," the organizer said.

"All right, boy, it's all up to you now," Eby said.

Once again, Art raised his rifle and took aim. He took a breath, let half of it out . . .

"Don't get nervous now," Eby said, purposely trying to make him nervous.

"No fair, Eby. Let the boy shoot without your blathering," someone said.

Art let the breath out, lowered his rifle, looked over at Eby, then raised the rifle and aimed again. There was a moment of silence; then Art squeezed the trigger. There was a flash in the pan, a puff of smoke from the end of the rifle, and a loud boom. The bottle that was his target shattered. Like the other bottle, the neck remained, though only about half as much of this neck remained as had been left behind from the first bottle.

"Yes!" Jennie shouted in pleased excitement. Quickly, she covered her mouth before Eby looked toward her. He wouldn't go easy on her if he knew she had been cheering for his opponent. Fortunately, the applause and cheers of the crowd covered up Jennie's response.

The organizer handed the money over to Art. "Looks like you won your bet," he said, "but the outcome of the shooting match is still undecided. Gentlemen, shall we go on? Or shall we declare it a tie?"

"We go on," Eby said angrily. "Put two more bottles up."

"Wait," Art said.

Eby smiled. "Givin' up, are you?"

"No," Art said. He pointed toward the cart. "We didn't finish them off. The necks of both bottles are still standing. I say we use them as our targets."

"Are you crazy?" Eby asked. "You can barely see them from here. How are we going to shoot at them?"

"I don't know about you, but I plan to use my rifle," Art said.

The others laughed, and their laughter further incensed Eby.

"What about it, Eby?" the organizer asked. "Shall we go on?"

Once more, Eby looked toward the cart. Then he saw that the neck from his bottle was considerably higher than the neck from Art's bottle. He nodded. "All right," he said. He raised his rifle, paused, then lowered it. "Only this time he goes first."

Art nodded, and raised his own rifle. "The one on the right," he said.

"No!" Eby shouted quickly. "You have to finish off the target you started. You have to shoot at the one on the left."

"I thought we could call our own targets," Art replied.

"You can. And you already did. Like you said, we didn't finish them off. You called the bottle on the left, that's the one you've got to finish."

"I think Eby's right," one of the spectators said.

"All right," the organizer agreed. "Your target is what remains of the bottle on the left."

"A hunnert dollars he don't do it," someone said.

"Who you goin' to get to take that bet?" another asked. "Ain't no way he can do it."

"What about you, mister?" Eby asked. "You want to bet whether or not you hit it?"

"No, I'll keep my money," Art said.

"Tell you what. You wanted the girl a while ago. I'll bet her against a thousand dollars you don't hit it."

Jennie felt a sudden flash of hope, followed by a feeling of guilt. If Art could hit the target and win her, she would be free of Bruce Eby. On the other hand, if he missed—and this target was very small—then he would lose the one thousand dollars, which was, in all likelihood, every cent he had. Part of her begged him to accept the wager, and yet she prayed that he would not.

Art looked over at Jennie and she saw that he was going to take the bet. She took a deep breath and held it. Could he hit the target? It was mighty small, and it was a long way off.

"What do you say, mister?" Eby taunted. "Is it a bet, or isn't it?"

"I don't want the girl to come to me."

Jennie felt a sudden draining of all the blood from her face. She had allowed herself to think that he might win her from Eby; now that hope was dashed.

"You don't want the girl? Then what do you want?" Eby asked.

"If I win, I want you to set Jennie free."

Jennie gasped, and her knees went weak. Could this be? Could it really be that for the first time in her entire life, she would be free?

"All right, boy, you hit that sawed-off piece of a bottle neck on the left there, and I'll set her free," Eby promised.

Art nodded. "You've got a bet."

Everyone expected to wait for a long moment while Art aimed, but to their surprise he lifted the rifle, aimed, and fired in one smooth, continuous motion. The bottle neck shattered. The reaction from the crowd was spontaneous.

"Did you see that?"

"Hurrah for the boy!"

"Who woulda thought . . ."

Jennie saw Eby raising his rifle, aiming it at Art. "Art! Look out!" she screamed.

Almost on top of Jennie's shouted warning, there was a loud bang, followed by a cloud of smoke. When the smoke rolled away, Eby was lying on his back with a large bullet wound in his chest. Turning quickly, Jennie saw another mountain man standing there with a smoking rifle. He had shot Eby.

"Clyde Barnes! Where did you come from?" Art asked.

"I decided to come on in early as well," Clyde said as he held his still-smoking rifle. "I couldn't let you have all the fun."

"Ever'one seen it," the organizer of the shooting match said. "Eby was about to shoot the boy when this fella shot him. We ain't got no judge nor law out here, but I say it was justifiable homicide."

"Hear, hear!" another shouted.

"Anyone say any different?"

There were no dissenters.

"Then let's get this piece of trash buried and get on with the Rendezvous. Oh, by the way," the organizer said, looking over toward Jennie. "I reckon we also heard the bet. Girl, you're free."

"Wait, you can't do it like that," someone else shouted.

Once again, Jennie felt a sinking sensation in her stomach. Was this all to be a cruel hoax? Was she destined to remain a slave? But if so, who would be her master? Eby was dead.

"What do you mean you don't do it like this?"

"Someone is going to have to draw up a letter of manumission."

"Manumission? What is that?"

"It's a letter that says this here girl has been given her freedom."

"Who signs the letter?"

"We all heard Eby wager the girl to this young fella. That means she belongs to him, until he gives her freedom. I reckon he'll have to sign it. Can you write your name, mister?"

"Yes," Art said. "I can write my name."

The man stuck out his hand. "The name is P. Edward Kane. I've done some lawyerin'. I can fix up the letter for you for two dollars."

Art took two dollars from his pocket and handed it to the man. "Here's my two dollars," he said.

"It'll need two witnesses," Kane said.

"I'll be one of the witnesses," the man who had shot Eby said. "The name is Clyde Barnes."

"And I'll be the other," another trapper said. "The name is Pierre Garneau."

The House of Flowers, St. Louis, Tuesday, June 22, 1824

Jennie held the precious paper in her hand. Showing this to Constable Billings would validate her claim to be a free woman. She held the paper to her breast and thanked the Lord for her freedom. Then, opening the paper up, she studied the three signatures: Clyde Barnes, Pierre Garneau, and the most important one of all, Art. Only Art. Even in this document, he had used the only name she knew him by. She thanked the Lord for Art too, for the man who had made her freedom, her new life possible.

The man she knew, she thought. She smiled. She knew him, all right; she knew him that night in what is sometimes referred to as the biblical sense. For that night, she had made a man of the boy, and he had made a woman of her, touching her soul for the first and only time in her entire life.

Four

It was just after midnight, about six weeks since Art had begun his trek from Rendezvous, and the campfire was now little more than a scattering of orange-glowing coals. Both Art and Dog were sleeping nearby. Art had made his encampment in a meadow at the river's edge, about one hundred yards from the edge of a thick forest. A full moon illuminated the scene in shades of silver and black.

The night had come alive with the sounds of nature: the whispering river, wind sighing through the trees, and night creatures from frogs to cicadas. Two men emerged from the trees, interrupting this peaceful scene.

"There it is, Cally! I see the boat!"

"Well, why don't you just shout it out, Angus?" Cally replied.

"I see the boat," Angus said again, much quieter this time.

"I see it too."

"What you think he's got on that boat?"

"I seen 'im from the ridge just afore he landed. Don't know for sure what he's a-carryin', but my guess would be beaver pelts."

"Beaver pelts?" Angus said. "When you ask me to come

along with you, I thought maybe we was goin' to rob a trader, carryin' whiskey and the like. What do we want with beaver pelts?"

"Beaver pelts is the same as gold back in St. Louis."

"How we goin' to get 'em to St. Louis?"

"Same way he was doin' it. We're not only goin' to take his pelts, we're goin' to take his boat. Get your gun out, make sure it's loaded."

"It's loaded, all right," Angus said as he pulled his pistol from his belt.

Dog growled quietly, then sat up, fully alert. The sudden movement awakened Art. Opening his eyes, he saw two men moving awkwardly across the open field, clearly illuminated in the moonlight. Dog growled again, standing with his back arched menacingly.

"I see them, Dog," Art said. Slowly he reached for his rifle and pulled it toward him, cocking it at the same time.

Dog stood up, but as yet made no move toward the men.

"Wait," Art said under his breath. Without moving, Art lay as if he were asleep, all the while watching the two men approach. When they got within twenty yards, Art suddenly sat up. "Now!" he said.

Dog leaped forward as if he were on springs. Within ten feet of the two men, he hunkered down on his hind legs, ready to pounce again. He growled, baring his fangs.

"You two boys better hold it right there," Art said. He did not have to shout, but spoke as if he were chatting with them in a parlor. "If you move again, Dog will rip open your throats."

"He—he can't get both of us," Cally said.

"What makes you think he can't? How long do you think it would take for him to rip out your windpipe?"

Still growling, Dog inched even closer. He had their

scents now, something his wolf-brain would never forget. They were as good as dead if he felt they posed a deadly danger to Art.

"No!" Angus said. "Call off your dog, mister. Call him off!"

"Put your guns down on the ground," Art ordered calmly. By now he was on his feet, walking forward, pointing his rifle at them.

"Suppose we just put our guns back in our belts and walk away," Cally said.

"Put them on the ground," Art repeated. "Only, do it real slow. You don't want to upset Dog now, do you?"

"No, no, we don't want to upset him," Cally said. "Do what he says, Angus."

Holding their guns, they started to bend down.

"Turn the guns around," Art said. "Hold them by the ends of the barrels."

"Mister, these things is loaded and charged," Cally said. "We'd be fools to hold them by the ends of the barrels."

"You'll be dead if you don't," Art said, moving his rifle menacingly to cover Cally.

"All right, all right," Cally said. First Cally, and then Angus, turned their pistols around so they were holding them by the ends of the barrels. Then, bending over, they put their guns down, all under the watchful eyes of Dog and Art.

"It's after midnight. Seems to me that's a little late to be making a sociable visit on a man's camp. So, what are you boys doing here?" Art asked.

"Nothing," Cally replied. "We just seen the boat tied up and was sort of wonderin' who you was and what you was doin' here."

"Who I am is none of your business," Art said. "And as to what I'm doing here, I was trying to get a little rest."

"What are you carryin' on that boat of your'n?"

"That's none of your business either," Art said. He made a waving motion with his rifle. "I expect you two boys better get on now."

"What about our guns?"

"Leave 'em."

"Them guns cost money, mister. We can't just leave 'em here."

"Come back for them in the mornin'. I'll leave 'em in the river."

"By the river?"

"In the river."

"They'll get all rusted."

"Clean them. Now, get." Art made another wave with his rifle, and the two men, with one final look at Dog, turned and started walking quickly back across the meadow. By the time they reached the tree line, they were both running.

Art laughed, then rubbed Dog behind the ears. "Well, now, Dog," he said. "You're turnin' into a pretty good partner to a man."

Blackfoot Village, Upper Missouri River, Monday, July 5, 1824

Because Wak Tha Go had a sister who was married to a Blackfoot Indian, he was welcomed in the village of the Blackfeet. This was good, because he was no longer welcome in the village of the Arikara. Four young men who had followed him when he led the war party on an adventure had been killed. The wives and mothers, the sisters and brothers of those who were killed were angry with Wak Tha Go.

In this way Wak Tha Go was eating dinner in the lodge of his sister when her husband, Yellow Dog, came to him.

"Crazy Wolf is holding a council now, and he wants you to come," Yellow Dog said.

"I will come," Wak Tha Go said. He finished the last of the piece of meat he was eating. Wiping his fingers on his chest, he followed the husband of his sister through the village and to the circle where the council was meeting.

They were seated around the fire. Wak Tha Go sat in the outer ring of the circle. If he sat in the inner circle, and had been asked to move back, it would have brought him dishonor. By sitting in the outer circle, it would bring him honor to be invited to move closer to the fire, which he fully expected to happen.

"Wak Tha Go," Crazy Wolf said. "Come, sit in the inner circle with the elders of this band."

There were a few grunts of recognition and respect as Wak Tha Go, his presence now honored by Crazy Wolf's invitation, moved to the inner circle.

"I will tell a story," Crazy Wolf said simply once Wak Tha Go was seated.

"During the geese-flying time, white soldiers made war on the Arikara people. They came in the night, while the people slept, and they killed many and set fire to the tepees and burned food and blankets. They also stole many horses, but Wak Tha Go, who is a brave warrior, did not forget what the white soldiers did, and he made war against them. But now the Arikara want war no more, and The Peacemaker has said that he will make peace with the white soldiers. But Wak Tha Go will not make peace with the white soldiers, so he has come to us, the Blackfoot people. So I say, from this day until there are no more days, Wak Tha Go will be a Blackfoot."

Crazy Wolf pointed to Wak Tha Go as he spoke, and the others smiled and congratulated him for making war against the white soldiers, and for coming to join them.

"Wak Tha Go, will you speak now?" Crazy Wolf said.

Nodding, Wak Tha Go stood, then turned to face the other Indians.

"I have heard that the Blackfeet turn away the white trappers who come to your land to hunt the beaver.

"I have heard that the warriors of the Blackfeet have fought bravely and well against the trappers while other villages and nations surrender to the white trappers.

"I have heard that there is no warrior more fierce than a warrior of the Blackfeet."

"Ai, yi, yi, yieee!!!" the others cheered.

"What would you have of us, Wak Tha Go?" Crazy Wolf asked. "You have abandoned your people because the Arikara want to make peace with the whites? Have you come to bring the word of peace from your people?"

"No," Wak Tha Go answered resolutely. "I have come to the Blackfeet because only the Blackfeet will make war. The Arikara are no longer my people. They are more rabbits than people. I belong to the Piegan Blackfeet."

"Show us that you are deserving," Crazy Wolf said. "Become a leader of our warriors."

"I will," Wak Tha Go answered, and his response was greeted by more cheering.

The council was not yet over, but Wak Tha Go left. He knew that it was better to leave while they wanted him to stay, than it was to stay when they wanted him to go.

He would lead a war party of Blackfeet warriors, and he would count many coups and he would steal many things. But what he wanted to do more than anything else was to kill Artoor, the white man he had seen on the boat. Wak Tha Go had learned Artoor's name from Tetonka, the Mandan who had traded with him.

St. Louis, Wednesday, July 21, 1824

He put in at LaClede's Landing in St. Louis after two months on the river. Even from the river, he could see that the city had changed a lot since he was last here many years before. Missouri was a state in the Union of States now, and St. Louis had grown from a frontier town to a bustling, prosperous city of nearly ten thousand people. That was a lot of people—too many people for someone like Art who had grown accustomed to life in the wilderness and going for days or weeks without seeing another human soul.

A friendly hand ashore took the rope Art tossed to him, and made the boat secure.

"You'll be wantin' to sell them furs, I reckon," the man said.

"You buying?" Art asked.

"No, Mr. Ashley does the buying. I just work for him."

"That would be William Ashley?"

"Yes, sir. You know him, I expect."

"I know of him. If he's the one buying, I'm selling."

"Very good, sir. If you'll permit me, I'll get the plews loaded and down to Ashley's office."

"I'd appreciate that," Art said, surprised to find someone so helpful upon his arrival. He hoped for his sake that the man was honest as well.

Fifteen minutes later the pelts were loaded onto an ox-cart and hauled down to Ashley's office. Art sat with his fur bundles, his legs dangling over the back as the cart rolled up Market Street. Dog followed along behind the cart, seeming not to mind the people and the traffic everywhere. Of course, the people gave Dog a wide berth.

St. Louis was a vibrant city, alive with the pulse of commerce and enterprise: the scream of a steam-powered sawmill, the sound of steamboat whistles from the river, the hiss and boom of the boats' engines, and the clatter of wagons rolling across cobblestone streets. To someone used to solitude so quiet that he could hear the flutter of a

bird's wings, the noise of civilization was almost unbear-
able.

The cart stopped in front of a two-story building. A
neatly painted sign out front read: FURS BOUGHT AND SOLD,
WILLIAM ASHLEY, PROP.

Even before Art dismounted, a dignified-looking man,
wearing mustard-colored trousers and a blue jacket, came
out of the building and began looking Art's load over. The
man's whiskers were neatly trimmed, his hands clean, his
eyes bright and direct.

"You've got some good-looking plews here," he said.

"Would you be Ashley?" Art asked.

"Indeed that is who I am, sir, William Ashley, at your
service." He bowed slightly, politely, but not in servility.

"Then you're the man Clyde told me to look up."

"Clyde?"

"Clyde Barnes."

"Ah, yes," Ashley said, smiling. "I know of Mr. Barnes.
How is he?"

"He's dead. Killed by Indians on our way downriver."

"I'm sincerely sorry to hear that. Blackfeet?"

"Arikara."

"I see. Well, the Blackfeet have always been hostile to
our fur-trading enterprise, but the problem with the
Arikara is more recent."

"Is it true that a couple of your men traded bad whiskey
to the Arikara for pelts?"

"Word does get around, doesn't it?" Ashley said. "Yes,
unfortunately it is true. The men were working for me. But
the idea of trading whiskey for plews was their own. I
don't do business that way, never have, and never will. Believe me, Mr. McDill and Mr. Caviness were severely
reprimanded."

"Reprimanded? What does that mean?"

"It means I gave them a good scolding."

"People have gotten killed over that, and more people are likely to get killed, and all you did was give them a scolding?"

"I have no authority to do anything more to them," Ashley said. "I'm not the law."

"I reckon not."

"What's your name, sir?" Ashley asked.

"Art," the young trapper said simply.

"Art? Art what?"

"Just Art."

"Well, I reckon if Art is enough for you, it's enough for me," Ashley said.

Since leaving home at an early age, Art had made a point of never using his last name. This way, he figured, he would never do anything that would bring dishonor to his family back in Ohio. He needn't have worried about such a thing, for so far in his young life, he had been the epitome of honorable conduct. It was the way of the man that the onetime runaway boy had become.

"That your animal?" Mr. Ashley asked, pointing to Dog, who stood at alert between the cart and Art.

"Not mine, but we have traveled a piece together."

"Tell you what, Art. Give me a day to get your plews counted and graded. Come on back tomorrow morning and I'll have your money."

"All right," Art agreed. He started to leave, then caught himself and turned back. "Do you suppose I could have twenty dollars now?" he asked.

Ashley chuckled knowingly. He had dealt with mountain men for a long time. "Want to take advantage of the big city, do you? Yes, of course you can. You can have much more than that, if you need it."

"Twenty is enough."

"Come on inside."

Art followed Ashley into his storehouse. As the door

opened, a little bell attached to the top of the door rang. Surprised, Art looked up at it.

Ashley chuckled. "If I'm in the back, that little bell lets me know when someone comes in," he explained.

The back of the store that Ashley mentioned was his counting and grading room. A counter separated the front of the store from the back, and through a door that led into the back, Art could see several long tables around which men were working.

Ashley went around behind the counter, took twenty dollars from a strongbox, then opened a ledger book and wrote Art's name in it. Beside Art's he wrote, "Twenty dollars on advance." He turned the book around and handed the quill pen to Art. "Make your mark here," he said.

"I can read and write," Art said.

"A mountain man who can read and write? I'm impressed."

"Mr. Ashley, do you know a man by the name of Seamus O'Connor?"

"Seamus O'Connor? It doesn't ring a bell with me."

"He owned a place called the Irish Tavern. I used to have friends who spent time there: a man named Tony, another named James O'Leary."

"Ah, yes, I remember them. O'Leary was a big strapping fellow. And the other—Tony, you say? They worked for Ed Gordon down at the wagon-freight yard."

"Yes!" Art said, smiling broadly. "That's them. Do you know where I can find them?"

Ashley shook his head sadly. "They're dead, son. Both of them."

"What? How?"

"They were unloading a riverboat when the boiler exploded. Killed Gordon and six of his men, including your two friends Tony and James."

"Oh."

"Sorry to have to be the one to tell you."

"That's all right," Art said. "Those things happen." He held up the silver coins. "Thanks for the advance."

With Dog alongside, Art left the store and walked on up Market Street, looking for the Irish Tavern. It was no more. In its place was something called the Joseph LaBarge Tavern. Art was standing in front of it, looking it over, when he heard a woman's voice call out from just inside the building.

"No, please, don't! It was an accident!"

"You bitch! I'll teach you to be clumsy around me!" a harsh voice said. The voice was followed by a smacking sound and as Art looked up, he saw a young woman propelled backward through the open front door. She fell on the porch, and a large, gross-looking man stomped out of the saloon behind her.

"Please," the young woman begged. "I didn't mean to spill the beer on you." She tried to get up, but as she did so, the big ugly man hit her again, knocking her back down onto the porch. She rolled over onto her hands and knees and tried to escape him that way, but he followed after her and kicked her. She cried out in pain.

Art stepped up onto the porch behind the man.

"I'll learn you to spill beer on me, you worthless whore. I'll kick your ass clear into Illinois," the man growled at the young woman, who was still cowering on the wooden planks of the porch.

"Sir?" Art said from just behind the man.

"What do you . . ." the man started to ask, but he was unable to finish his question because as soon as he turned toward Art, the young mountain man brought the butt of his rifle up in a smashing blow to the man's face. The blow knocked out two of the man's teeth, broke his nose, and sent a stream of blood gushing down across his mouth and into his beard. If he hadn't been ugly before, he certainly was now. His eyes rolled up into his head, and he dropped heavily to the porch.

The young woman, now on her knees, looked on in shock and fear as Art reached his hand for her.

"Ma'am, may I help you up?" he asked.

The woman made no effort to take his hand.

"Don't be afraid. No one's going to hurt you anymore," Art said. His hand was still extended toward her.

Hesitantly, the woman took his hand, and Art pulled her to her feet.

"I—I didn't mean to spill the beer," she said. "But he grabbed me as I walked by. I was startled. I couldn't help it. I tried to explain and apologize, but he wouldn't listen."

"Ma'am, you don't owe an explanation or an apology to anyone," Art said reassuringly. "Least of all to a pig like him. Why don't you come back inside and sit down until you feel better."

"Thank you," the young woman said.

Art led her back toward the front door of the saloon, which was still open, and now crowded with many patrons who, drawn by the commotion out front, had come to the door to see what was going on. They made way for Art, the woman, and Dog.

"Hey!" the man behind the bar called. "You can't bring your dog in here."

"He's not my dog, and I'm not bringing him anywhere, he's just with me."

"Get him out of here."

"You get him out," Art said.

"You two, get him out," the man behind the bar said, pointing to a couple of the patrons. The two men started toward Dog, but he bared his wolflike fangs at them and growled. They stopped in their tracks.

"Get him yourself, LaBarge," one of them said.

LaBarge came out from behind the bar, looked at Dog, then shrugged. "He can stay if he don't cause no trouble," he said.

The others laughed.

Art walked all the way to the rear of the saloon, then chose a chair that put his back to the wall and gave him a good view of the entire room. Dog trotted along with him, then curled up alongside. Art was sitting next to an iron stove. The stove was cold and empty now, but still smelled of smoke and charcoal from its winter use. Once again, the proprietor, LaBarge, came out from behind the bar.

"Carla, I expect you'd better get back to work now," LaBarge said.

"Yes, Mr. LaBarge."

"Give her a chance to catch her breath," Art said.

"You paying her wages, mister?" LaBarge asked.

"No."

"I am. So she'll do what I say. Get back to work, Carla. And be more careful 'bout spilling beer on the customers."

"Yes, sir," Carla said. Looking at Art, she smiled. "What can I get you?"

"A beer."

"It's on the house," LaBarge said.

"Thanks."

"I reckon you done what you thought was right, hittin' Shardeen like that. But it's goin' to get you kilt. Shardeen ain't a man you want to mess with."

A moment later Carla brought Art his beer and, smiling shyly, set it in front of him. From the folds of her dress, she removed a couple of boiled eggs, wet from the brine in which they were stored. "These here two hen's eggs is from me," she said.

"Thank you, Carla," Art said, smiling up at her.

Carla walked away, and had just returned to the bar when the front door burst open and the man Art had encountered, the one LaBarge had called Shardeen, rushed inside. He was carrying two charged pistols, one in either hand.

"Where is that son of a bitch!" he yelled angrily. His nose was flattened almost beyond recognition, his eyes were black and shiny, and his beard was matted with blood.

When Shardeen entered, everyone else in the saloon scattered, moving so quickly that chairs tumbled over and tables were pushed out of the way. Art's rifle was leaning against the wall behind him. It was loaded, but not primed, so even if he could get to it, it wouldn't do him any good at this moment.

Seeing Art in the back of the saloon, Shardeen let out a loud bellow and shot at him. There was a flash of fire and a puff of smoke. The bullet crashed into the smokestack of the stove, sending out a puff of soot. With a shout of frustrated anger over his miss, Shardeen raised his other pistol and fired it as well. This one slammed into the wall behind Art. Art had not moved a muscle since the big man had entered the tavern.

Dog jumped up and growled at Shardeen.

"No, Dog," Art said quietly. "I'd better handle this myself."

With both pistols empty, Shardeen pulled his knife and, with an angry roar, rushed across the room toward Art. Now Art moved. He pulled his own knife and waited for him. At the last moment, Art danced to one side, rather like a bullfighter avoiding a charge, and like a bullfighter, thrust toward Shardeen. His knife went in smoothly, just under Shardeen's rib cage. With a grunt, Shardeen stopped, then staggered and fell. Art twisted his knife so that, as Shardeen went down, the brute's own weight caused the blade to open him up, spilling blood and steaming intestines. Art pulled the knife out. Shardeen fell face down on the floor, flopped a couple of times like a fish out of water, and then was still.

"Is he dead?" Carla asked. She had fled, in terror, to the back corner of the room, but peeked out.

"I reckon he is," Art said, pouring beer on his hand to rinse away the blood.

"Get him out of here," LaBarge said.

"Hold it!" a voice called from the front. The order came from a member of the St. Louis Constabulary, the militia group that Mayor Lane depended upon to maintain order in the city. "You people just leave him right where he is until I find out what happened here."

"Shardeen got hisself kilt, that's what happened," LaBarge said. "And if truth be told, there ain't nobody in St. Louis likely to shed a tear over the sonofabitch."

"I agree that if anybody in this town needed killin' it was Shardeen," the constable said. "But just bein' downright mean don't give someone the right to kill him. Who did it?"

"I did," Art said.

"And who might you be?"

"Art."

"Art? Art what?"

"Art's enough."

"No it ain't enough, mister. Not when murder's concerned."

"Oh hell, John," LaBarge said to the constable. "Art didn't murder Shardeen. He killed him in self-defense. Ever'one in here will testify to that."

"That's right, Constable," one of the customers said. "Shardeen come in here a-blazin' away at this young fella."

"Who are you?"

"The name is Matthews. Joe Matthews."

"You're saying Shardeen shot first?"

"He didn't shoot first," Matthews started, but he was interrupted by the constable.

"Well if Shardeen didn't shoot first, how can it be self-defense?"

"You didn't let me finish. He didn't shoot first. He was the only one who shot."

"That's right," LaBarge said. "And if you'll take a look over there, you'll see where them two bullets went. One into the wall and the other one into my stovepipe. Which, incidentally, I'm going to have to replace before next winter, so if ol' Shardeen has any money in his pocket, by rights it should come to me."

"How'd you kill him if you didn't shoot him?"

"With a knife," Art replied.

"After Shardeen come at him with a knife," Matthews added quickly.

"All right, maybe you'd better come with me," the constable said. As the constable started toward Art, LaBarge put his hand out to stop him.

"Now, hold on there, John. I done told you it was self-defense, and there ain't a man present but won't back me up. You got no call to be takin' him in."

"Hear, hear!" some of the others shouted.

"I got Mayor Lane to worry about," the constable said. "I've got to answer to him."

"All you got to do is tell him that you investigated it and found it to be self-defense, pure and simple," LaBarge said. "Besides which, the mayor is so tied up with this here General Lafayette fella comin' to town, that he don't want to be bothered with somethin' like this, and you damn well know it."

The constable stroked his jaw for a moment as he considered LaBarge's words. Everyone in the saloon stared at him, waiting for his answer. Finally, he nodded in resignation.

"I reckon you're right," he said. "A jury is sure to find

him innocent, so why go to the bother? Ain't goin' to be no charge here."

Every patron in the saloon erupted in a loud cheer.

"Now," LaBarge said, pointing to Shardeen's body. "Someone get this trash out of here."

Five

After leaving LaBarge's Tavern, Art passed by Chardonnay's, a restaurant that advertised itself as "St. Louis's finest dining establishment." It had been a long time since he had eaten a meal he didn't cook himself, and even longer than that since he had eaten in a restaurant, let alone a fancy "establishment" like this one. Opening the door just a crack, he took a sniff. Whatever they were cooking smelled awfully good to him.

"Dog, I expect you'd better not go in here with me," he said. This place was very different than LaBarge's, for sure.

Dog looked up at him as if challenging him.

"Don't look at me like that. This just isn't a place for dogs, that's all. Why don't you just wait for me over there, and I'll bring you something to eat."

Shaking himself in a way that caused his loose skin to make a flapping sound, Dog walked over to the corner of the porch, made a few quick turns, then settled down. His eyes were closed even before Art went inside.

A well-dressed, dignified-looking man came to his table. "May I take your order, sir?" he asked in an affected, cultured voice.

"What's good?" Art asked as he looked at the menu.

"Sir, I assure you everything on our menu is without parallel."

"That means it's good?" Art asked.

"Indeed it does, sir."

"All right then, I'll have pork chops, fried potatoes, and a half-dozen hen's eggs."

The waiter looked chagrined. "I beg your pardon, sir. Did you say pork chops, fried potatoes, and eggs?" he asked.

"Yes."

"Excuse my asking, sir, but why would you come here to order such pedestrian fare? We have rack of lamb, pork tenderloin, coq au vin, and many other viands not served by any other restaurant in the city. You can get what you just ordered at any cheap hotel in town."

"You do have pork chops, potatoes, and eggs, don't you? Hen's eggs now, not those nasty things from a guinea."

"Yes, of course we have those things, but . . ."

"And biscuits?"

"Our bread is baked fresh daily."

"Biscuits?" Art repeated.

"Yes, sir. We can prepare biscuits."

"Good. I'll have biscuits. And pie. Do you have any pie?"

"Apple and pecan."

"All right."

"All right?" the waiter asked, confused by his answer.

"All right, I'll have apple and pecan."

"Sir, you do understand, do you not, that by apple and pecan, I'm referring to two separate pies. I don't mean something like apple-pecan pie."

"Yes, I want one of each."

"Very good, sir."

"I'll have beer with my dinner, and coffee with my pie," Art concluded.

"Yes, sir," the waiter said. "I must say, sir, your appetite is quite prodigious."

"That's all right. I don't reckon it's catchin'," Art said.

He wasn't sure whether he was having fun, but he knew that the waiter wasn't.

"Indeed, sir," the waiter replied without a smile.

Art watched the waiter until he disappeared into the kitchen. Out of the corner of his eye, he saw someone standing just inside the front door, looking at him. It was a woman.

"Art?" the woman said.

At first, Art couldn't see her features clearly, because she was standing in silhouette. He put his hand up to shield his eyes. Realizing that she wasn't clearly visible, the woman moved out of the bright light.

"Do you recognize me now?" she asked. The woman was quite pretty, with dark, almost black hair, brown eyes, and a clear, olive complexion.

"Jennie?" Art said, recognizing someone from his past. "Jennie, is that you?"

With a happy little laugh, Jennie hurried to him. Art stood and they embraced.

"Yes, it's me. I thought I would never see you again," Jennie said.

"Sit down, sit down," Art told her. "Have dinner with me."

"Oh, I don't know," Jennie demurred. "I've never been in here before. This is a pretty fancy place. I'm not sure I would be welcome."

"You're welcome anywhere I'm welcome," Art said.

Hesitantly, and looking around as if expecting to be tossed out at any moment, Jennie sat at the table with Art.

"When Carla described the person who came to her rescue, I thought of you. Then when she said that the only name you gave the deputy was Art, I knew it was you. So I checked with Mr. Ashley, and he said he saw you come into Chardonnay's. I just had to come in here to see for myself."

"I'm glad you did," Art said. "I'm really happy to see you, Jennie. How are you doing? What are you doing in St. Louie?"

"I own my own whorehouse," Jennie said proudly and without irony. "Carla, the girl you helped, is one of my boarders."

"I thought she worked for LaBarge."

"She does. She just works for me part-time—but not as a, well . . . you know what I mean, I think. What are *you* doing in St. Louis?"

"I brought in my winter's trapping," Art said. "I could have sold it at Rendezvous, but I decided to bring the plews in myself this time."

"Rendezvous," Jennie said. "Oh, I remember those. They were always exciting, and could have been fun if I hadn't been hauled around as Eby's slave."

At that moment the officious waiter came out of the kitchen carrying Art's order on a tray. Seeing Jennie, he stopped. "What are you doing here?" he asked.

"She is with me," Art said. "She would like to order. I've invited her to eat with me."

"No," the waiter said. "Absolutely not. I do not allow her kind in here."

"You do not allow?" Art asked. "I thought you were just the waiter. What does the owner say?"

The waiter smiled. "The owner is my father-in-law. He would say exactly what I am saying. Prostitutes are not allowed in here."

Jennie reached her hand across the table and put it on Art's hand.

"It's all right, Art," Jennie said. "I told you that I wouldn't be welcome. I'll leave now. I don't want to make any trouble."

"Oh, there's no trouble," Art said easily. He stood. "I'll leave with you."

"But sir, you aren't being asked to leave," the waiter said.

"As far as I'm concerned, I was," Art said. "I told you the lady was my friend."

"But what about your food?" the waiter said.

"You eat it."

The waiter looked at the pork chops, fried potatoes, and half-dozen eggs.

"Oh, sir, I couldn't possibly eat . . . this," he said, screwing his mouth up distastefully.

"Then feed it to the pigs," Art said. "Come, Jennie." He started toward the front door with her.

"But you haven't paid for your meal," the waiter called to him.

"What meal? You don't expect me to pay for a meal I haven't eaten, do you?" Art called back.

Jennie laughed. "Why don't you come with me?" she asked. "I'll fix you the best meal you've ever eaten."

"Miss Jennie, I'll just take you up on that," Art said.

As they stepped out the front door of the restaurant, Dog stood up and started toward them.

"Oh!" Jennie said, recoiling back against Art.

Art chuckled. "Relax, he won't hurt you."

"What is that? A wolf?"

"No, Dog is a dog."

"Dog is a dog?"

"Yes. His name is Dog."

"Why would you name him something like that?"

"That's the name he picked out for himself," Art said without further explanation.

"Well, I certainly don't understand men—or dogs, in this case," she said with a slight laugh.

Art finally got his pork chops, fried potatoes, eggs, biscuits, and gravy, and he was positive the meal was better here than it would ever have been at that fancy restaurant. Jennie not only cooked his supper for him, it was obvious that she enjoyed doing it.

"It's nice having someone to cook for," Jennie said as she took a steaming apple pie from the oven.

"It's nice having someone to cook for me," Art said.

"Is it?"

"Yes, of course it is." He looked into her dark eyes and liked what he saw there. He remembered every moment he had been in her presence, everything that had happened to them together.

"Dog seems to be enjoying his meal," Jennie said. Dog was eating from a plate she had put on the floor for him. "You, me, Dog, it's almost like a family, isn't it? I mean we could . . ." Jennie stopped in mid-thought and looked at Art with a wistful smile. Her eyes were deep and pensive and Art looked directly into them. Then he turned away quickly, as if ashamed of the fact that he had gotten a momentary glimpse of her unguarded soul.

Realizing that she had gone further then she intended, she changed the subject. "Uh, do you want some more coffee?"

Art held out his cup. "Yes, I'd love some," he said. "Thank you."

Art ate ravenously, enjoying the meal as much as any he had ever eaten, appreciating it as much for Jennie's company as for the food itself. Her voice, her laugh washed over him like a rain shower. And the food was delicious.

"Oh," he said after he had put away his third piece of pie. "I have something for you."

Jennie looked surprised. "You have something for me? But how could that be? Did you know you were going to see me here?"

"No," Art said. He smiled. "Finding you here was a very happy accident."

"Then I don't understand. What do you mean you have something for me?"

"It's something that a friend of mine bought," he said. "And his last wish was that I give it to a pretty girl. Well, you are the prettiest girl I know."

"Why, thank you, Art," Jennie said, beaming over the compliment. "But what do you mean, his last wish?"

He told Jennie about Clyde, how Clyde was one of the two men who had rescued him many years ago, and how Clyde had been coming to St. Louis with him. He told also of the Indian attack that had cost Clyde his life.

"I know who Clyde is," Jennie said, wiping away a tear. "He is the one who saved your life by shooting Bruce Eby. His name is also on my letter of manumission. He was one of the witnesses, along with Pierre Garneau."

"They were good men, both of them," Art said. He pulled the dress from his pack and showed it to her.

"Oh, Art!" Jennie said. "It is beautiful!" She reached for it. "Can I?"

"Of course. It's yours."

Jennie held it up to herself. "I don't think I've ever seen anything as beautiful," she said. She held up her finger. "Wait, I'll be back."

Jennie disappeared for a few minutes, then returned, wearing the dress. She had removed her heavy "professional" makeup. Now, in the simple and beautiful Indian dress of white doeskin, Art could see her for what she really was—the girl he remembered her to have been some dozen years before. He felt a catch in his breath.

"Jennie," he said quietly, the words almost caught in his throat. "You look like a queen."

Jennie laughed, then did a pirouette and a curtsy. "Why, thank you, kind sir," she said. "And thank you for this dress. I will treasure it, always."

Thursday, July 22, 1824

St. Louis was too noisy. It seemed to Art that there had been something going on all night long, from boat whistles, to bells, to people laughing and yelling in the saloons and dram shops. Then, shortly after sunrise, the sawmill started again, its terrible screech filling the morning air. Though he had barely managed to sleep through all the other noise, this one woke him up.

Art, bare from the waist up, stood at the second-floor window, looking out on the busy street below. Across the street, a shopkeeper was sweeping his front porch, the broom making a scratching sound against the planking. A fully packed wagon clattered by while, somewhere nearby, a carpenter was hammering vigorously.

"Good morning," Jennie said. Coming up behind him, she put her arms around him and leaned into his back. By that action, Art realized that she was naked. "Do you want some breakfast?" she asked.

"Uh, maybe later," Art said, turning toward her.

With her now-familiar happy little laugh, Jennie led him back to the bed they had shared the night before. Dog, lying curled up over in the corner, didn't even open his eyes.

"I never knew anyone who could eat as many eggs as you can," Jennie said with a laugh as she put two more onto Art's breakfast plate.

"I like hen's eggs," Art said. "And there aren't that many chickens in the mountains, so anytime I get into town, I eat as many as I can."

"It's a good thing you don't live in town. You'd keep a whole henhouse busy just laying eggs for you."

Art broke the egg, then sopped up the yellow with a biscuit.

"No chance of me ever living in town," Art said. "I couldn't stand the noise. And as for hens . . ." He just grinned.

"Most folks who live here just sort of blank it out of their minds," Jennie said. "It gets to where you don't even hear it anymore."

"For you maybe, not for me."

"How long are you going to stay in town?"

"Only another day or two," Art replied. "I'll need to get supplies and some livestock and start back for this winter's trapping."

"So, you're going to go back into the mountains all alone?"

"Yes. That is, I'll be alone unless Dog comes with me."

"Is Dog going with you?" she asked pointedly.

Art looked over at Dog, who, having eaten his own breakfast, was lying on the floor with his chin resting on his two front paws. "I don't know, that's up to Dog."

"You say you couldn't live in the city because of the noise. I don't know how you can spend an entire winter in the mountains all by yourself. I know I certainly couldn't."

"It's nice up there," Art said. "The stars are so big and bright that you get the feeling you could reach up and pull one down. And the silence is wonderful. After the first snow, it is so quiet that you can hear the wind singing through pine boughs half a mile away."

"You can keep your silence. I prefer civilization."

"Well, I reckon that's why God didn't make everything the same color," Art said. Finishing his eggs, he stood up. "I'd better see to my supplies."

"You don't have to leave, you know," Jennie said. "You could stay here in St. Louis. Or we could go somewhere else, down to New Orleans maybe."

Art looked at Jennie for a long time before he opened his mouth. Just as he started to speak, Jennie put out her hand to stop him.

"No, don't," she said. She shook her head and bit her bottom lip.

"Don't what?"

"Don't say what you were going to say."

"How do you know what I was going to say?"

"I just know, that's all. You were going to tell me that there could never be anything between us."

Art took Jennie's hand in his.

"I wasn't going to say that, Jennie. There is something between us, and there always will be. But I can't live in the city, and you wouldn't survive in the mountains. The Indians have a saying. A fish and a bird might fall in love, but where would they live?"

Jennie's eyes flooded, then a tear slid down each cheek. She forced a smile through the tears.

"Which one of us is the fish?" she asked. "And which is the bird?"

"You're the bird," Art said. "A beautiful bird." He raised Jennie's hand to her own cheek and caught each of the tears with the tips of her fingers. Then he moved those fingers to his lips, where he kissed them.

Jennie nodded, struggled to speak. "Art, will you come back? Will I see you again?"

"I'm sure of it," Art said.

Jennie said, "I think you will be back too. And until you do return, I will always have last night to remember you—to remember us by."

* * *

The strange small doorbell jingled as Art stepped into William Ashley's furrier establishment. Ashley came from the back of the building. He was as dapper and precise as he had been at their first meeting.

"Well, if it isn't my friend with no last name," Ashley greeted. "Come for your money, I suppose?"

"Yes, sir."

"Well, I've got it right here," Ashley said. He opened a ledger book and ran his finger down the column until he came to what he was looking for. "They were nearly all top-quality plews, by the way. Out of one hundred eighty-three, only thirty-seven were less than first-class. That leaves one hundred forty-six at five dollars and ten cents each, coming to seven hundred forty-four dollars and sixty cents; thirty-seven at three and a half dollars each, for one hundred twenty-nine dollars and fifty cents, minus the twenty-dollar advance brings it to a grand total of eight hundred fifty-four dollars and ten cents. How do you want that, in cash, credit, or a bank draft?"

"Credit?"

"That means I'll keep it on the books for you until you leave. That way you won't be carrying so much money around."

"Oh," Art said. He stroked his jaw as he studied Ashley for a long moment.

Ashley chuckled. "Look, if you're worried about me cheating you out of the money, why don't I just give it to you now."

"Oh, I'm not worried about you cheating me," Art said. "I think I could convince you to give me what is mine."

This time Ashley's chuckle was an out-and-out laugh. "I reckon you could, Art, I reckon you could. I heard about the little fracas between you and Shardeen down at LaBarge's Tavern yesterday. Fact is, the whole town has heard of it in gruesome detail. You don't strike me as the kind of person a man would want to cross."

"I wouldn't take too kindly to it," Art agreed. "I tell you what, give me another twenty dollars. I'll collect the rest later."

Ashley counted out twenty more silver dollar coins, made another entry in the book, then handed them over to Art.

"Now don't spend that all in one place," he quipped.

"Why not?" Art replied, not understanding the joke that was tired even in those days.

Ashley laughed, shook his head, and held up his hand. "Never mind. It's your money, you can spend it any way you want to, with my hearty congratulations."

When Art left Ashley, he saw quite a crowd gathered down by the waterfront and, wondering what it was, walked down to see.

"It's the Marquis de Lafayette," someone told him. "You know, the French hero who helped us gain our independence from England?"

"I've heard of him," Art said. "But I didn't know he was still alive."

"He's sixty-seven years old," Art's informant told him. "I read about him in the newspaper."

"What's he doing in St. Louis?"

"He's touring America. From here, he is going to go downriver to New Orleans."

Nine carriages were waiting at the riverfront to carry the Marquis de Lafayette and his party of dignitaries to the home of Major Pierre Chouteau, where Mayor William Carr Lane would present the great Revolutionary War hero and confidant of George Washington with the ceremonial keys to the city. Lafayette's boat had been spotted down-river, and a fast rider had brought the news to St. Louis. As a result of the early warning, not only the carriages of the official party were on hand, but so were a couple thousand St. Louis citizens, resulting in the crowd Art had encountered.

A preacher, wearing a long black coat and a stovepipe hat, was working the crowd. He had a hooked nose and a protruding chin so that it wasn't too hard to imagine the chin and nose actually touching each other. He was rail-thin. As he spoke, he stabbed at the air with a bony finger.

"Hell and damnation, eternal perdition waits for every one of you. This is a city of sin and debauchery, a den of iniquity! Turn your backs on temptation, order Satan to get behind you. For if you fail to do this, if you close the door to God's holy word, worms will eat your rotting body and maggots will gnaw at your innards."

The preacher delivered his sermon in a loud, singsong voice, pausing between every sentence for an audible gasp of air.

"I am the way and the life, says the Lord, and only by me will you be saved!"

The sound of an approaching boat whistle could be heard over the preacher's sermon.

"Here he comes!" someone shouted.

Everyone rushed down to the wharf, including those who had been listening to the preacher, but the preacher was undaunted. He continued his delivery with as much zeal as he had displayed when he was surrounded by a large audience.

Art joined the others who had gathered to watch the arrival of the Frenchman who had come to help the Americans during the Revolutionary War. Lafayette was old, with a shock of bright-silver hair, but he stood erect and moved with a sprightly step down the gangplank and onto the riverbank. He was met by Mayor Lane, who escorted him to the first in the line of carriages.

"Thank you, General!" someone in the crowd called, and all, including Art, began to applaud.

Lafayette waved at the crowd as his carriage departed. The team of matched white horses pranced saucily, making hollow clops on the cobblestone street.

As the crowd began to dissipate, Art decided to go check on his furs. The preacher was still going strong, renewed and invigorated by the fact that he had regained much of his audience.

Six

Art spent the better part of the day just wandering around town, finding some parts of St. Louis that were familiar to him, and marveling at the tremendous growth of the city since he was last here. Mid-afternoon found him back down by the riverfront, where he saw the same preacher he had seen in the morning. The preacher was still going strong, railing loudly against all the sins of man and underscoring those sins with very vivid descriptions of them.

Art stayed to listen for a few minutes, marveling at the strength of the preacher's voice, then turned away to continue his survey of the town. That was when he heard it.

KABOOM!

The explosion was so loud that it shattered windows all over St. Louis. The shock wave rolled through the town, and Art could feel it in his stomach.

"What was that?" someone called.

"It come from Dunnigan's store. Look down there!" another said.

When Art looked in the direction pointed, he saw a huge cloud of smoke billowing up from one of the buildings. Fire was leaping from the roof.

"We better get down there. Those folks are going to need help," another shouted.

A crowd gathered quickly around Dunnigan's store, and Art went with them, watching as the building burned furiously. From up the street he heard the sound of a clanging bell and galloping horses.

"Here comes the fire engine!" someone shouted.

"Ain't nothin' left they can do," another said.

The team pulling the fire wagon came to a halt in front of the burning building. The driver and his assistant jumped down from the wagon seat and began playing out the hoses.

"You men . . . get on the pumps!" the driver shouted and a half-dozen men, three on each side, began pumping the handles to build up the pressure. Within a shorter time than Art would have imagined, a powerful stream of water gushed from the hose toward the fire. Others present grabbed buckets and began replacing the water in the tank that was pumped out by the men on the pump handles.

After several minutes of diligent application of the water, the men gained control of the fire. The flames drew down, then disappeared altogether. After several more minutes, even the large billows of smoke were gone, replaced by a few smoldering embers. The building was totally destroyed, but quick action had prevented the fire from spreading to the adjacent buildings.

In LaBarge's Tavern that evening, Art learned that, in addition to the storeowner, Danny Dunnigan, four other men had lost their lives in the explosion and fire.

"One of 'em must've been smokin' a pipe," someone said. "You'd think a fella would have better sense than to smoke a pipe while he was workin' around gunpowder."

"McDill, I done seen you smokin' around gunpowder lots of times," someone said.

At the mention of the name, Art looked up to see who McDill was. McDill, he knew, was one of the two men who had created the problem with the Arikara.

McDill was a big man with a flat nose and a scar that

hooked down across his left eye, causing a deformation of the eyelid before it disappeared into a bushy, red beard.

"Well, I'll tell you this," McDill said. "I got me enough sense to know how to do it without gettin' my fool head blowed off, which is more than you can say for Thompson now, ain't it?"

"Thompson was one of the men killed?" another patron asked. "George Thompson?"

"One and the same."

"Why, Thompson was supposed to lead Ashley's trading party, wasn't he?"

"He was supposed to," McDill said. He chuckled. "But I don't reckon he'll be doin' that now."

"Who you think Ashley will get to lead the party, now that Thompson's got hisself killed?"

"Well, I reckon it'll either be me, or Ben Caviness there," McDill said. He pointed to one of the men who was sharing his table. That man was nearly as big as McDill, but dark-haired and clean-shaven. "Either one of us could do the job all right."

"Better'n all right," Caviness said, his massive arms crossed against his chest.

Ben Caviness, Art knew, was the other man who had traded whiskey to the Arikara. The damage he and McDill had done had set back relations between the Indians and the whites, possibly for good. At least it would take some sincere talking and trading to win back the trust of the tribes who had once been friendly to the white fur trappers.

"Percy McDill, there ain't no way in hell William Ashley is goin' to let either one of you lead that party," a patron said. "Ever'body knows you two is the ones that caused all the troubles with the Indians last year."

"'Twas a misunderstandin' is all," McDill said. "There wa'nt nothin' wrong with that whiskey. Only mistake we made was in givin' whiskey in the first place. Indians can't handle whiskey. I know that now."

"Yeah, you know it now, but it took a war for you to learn your lesson."

"Wasn't that much of a war," McDill said. "And in the long run, it was probably a good thing."

"How can a war be a good thing?"

"It taught the Indians better than to mess with us," McDill insisted. "They's slow learners anyhow, seein's they ain't got no proper schools and such. So they need to be teached proper."

"Yeah, well, that ain't the way I look at it, and I don't think that's the way Ashley looks at it either. You notice, he didn't send nobody out to Northwest to buy furs this year. Like I say, there's no way he's goin' to make you head of his trapping party."

"I'd like to know just who it would be then, if not me or Caviness," McDill said. "Who? Matthews? Montgomery? Hoffman?" McDill snorted what may have been a laugh. "Them three is greener than a spring sapling. Couldn't none of 'em find their way up the river and back. Me 'n Caviness is the only ones that's made the trip more'n one time."

"I'm afraid McDill may be right," another said. "I reckon when it comes right down to it, Ashley won't have no choice but to put one of the two of 'em in charge."

Caviness laughed, speaking at greater length than he had in a long time. "Why so glum? You gotta find the furs if you want to make any money, and best way to do that is go with someone that knows what he's a-doin'. Very few of us around anymore, what with Injuns murderin' and accidents a-happenin'. Come on, boys, me 'n McDill will set all of you up to a drink."

After that oration, several crowded up to the bar to get a refill.

Art, who was sitting by the stove that still had Shardeen's bullet hole in the pipe, watched the whole thing with little interest. He noticed, however, that the two men sitting at the table next to him made no effort to join the others at the bar. One of the two men was the one who had spoken up for him yesterday, when the constable was investigating the incident with Shardeen. His name, Art remembered, was Joe Matthews. The other man at the table with Matthews was the one who had challenged McDill when McDill suggested that he or Caviness would lead the trapping party.

"I'll say this," Matthews said, speaking quietly to his table companion. "There ain't no way I'd go up the river with either one of them no-'count bastards in the lead. Ain't neither one of them worth a bucket of warm piss."

"Yeah," the other agreed. "If they didn't get you lost, they'd more'n likely get you kilt by Indians. Besides which, they're goin' to make life miserable for anybody that's under them."

"Still, McDill is right. There's no one else in St. Louis, right now that Ashley can get to lead the party. The good ones has already left."

"Gents," Art said. "Since you two aren't drinking with McDill and Caviness, maybe you'd let me buy you a beer. Least I can do, in thanks for your speaking out for me," he added to Matthews.

"Well, that's very generous of you, mister," Matthews said.

"I remember your name is Matthews," Art said. He looked at the man with Matthews.

"The name is Montgomery," he said. "Don Montgomery."

Art signaled to Carla and she brought three beers to the table.

"I take it you men aren't too fond of McDill and Caviness," Art said as they began drinking.

"Fond of them? I doubt their own mothers are fond of those two. Do you know them?"

Art shook his head. "No. But I had a run-in with a couple of Arikara because of them."

"You're lucky you still have your scalp," Matthews said.

"Was the fella right when he said Mr. Ashley wouldn't have any choice but to make one of them two the head of his party?" Art asked.

"Yeah," Matthews said disgustedly. "I'm afraid he was. All the good ones have left already."

"Too bad," Art said. He sat in silence for a couple of minutes, then finished his drink. "It's been nice talking to you," he said. The two men watched him leave, then fell to talking between themselves again.

Departing the tavern, Art walked back down to William Ashley's fur trading post. Seemed he couldn't stay away from the place. Again, the little tinkling bell over the doorway announced his entrance.

Almost instantly, William Ashley appeared from the back room where he had been working. He smiled at Art, as if he were genuinely glad to see him.

"Well, if it isn't the man called Art."

"Hello, Mr. Ashley," Art said.

"What can I do for you, Art?"

"It's time for me to get my supplies laid in for the winter," Art said. "But . . ."

"But what?"

Art made a motion in the general direction of the burned-out store. "Dunnigan's store got burned down. And Dunnigan was killed in the fire. Don't know where I can get outfitted now."

"I can outfit you, Art. I have all the things you'll need right here. Including livestock."

"Is that a fact? Well, I may just have to take you up on that." Art frowned and frankly eyed the successful fur trader. "Though I reckon, now that Dunnigan's place is gone, you'll be wantin' to charge a body an arm and his leg to do business with you."

"Well, a fella has a right to make a reasonable profit," Ashley said. "But I won't hold you up none, I promise you that." He opened the ledger book and took a quill pen from the inkwell. "You just tell me what you need and I'll . . ." Ashley stopped in mid-sentence, then closed the ledger book and stared at Art for a long moment. "On second thought, I've got a proposition for you. I won't charge you anything at all if you'll do a favor for me."

"What kind of favor?"

"I want you to lead the trapping party upriver," Ashley said.

Art chuckled. "The way they're talking over in the tavern, you'll be asking McDill or Caviness to lead the party."

"Well, truth to tell, I figured I was goin' to have to ask one or the other. What with Thompson dead, they're near 'bout the only ones left in town that could find their way upriver and back without wearing a quiver of arrows in their backs. But they are a couple of the biggest no-accounts that ever drew a breath, and I hate the thought of putting either one of them in charge."

"Why would you ask me to lead the party?" Art asked. "You don't know anything about me."

"I know you brought in the largest catch of any single man this season," Ashley said. "And they were all fine pelts too. I've been through 'em all. Most folks will try and pass off ten or twenty bad pelts, but you culled them out, had all the lower-quality plews together. That's plumb unusual in my experience. Why'd you do that, Art?"

"I figure if a man wants honest treatment, then he needs to be honest." The young mountain man had remembered the lessons taught to him by his father and mother, and even some of the preaching he had heard in church of a Sunday many years ago.

"That's a good policy. But it's not just the pelts you brought back that makes me think you would be a good man. I checked around on you, Art. There's some fellas in town say they remember you from the war. They say you was at New Orleans with Andy Jackson."

"That I was." It was the experience of a lifetime, and Art had been but a boy, fighting in a man's war. He drank up knowledge of men and weapons like a sponge, which had stood him in good stead in the later years.

"And they say you was made a lieutenant even though you was only fifteen years old."

Art chuckled. "I don't know that I was a real lieutenant," he said. "I think they may have just done that to be nice."

"Well, real or not, everyone who's ever heard of you has nothin' but good things to say about you. Plus, there's no denying that you can handle yourself if it comes down to it. Your run-in with Shardeen yesterday proved that. That's all I need to know that I'd like you to lead my trading party upriver."

"I'd like to do it for you, Mr. Ashley," Art said. "But I work alone." It was truer than Ashley or any man could ever know, just how alone a man he was. Except maybe now that he had Dog in his life . . .

"Oh, don't misunderstand me, Art. I'm not asking you to trap with the team. You can still work alone. All I want you to do is to lead my party upriver and"—he paused for a moment before he continued—"make peace with the Indians."

"I beg your pardon?"

Ashley stroked his jaw. He could see he had the mountain man's interest, but he needed to convince him that only he was the right man for this job. "You see, Art, that's the whole of it. Truth to tell, McDill or Caviness either one could lead the party upriver, but because of what happened with the

Arikara last year, there's likely to be even more Indians now that don't want us comin' into their territory. I need somebody that can parlay with them, work out a way that our men can trap in their country without getting their scalp lifted. I sure can't count on McDill or Caviness for that."

"I don't know," Art said, considering every angle of this proposition, and not liking it much. "There's a lot of Indians up that way: Poncas, Sioux, Cheyennes, Mandans, even the Arikaras that I could probably deal with. But there's also Blackfeet, and they are about the gol-darned orneriest people there are in creation."

"Do this for me, Art, and I'll outfit you for free. A horse and two mules, food, gunpowder, lead, matches—anything and everything you need, I'll furnish. And I'll let you pick out your own livestock. Then, once you get the party upriver and make peace with the Indians, why, you can go off on your own. And because I'm giving you your personal outfit free, every pelt you bring back will be pure profit for you."

"Same price as you're payin' now?"

"No guarantees—don't know what the market will bear—but I can assure you I won't cheat you, never would."

"If I agree, when do we leave?"

"Leave whenever you want to. You'll be in charge," Ashley said.

"All right. Have your party gathered up, ready to go by sunrise tomorrow morning."

Ashley smiled broadly, then extended his hand. "Thanks," he said. "I'll start getting your supplies together."

"Mr. Ashley, you're a respected businessman in St. Louis. I expect you know just about everyone and everything about the town, don't you?"

"You mean, am I a busybody who sticks his nose into everyone's business?"

"No, I didn't mean that."

Ashley chuckled. He took a pipe from a collection he

kept on his desk, and began to fill it with fragrant tobacco. "I know you didn't. I was just funnin' with you, that's all. Yes, I know quite a bit about what is going on in this ragamuffin town that some people call a city. Why do you ask? Do you have a question about someone?"

"There's a girl here in town . . ."

"My, you work fast," Ashley said, interrupting Art. Clearly he was impressed with the young man. "You've only been here a few days and you've already met a girl?"

"Well, the fact is, I've known her for a long time," Art said. "I would just like to know how she's getting along."

"I'll tell you if I know. What's her name?"

"Jennie."

"Jennie? What's her last name?"

"She doesn't have a last name."

Ashley laughed again. "Art, what is it about you and last names? You don't have a last name, now you're asking me about a young woman who also doesn't have a last name. Jennie, you say? Well, there must be a dozen women and girls in this town named Jennie."

"This Jennie lives in a big white house over on Chestnut Street."

"Well, that narrows it down a bit," Ashley said. The smile left his face. "Wait a minute, a big white house on Chestnut, you say? Are you talking about the House of Flowers?"

"I dunno. The House of Flowers?"

"The House of Flowers is a big white house on Chestnut Street run by a girl named Jennie. But it's a . . . uh—"

"Whorehouse?" Art asked.

"Well, I wasn't going to say that exactly, but yes. It is. Is that the one you mean?"

"Well, yes, that's the one I mean. Didn't know it was called that. How does the town treat her?"

"She's a whore. How is the town supposed to treat her?"

"She's a good woman," Art said. Before Ashley could reply, Art held up his hand to stop him. "I know she's a whore, but she didn't have much choice in that. But inside, she's got a good soul, and I wouldn't want to see her hurt in any way."

"Well, as far as I can tell, she isn't being mistreated," Ashley said. "She sort of minds her own business, so the only people who ever take note of her are the people who are her customers."

"She must be doing pretty well to own that big house," Art said.

"Yes, well, that's another matter. There are some who say she might have bitten off more than she could chew when she bought that house. You see, she couldn't buy it outright, so the bank holds the paper on it. And from what I understand, some of our . . . so-called decent folk . . ." Ashley just about choked on the word "decent." He went on. "Well, the good citizens of the city of St. Louis are trying to get the bank to foreclose."

"Why?"

"Why? Well, because St. Louis is becoming a very important city, and there are those who feel that having something like the House of Flowers is bad."

"Who are the ones that say this?"

"Well, one name that comes to mind is Mrs. Sybil Abernathy. She is President of the Women's Auxiliary of the St. Louis Betterment League. Betterment League," he snorted. "A genuine bunch of busybodies is what they are. Put me to shame in that department." He tried to make light of an unpleasant situation.

"Is Jennie behind in her payments?" Art persisted.

"Oh, I'm sure she isn't. Duane Abernathy, Sybil's husband, is chairman of the board of directors of the bank. Believe me, if Jennie was late in her payments, he wouldn't hesitate to throw her out on her you-know-what."

"Then I don't see how anyone can do anything against her."

"One would think so," Ashley replied. He looked at the younger man and saw the naïve kid who still resided inside the tall, strong, weathered exterior. Still, it made Art that much more likable and trustworthy. "But there is a clause in her contract that would allow the bank to call in the note at any time."

"Can a bank do that? I mean if you are paying on time?"

"Yes, as long as that clause is in the contract. And that clause is put into many loans that the bank considers at risk. Whorehouses are considered at risk. Though why they are, I don't know. They always seem to do a brisk business."

"How much does Jennie owe, do you know?"

"I think it's around five hundred dollars or so."

"Pay it off," Art said.

"I beg your pardon?"

"I want you to take five hundred dollars, or however much it takes, from my account here, and pay off Miss Jennie's loan."

"Art, that's a helluva lot of money. Are you sure you want to do that?"

"Yes."

"Well, if you are going to do that, why don't you just take the money yourself and give it to her?"

Art shook his head emphatically. No question in his mind about this. "No," he said. "I'd rather do it this way. That is, if you will do it for me. And I don't want her to know that the money came from me."

Ashley paused for a moment; then he nodded in complete understanding. "Yes, of course I'll do it for you," he said. "You are a rare man, Art. A rare man indeed. And the rest of the money in your account?"

"I'd like for you to just keep it on your books."

"You mean you want me to act as a bank for you?"

"Yes, if you don't mind."

Ashley smiled. "I don't mind at all. Fact is, I do run sort of a bank here. You won't be the only one to leave your money on the books."

"Thanks," Art said. "I appreciate that, Mr. Ashley."

The two men shook hands, and without another word Art left Ashley's place and wandered back down to the waterfront, where again the same talkative preacher was holding court. Dog, who had trailed Art at a close distance throughout the entire day, stayed with him every step. Art always kept him within sight from the corner of his eye, but didn't seek him out or pet him or feed him. Dog was a survivor, for sure. Now, Art stopped to listen for a few minutes to the longest nonstop sermon he had ever heard—and he remembered a few from his childhood.

"These here new-fangled steamboats is an abomination to the Lord!" the preacher said in his singsong voice. "I say now that all God-fearin' people should rise up against them, for surely they will mean the end of us all.

"Steam wilts the grass, so the horses and cattle cannot feed. The noise of those infernal engines keeps the chickens from layin', puts the pigs off'n their feed, and makes our womenfolk barren."

He held up a Bible and pointed to it.

"And it also poisons the water, for listen to this." The preacher opened the Bible and began to read. "From the Book of Revelation, 9:11. 'The waters became wormwood, and many men died of the waters because they were made bitter.'"

He slammed the Bible shut, then stabbed at the air with a long, bony finger. "Hear the word of the Lord!" he shouted.

Chuckling quietly and shaking his head, Art walked away. The preacher was still railing behind him.

Returning to LaBarge's Tavern, Art took the table that

had become his during his time in St. Louis. He was eating a supper of beans and bacon when a shadow fell across his table. Looking up, he saw McDill and Caviness staring down at him.

"Something I can do for you gentlemen?" he asked.

"I'm told you plan to lead the fur-trapping party out of here in the morning," McDill said.

"That's right."

"Well, you ain't goin' to do it."

"Oh? Why not?"

" 'Cause by rights that job belongs to me 'n my partner here," McDill said. "So if I was you, mister, I'd just get on out of town tonight and forget about the fur trapping party."

"Sorry. I've already given my word to Mr. Ashley," Art said easily. The more he saw of these two, the less he liked.

"Maybe you don't understand what I'm tellin' you, boy. I'm tellin' you you ain't goin' to lead no fur-trapping party."

"McDill, why don't you and Caviness back away and leave that fella alone?" someone asked. "If Mr. Ashley chose him, it's good enough for me."

"Yeah, me too," another said.

"That goes for all of us," another added.

"Matthews, Montgomery, Hoffman," McDill said, scoffing. He pointed at them. "Once we start up the river tomorrow with me 'n Caviness in charge, I'm goin' to remember your sassy mouths."

Each of the three men took a step back.

"What's your name, mister?" Caviness asked.

"My name is Art. Oh, and this is Dog."

So far, Dog had not raised his head.

"Art? That's all? Your name is just Art?"

"That's enough for me."

McDill snorted what might have been a laugh. "Art and Dog," he said. He looked at Caviness. "Hey, Ben, which one of these two is a real dog?" he asked. He and Caviness laughed at his joke. McDill hiked up his trousers as if he were about to do something—but he didn't make his move yet.

"You know what I think?" Caviness chimed in. "I think we ought to just whup old Art here, just to show him who his master is. Don't think he's very smart."

"Yeah," McDill said. "What do you say, Art? Shall we show you who your master is?"

"There are two of you," Art said.

McDill flashed an evil smile. "Well, then, we'll just take turns with you. First one of us will whup you, then the other. How does that sound?"

"That sounds fair enough. Who is going to be first?" Art asked easily.

"Who is going to be first? What difference does that make?" Caviness asked.

Art smiled up at them. "Oh, it makes a lot of difference," he said. "You see, under this table, I'm holding a charged pistol. I intend to shoot whoever is going to be first, then I'll let Dog deal with the other one. Dog," he called sharply.

Dog woke up, sat up, and seeing that Art was being confronted by two men, let out a low intense growl.

"Wait a minute now," McDill said, taking half a step backward.

"Come on, gentlemen, make up your mind. Who is going to be first?"

"You . . . you ain't got no charged pistol under that table," Caviness challenged. He had held his ground, but stood there with some uncertainty, looking back and forth between McDill and Art.

"Try me," Art said. He moved not a muscle, kept both men within his range of vision. Only his jaw clenched, and his enemies could see that.

"McDill? Caviness?" LaBarge called from behind the bar.

"You stay out of this, LaBarge. This here ain't none of your concern," McDill said in as blustery a voice as he could manage.

LaBarge laughed. "Oh, I ain't plannin' on getting into it," he said. "But I was just wonderin' if you had any last wishes. I mean, after he and Dog kill the two of you, is there anyone you want me to write?"

Matthews laughed. "Are you joking, LaBarge? There ain't nobody who will miss either one of them after they're dead."

"You're probably right," LaBarge said. "I just wanted to give them a chance." He took a wet towel and began to damp down the bar surface, but kept an experienced tavern keep's eye on the situation.

"I don't believe he's holdin' no charged pistol under that table," McDill said.

"I don't either," Caviness said, though not quite as forcefully as before.

"You go first," McDill said.

"Me go first?" Caviness replied. "Hell, no, I'm not going first. You go first."

The two men stood there for a long moment, staring at Art, who was looking, without wavering, back into their eyes. By now the rest of the tavern realized that a potential life-or-death confrontation was reaching some sort of climax. A few chairs scraped along the rough-planked floor as men prepared to evacuate the battlefield if need be.

"I seen him yesterday," a voice said. "He was cool as a cucumber while Shardeen emptied both his pistols at him. Then, when Shardeen come at him with a roar, that fella never flinched. He just stood there waiting, and the next thing you know ol' Shardeen was deader'n a polecat in a wagon rut."

Caviness began to sweat, and McDill licked his lips nervously.

"Ah," McDill said with a dismissive wave of his hand.

He tried to force a smile. "We was only funnin' with you, Art," he said. "If you're goin' to be leadin' us tomorrow, we just wanted to know that you've got the makin's, that's all. We didn't mean nothin', did we, Caviness?"

"No," Caviness said. "We didn't mean nothin'. Uh, would you call your dog off now?"

"He's not my dog," Art said. He looked over at Dog and nodded. Dog eyed Art, then the two bullies, and gave up his threat position; he lay down again with one eye shut, the other open wide.

"If you're planning on going on this trip, be in front of Ashley's at sunrise tomorrow," Art said.

"Yeah, yeah, we'll be there. You, uh, can put away your pistol now," McDill said.

"Oh, yeah," Art replied. With a smile, he brought his hand up from under the table. He was holding a fork. "As it turns out, you were right. I wasn't holding a pistol."

Everyone in the tavern began to laugh then, as much from a release of tension as from the humor of the situation. LaBarge unthinkingly used the soiled towel to mop his own brow.

"Why you . . ." McDill sputtered.

"Come on, McDill, Caviness," Hoffman said. "He got you, that's all."

"Yeah," Montgomery added. "He got you good."

Scowling, McDill and Caviness turned and marched out of the tavern, chased by laughter, whistles, and catcalls.

Art, the mountain man, returned to his meal, using the fork-pistol to shovel in the food that would be his last city meal for a long time to come.

Seven

It was just before sunrise, and in the east the sky was pearl-gray, laced with streaks of pink. The Mississippi River was glowing a silver-blue, as if it had its own internal source of light. Roosters were crowing, and in the backyard of a nearby house a cow bawled to be milked.

Although Art had told everyone to be in front of Ashley's place by sunup, they all arrived even before the sun rose. Art, who had picked out his livestock the night before, now saddled his horse, then checked the harness on his pack mules. Neither of his mules was heavily loaded now, as they were carrying only the supplies he would need for the winter, as well as some trading material for the Indians. Ashley had furnished a goodly amount of trade goods, so much that these items were equally distributed among all the mules in the party.

After Art checked his own animals, he went down the line looking at the others, and meeting the men who would be traveling with him.

"What's Ashley doing, giving the Indians all this stuff?" McDill asked as he worked on his animals. "We give them all this stuff this time, they're going to expect it every time. And if we show up empty-handed, there's going to be hell to pay."

"Yeah," Caviness replied. He too was working on the loads of his mules. "If we had any kind of leader, he'd tell Ashley what a fool he's makin' of himself."

Art knew that McDill and Caviness were talking for his benefit, but he paid no attention to them. Instead, he just looked over the harness and the load. The loads were skillfully packed, evidence that McDill and Caviness knew the business. Art hoped he would have no more trouble with them.

Third in line was Don Montgomery, followed by Joe Matthews. Montgomery and Matthews were first cousins, about twenty-two years old. They were a little green, but they seemed willing enough. Last was Herman Hoffman. Hoffman was a big Hessian, and at fifty, the oldest of the group. Hoffman had fought in the Napoleonic Wars, and any misgivings Art might have had about whether or not Hoffman would follow a much younger man were dispelled when Hoffman spoke. Hoffman was a military man, used to the structure of command, and in his mind, Art was his commander, pure and simple.

"Have you been trapping before?" Art asked.

"Nein," Hoffman said. He held out his large, rough hands. "But I am strong and good worker. I will do what you tell me and I think all will be fine."

Art smiled. "I think all will be fine as well."

Looking down the street, Art saw William Ashley moving toward them, having walked up from his home. Although the sun had not yet risen, there was enough light for Art to recognize him from some distance away. Reaching the group, Ashley lit his pipe before he spoke.

"Well, Art, you have your party together, I see. Have you met all of them?"

"Yes. McDill, Caviness, and the others."

Ashley chuckled. "Yes, I heard about your little run-in with those two last night. But from what I hear, you handled it very well. I don't think you'll be having any more trouble from those two. And they are good trappers. I probably would have had one of them lead the group if you had refused. It's just that they . . . well, you saw how they are last night. And this is as much a peacemaking trip as anything else. After what happened last winter, I don't think I could trust either one of them to make a lasting peace with the Indians."

"No, I wouldn't think that very likely," Art agreed.

Ashley took a letter from his pocket and handed it to Art. "This is a letter to Joe Walker," he explained. "Joe is in command of a fort built by the American Fur Company. We may be competitors in business, but they'll have as much an interest in having peace with the Indians as we do, so I reckon Joe will treat you all right when you get there. Also, if you need to replenish any of your supplies, this letter promises that I'll make it good to them."

"Thanks," Art said, taking the letter and putting it into his saddle pouch.

By now several early-rising St. Louis citizens had turned out to watch the departure. While this was neither the first, nor would it be the last fur-trapping party to leave the city, it was the largest and it was being sent out by William Ashley, the most important fur trader in St. Louis.

"Sun's up," Art said, looking across the river. "I expect we'd best be going."

"Good luck to you, Art," Ashley said, reaching out to shake Art's hand. Then he called to the others. "Good luck, good trapping, all you men!"

"Mount up!" Art commanded as he swung into his saddle. Twisting around, he waited until Hoffman, the last man, was mounted. "All right, let's go!" He waved the party forward.

The convoy of eighteen horses, six men, and one dog stretched out for nearly a block as Art led them forward.

He planned to go north to the Missouri River, then turn and follow that river all the way to its head.

From her bedroom window on the second floor of her house, Jennie watched Art and the others leave. She had thought he might come to her again last night, hoped that he would, and purposely turned away customers so she would be ready for him. But he didn't show.

When she finally realized, well after midnight, that Art wasn't going to come see her again, she was angry and hurt. But as she considered it, the anger and hurt left, to be replaced by a terrible sense of sorrow and longing for what she knew could never be.

"Oh, Art," she said quietly. "Why couldn't we have met at another time and another place—you a farmer, and I an innocent young girl?"

"Miss Jennie?" one of her working girls called from downstairs. "Miss Jennie, will you be coming down to breakfast?"

"Yes, Lily, I'll be right there," Jennie called back. Before she turned away from the window, she kissed her fingers and blew the kiss toward Art, who was now so far up the street that she could barely see him.

"Go with God, dear Art," she said quietly.

The River Bank of St. Louis had assets of nearly one million dollars, and that figure was proudly displayed on the front window of the building. In keeping with its success, the bank occupied one of the most substantial buildings in St. Louis. Built of brick and stone and iron grillwork, it sat squarely on the corner of Fourth and Market.

Although the bank was owned by a consortium of St.

Louis businessmen, it was managed by its chief teller, Theodore Epson, a New Yorker who had been hired by the Board when the bank was opened. Epson arrived every morning exactly one hour before the bank opened. During that quiet hour, he would go over all the transactions from the day before, often finding a mistake one of his tellers had made.

Epson enjoyed finding mistakes, because it gave him an opportunity to berate the hapless teller who made it. It also gave him a sense of self-satisfaction and reinforced his personal belief that, without him, the bank would fall into insolvency.

One of the most difficult tasks Epson had was in controlling the loans granted by the bank. It seemed that every board member had a close, personal friend who had fallen into financial difficulty and could survive if only they could secure a loan. Epson tried to explain to the board member concerned that the bank was not in the business of lending money to help people, but was in the business of lending money to make more money.

On the other hand, a few of the board members were after him to deny some of the more solvent loans. One example was the mortgage note the bank held on the House of Flowers. Mrs. Abernathy and her Women's Auxiliary League for the Betterment of St. Louis had done their job well, and now there were many St. Louis citizens protesting against Jenny and her House of Flowers. There were many who wanted Jenny's note called and her loan terminated, because they considered her business to be unsavory.

"Unsavory it might be," Epson told them. "But it is certainly a profitable business. Would that all our accounts paid as promptly as the House of Flowers."

Closing the book of yesterday's transactions, Epson checked the Terry clock that stood against the wall, and saw that it was less than a half minute until time to open. He walked over to the front door, raised the shade, and saw several people standing just outside the door. The man first in line expected Epson to open the door at that precise moment, but it wasn't yet time. Epson remained standing behind the glass, staring at the clock.

"Let us in, Epson! It's time to open the door!" someone shouted.

Holding up his finger, Epson shook his head, indicating that it was not yet time. As the crowd grew more frustrated, Epson continued to stare at the clock. The moment the minute hand reached the twelve, the clock began to chime. Then, and only then, did Epson reach for the door.

"Well, it's about time!" one of the customers said, his irritation clear in the tone of his voice.

"You know the hours, Mr. Warren," Epson said. "Our bank opens its doors promptly at nine o'clock. Not one minute sooner and not one minute later."

The customers poured into the bank, then hurried to the two teller cages. Epson watched with a sense of smug satisfaction, then returned to his desk. He had been there for no more than five minutes when William Ashley arrived. Stepping inside the bank, Ashley looked around for a moment, then came straight to Epson's desk.

"Mr. Epson, I wonder if I might have a word with you?" Ashley said.

"Certainly, Mr. Ashley," Epson replied, standing to greet him. "It is always a pleasure to greet one of our fair city's most powerful businessmen. How are you doing, sir?"

"I'm doing fine, Epson," Ashley said.

Epson's eyes squinted and he continued the conversation in a somewhat more guarded tone. "I must say I'm a little surprised to see you, though. I've been given to understand that you have started your own bank for the fur trappers."

Ashley shook his head in the negative. "Not at all," he

said. "All I'm doing is keeping some of my trappers' earned income on the books for them."

"Isn't that what a bank does?"

"I suppose. But I'm only doing it as a favor for my trappers. Most of them don't like to carry any more money than they need."

"Nobody does," Epson said. "That's what banks are for. You could steer some of your accounts our way, you know."

"Yes, I know," Ashley replied. "And I fully intend to, over a period of time."

"Really?" Epson asked, brightening. "So, have you brought me a deposit today?"

"Not a deposit, but a payment."

"A payment? I don't understand. A payment for what? You don't have a loan here."

"It isn't for me. It is for one of your customers. It's more than a payment, actually. I intend to pay off the entire mortgage."

"Why would you pay off someone else's mortgage" Epson asked. He frowned. "Wait a minute. Have you made the loan yourself? That's it, isn't it? You're paying off the loan because you have made it yourself. You *are* going into banking."

"No. All I'm doing is paying off the loan on behalf of an interested party."

"I see. And what loan are you paying off?"

"I'm paying off the loan on the House of Flowers."

"You are paying off the whore's loan?

"Yes."

"I don't understand. Why would you do such a thing?"

"I assure you, sir, I am not paying the loan from my own funds. I am doing so on behalf of an interested party. He doesn't want this Miss Jennie to know that he is doing it."

Epson stroked his jaw as he studied Ashley. "Are you saying that she doesn't know her loan is being paid off?"

"That's right."

"I am curious. Who is her benefactor? Some business-man in town?"

"I don't believe I'm at liberty to say who it is," Ashley said. "I wasn't told that I couldn't tell, but I wasn't given permission to tell either. Therefore I feel ethically bound to keep his identity a secret."

"Ha!" Espson said. "I was right, wasn't I? It is some local businessman. And of course he would come through someone else, if he wanted it kept secret. Like as not, it's one of the same men who, in public, call for that house to be closed, while in private, are her biggest supporters. Who is it? The mayor?"

"I told you . . . I don't believe I'm at liberty to say. It doesn't matter anyway. All I intend to do is pay off the note. Now, are you going to accept the money, or what?"

"Yes, yes, of course I'll accept the money."

Later that same afternoon, Jennie herself called at the bank. Seeing her the moment she stepped through the door, Epson went over to meet her.

"Yes, Miss Jennie," he said. "Is there something I can do for you?"

"I wonder if we could speak in private for a few moments?" Jennie asked.

"Yes, of course we can. Come over here to my desk. We can talk there without being overheard."

There were no other women in the bank, but there were several men customers, most of whom knew who Jennie was, many of whom had been paying customers at the House of Flowers. It would have been easy to pick out the ones who were the customers, for while the others stared at Jennie in unabashed curiosity, her customers looked away pointedly, pretending as if they didn't even see her.

Epson led Jenny through the gate of the small, fenced-in area that surrounded his desk. He offered her a chair, then sat as well.

"Now, Miss Jennie, what is it that we can only discuss in private?"

"Recently, some people have been attempting to close down my business," Jennie said.

Epson scratched his cheek with his forefinger. "Ah, yes," he said. "You would be talking about the Women's Auxiliary of the St. Louis Betterment League."

"You know about it?"

"Yes."

"Then you also know that chief among these women is Mrs. Abernathy."

Epson nodded. "Sybil Abernathy, yes."

"Doesn't her husband have something to do with this bank?"

"Yes indeed, he is the chairman of the board of directors of the bank."

"I thought as much." Jennie opened her portmanteau and fished out a piece of paper. "According to the contract, even if I am not in arrears, the bank can call in the remainder of my loan at any time. Is that right?"

"Yes, but . . ."

"That's what I thought. That's why I want to pay off the entire loan today. That way there will be no chance for the bank to foreclose." Jennie began writing a bank draft. "I believe the amount is four hundred and seventy-five dollars."

Epson was silent for a long moment, and Jennie looked up at him questioningly. "Am I not right?" she asked.

Epson wondered what he should do. He had accepted the money from William Ashley to pay off her debt, but was instructed not to tell Jennie.

"Mr. Epson, is four hundred and seventy-five dollars correct?"

"Uh, yes," Epson said. He would take the money now, and decide later what to do.

Jennie wrote the draft and handed it to him.

"I'll, uh, take care of this for you," Epson said.

Jennie smiled at him. "Thank you," she said. "I may be worried for no reason at all, but Mrs. Abernathy seems to be quite a determined woman, and I fear she may convince her husband to exercise the foreclosure clause in the contract. I would rather just own the house free and clear so that there is no question."

Epson nodded again. "Yes, I'm sure you are doing the right thing," he said. He picked up the draft and put it in his pocket. "I'll have the title delivered to you."

"Thank you again," Jennie said, getting up from her chair. Epson stood quickly, then walked with her to the door. He stood in the door and watched as Ben helped her climb into her carriage. Then he returned to his desk and sat there for a long moment, contemplating what he should do.

Opening one drawer of his desk, he removed a letter he had received from a bank back in Philadelphia.

"So, in conclusion, Mr. Epson," the letter read, "our bank is prepared to offer you a rather substantial salary should you accept the offer to become our chief of tellers. Please let us know, soonest, should you be interested."

Epson studied the letter for a long moment before he returned it to the desk drawer.

"Mr. Epson?"

Looking up, Epson was startled to see one of his tellers standing there. He had not noticed the teller's approach.

"Yes, Mr. Franklin?"

"I noticed the lady customer with you. Is there some business transaction you would like me to take care of?"

"Uh, no," Epson said. "Nothing at all. She just had a few

questions she wanted answered. Please return to your teller's cage."

"Very good, sir," Franklin said.

By nightfall Art and his party were already fifty miles upriver. They were still in the settled part of Missouri, and when they made camp that night, they were within sight of a farmhouse.

"After it's dark, me'n Caviness will go down there and get us some eggs," McDill offered.

"Why would you wait until after dark?" Art asked.

"What do you mean, why? Wouldn't you love to have some fresh hen's eggs with your breakfast come mornin'?"

"That would be good," Art agreed.

"Me too, but I don't want to get shot in the ass by some farmer for stealin' 'em," McDill replied, as if he were explaining something to a child.

"I see," Art said, masking his disgust. "You were planning on stealing the eggs."

"Of course I was planning on stealing them. You don't think he's goin' to just give them to us, do you?"

"No," Art said. "But he may sell us some."

"Sell us some? You mean you want to buy eggs?"

"Yes."

McDill and Caviness laughed. "This here will be my seventh trip up the river," McDill said. "And I ain't yet bought a hen's egg, or a chicken."

"Well, we're going to buy them this time," Art insisted.

"Huh. I reckon next thing you'll have us doin' is sayin' our prayers and singin' church hymns," Caviness said.

"A few prayers and hymns wouldn't hurt either one of you," Art replied. "But you'll not be getting them from me. All right, I'll go down and buy us some eggs. Who wants them?"

"I do," Montgomery said. Matthews and Hoffman also wanted some.

"I reckon a fip apiece will be enough to buy us a couple dozen."

"A fip? You ain't getting' no five cents from me," McDill announced.

"Fine," Art replied. "You aren't getting any eggs."

Art collected from Montgomery, Matthews, and Hoffman.

"Uh, I'd like some eggs," Caviness said, pulling a coin from his pocket.

"You, Ben?" McDill asked.

"Well, five cents ain't that much, Percy. And I be damned if I'm goin' to sit here in the morning watching everyone else eat eggs while I don't have none."

McDill waited for a moment, then sighed. "All right, all right," he said, handing a coin to Art. "I'll go along with it. But I'll be damned if I don't think this is about the dumbest thing I've ever seen, payin' good money for eggs when they're that easy to steal."

With the money collected from the others, plus his own, Art saddled his horse. Dog came over, ready to go with him.

"Dog, I'll be back soon. You stay here and watch my things," Art said.

When Art swung into the saddle, Dog stayed behind and watched him. Not until Art was out of sight, did Dog go over to where Art had made his own camp. Dog did a couple of circles on the bedroll, then lay down.

"The way this fella is acting, he's prob'ly going to say we have to pay the Indians for whatever beaver we trap," McDill complained.

"My pa is a farmer," Matthews said. "It's hard, honest work. I don't think he would appreciate someone stealing from his henhouse. Besides, five cents isn't too much to pay."

"I agree," Montgomery added. "Buyin' eggs is better'n getting shot for stealin' 'em."

"What about you, Hoffman? Everyone else is putting in their two cents worth. What do you think?"

"I think Art is our leader," Hoffman said. "We signed on to obey, we should obey."

"Ahh, he's got all of you buffaloed," McDill said with a dismissive wave of his hand. He looked over toward Art's bedroll and packs. "Wonder what he's brought with him."

McDill started toward Art's packs.

"What are you doing?" Matthews asked.

"I'm going to look through his packs."

"You got no right to do that."

"You going to stop me?" McDill challenged.

Matthews shook his head.

"I didn't think so."

Matthews grinned. "I don't have to stop you. He will." He pointed to Dog.

"Ha. That dog's not going to do anything. He knows me now. Don't you, Dog?" McDill said as he started toward Art's packs.

Dog stood up and watched him.

"See, he's not going to . . ."

That was as far as McDill got before Dog darted quickly to intercept McDill. Putting himself between McDill and Art's packs, Dog bared his fangs and growled.

Matthews and the others laughed.

"You still want to mess with Art's things?" Matthews asked.

"I wasn't goin' to do nothin' but see what all he was carryin'," McDill said.

"I think maybe you should go back to your own bedroll now," Hoffman suggested.

"Come on, Percy," Caviness said. "If that dog decides to

go after you, he'll have your windpipe pulled out before we can stop him."

"Ha, what do you mean before we can stop him?" Montgomery asked. "I don't intend to even try to stop him."

"All right," McDill said. He pointed at Dog. "But me and you's goin' to have an accountin' one of these days."

When Art approached the farmhouse he saw a tall, bearded man standing on the front porch. The man was dressed in homespun and holding a rifle.

"Somethin' I can do you for, mister?" the farmer asked.

"I'd like to buy a couple dozen eggs, if you've got any for sale," Art said.

The farmer looked surprised. "Did you say you wanted to *buy* eggs?"

"Yes, sir, I did. If they're not too dear, that is."

The farmer stroked his beard for a moment. "You a fur trapper, are you?" he asked.

"I am."

"Uh-huh, I thought so. They been comin' through here right regular over the last few weeks. You're the first one asked to buy eggs, though. The others tried to steal 'em."

"Tried?"

"They's one of 'em buried over there," the farmer said. "I yelled at him to get out of here an' leave my hens alone, but he turned and shot at me. So I shot back. It's a fearsome thing, killin' one of God's own, but I didn't have no choice in the matter."

"It doesn't sound like you did."

"So, you're wantin' to buy yourself a couple dozen eggs, are you?"

"Yes, sir, if you have any to sell."

"I got 'em. What about twenty cents for two dozen eggs?"

Art thought of the money he had collected. He didn't

know how he would divide ten cents up among six men. He could keep the money and no one would be the wiser, but he didn't want to do that. "What about three dozen for thirty cents?" he asked.

The farmer nodded. "I reckon I can do that," he said. "Come around back with me, you can help me gather 'em. But you better stay close to me."

"Stay close to you?"

"Over there," the farmer said, nodding. When Art looked in the direction the farmer had indicated, he saw two dogs, both of them bigger than Dog. Though they weren't growling, they were looking at him with dark, intense eyes. "If'n you had tried to come in here without me, them dogs woulda been on you."

"They look mighty fierce."

"They are fierce," the farmer said. "That's why they ain't nobody got away with any of my eggs yet."

"I can see that," Art said. "I've got a dog that's been followin' me around lately. He's come in handy a time or two."

"Dogs is good things for a body to have," the farmer said. He gathered up the eggs, wrapped them in a cloth bundle, then, held his hand out palm up.

"Here you are," Art said. "Thirty cents." He dropped the coins into the man's palm. The farmer wrapped his hand around the coins, then handed the eggs to Art.

Carrying the three dozen eggs carefully in a cloth bundle, Art returned to the campsite.

"Three dozen for thirty cents?" Montgomery asked. "You made a pretty good bargain."

"Ha," McDill said. "I could've gotten 'em for nothin'. You should've let me do it my way."

Art smiled. "Yes," he said. "Now that I think about it, I should have let you try."

* * *

Junction of Platte and Missouri Rivers, Saturday, August 14, 1824

There were so many people gathered at the junction of the Platte and Missouri Rivers that it resembled a small town. Tents and temporary shelters had been erected, some of which were made of logs, chinked with mud, to take on a more permanent look. Several keelboats were tied up, or pulled ashore, awaiting future employment. There were even a few squaws and children of some of the mountain men, thus giving the encampment even more of the look, feel, and sound of a nearly civilized city.

The more substantial structures belonged to employees of the Eastern fur dealers. These men would buy the pelts here, at a reduced price, then boat the pelts back downriver next spring. Until such time as there were furs to buy, though, they supplemented their income by providing liquor and goods from stores they had brought with them.

Most of the goods the mountain men bought weren't paid for at the time of purchase, but were put on an account. The account was settled when the trappers brought in their winter's catch. The representatives of the fur dealers would merely deduct from the pelt count so that, while a trapper might bring in fifty pelts, his indebtedness could cause him to be credited with only twenty-five or less.

As Art led his party into the encampment, he was greeted by hellos from dozens of other mountain men.

Art returned the greetings, then swung down from his horse. He looked back toward the ones who had come in with him. "Get your horses unsaddled, and take the load off your mules," he called. "We're going to be here for a while."

"How long are we going to be here?" McDill asked.

"Two, maybe three days," Art answered.

"If I was leadin' this outfit, we wouldn't spend no

more'n a day here. I think we should get on up into the mountains, get us a head start on the others."

"You want to go ahead on your own, McDill, go ahead," Art said. "I'm not keeping you." Art had already unsaddled and ground-staked his horse, and was now quickly and skillfully relieving his mules of their burden.

"I didn't say nothin' 'bout goin' on by myself," McDill replied.

Art walked over to a fallen tree trunk where a couple of men were sitting. A small campfire blazed in front of the downed tree, and one of the men tossed a few cut-up branches into the fire. McDill and the others were still working with their loads. Dog went with him.

"Hello, Art," the older of the two said. This was Jeb Law. Before Art went out on his own, Jeb had wintered in once with Art, Pierre, and Clyde.

"Hello, Jeb," Art replied. "Ed," he said, nodding to the younger of the two.

When Art sat, Dog settled down in front of him.

"How'd you come by the wolf?" Jeb asked.

"I didn't come by him, he come by me," Art said. "He just sort of attached himself to me."

"You gotta watch makin' pets of wolves. They don't ever get over their wild."

"I figure he's at least as much dog as he is wolf, and the dog part is pretty smart."

"Say, where at's ol' Clyde?" Jeb asked. "Did he decide to stay back in St. Louie?"

Art shook his head. "Clyde didn't make it," he said. "We was jumped by some Arikara. Clyde was killed."

"Oh," Jeb said. "That's a damn shame. Clyde was a good man."

"Yes, he was."

Jeb picked up a jug of whiskey from behind the log, and offered it to Art. Art pulled the cork, hefted it to his shoulder, and took a couple of drinks. When he brought the jug back down, he opened his mouth to suck in some air.

"Whooee," he said. "Where did you come by that poison?"

"McGhee's sellin' it," Jeb said, speaking of one of the furrier agents. "It's not so bad, once you get used to it. I think he puts a little mule piss in it to add to the flavor."

"That explains its kick, then," Art said.

Jeb laughed out loud. "Its kick. Hey, that's a pretty good one."

"You get your furs sold in St. Louis?" Ed asked.

"Yes. I sold them to William Ashley."

"I figured you'd go to him. Get a good price, did you?" Ed asked.

"I did."

"Might think on doin' that myself this year."

"It's not an easy journey," Art said.

"No, I reckon not, what with it getting Clyde killed and all," Ed replied. "Still, it might be worth it for the higher price."

Jeb nodded toward the men who had ridden in with Art. "So, what's with these men?"

"I made a deal with Ashley to lead these fellas up to the head of the Missouri. I will also be making peace with the Indian tribes."

"Makin' peace with the Indians, huh? Well, I reckon if anyone should try and make peace it's Ashley. It was his men got 'em all riled up in the first place."

"It was a couple of men who were working for him," Art said. "But it wasn't none of Ashley's doin'."

"A couple of men workin' for him, huh? Well, I'd like to get my hands on them two, let 'em know what I think of 'em."

Art chuckled. "If you're serious 'bout getting your

hands on them, there they are." He pointed to McDill and Caviness.

"What? You mean that's them?"

"Yep."

"Well, all I can say is, they got some brass comin' out here now, after all the trouble they caused. Was they part of the deal you made with Ashley?"

"Yes," Art answered. He told Jeb and Ed of the arrangement he'd made with William Ashley, in which he would lead Ashley's trapping party up to the headwaters of the Missouri, and would also parley with the Indians in an attempt to make peace.

"Why would you agree to such a thing?" Jeb asked.

"Well, if we don't have peace with the Indians, we're going to wind up spendin' so much time lookin' back over our shoulders that we won't get any trapping done," Art explained. "I don't want to see any more of my friends get killed. And Ashley agreed to outfit me, including livestock, if I would do it. So, here I am."

Jeb nodded, then pulled a pipe from his pocket. He stuck a long stick into the fire, captured a flame, and lit the fire. "Well, I don't blame you none, I reckon. Sounds like a pretty good deal to me." Jeb took several puffs from his pipe. Not until the bowl was smoking did he continue. "Parleying with the Indians might be a little harder than you think, though."

"Why's that?"

"According to the squaws, a good number of the Arikara has gone to live with the Mandan. And you know how Indians is. The enemies of their friends are also their enemies."

"What about the other tribes? The Ponca, the Sioux?"

"Haven't heard anything from them. They might open their lodges to you. On the other hand, they may scalp you as soon as they see you. You're up here now. If I was you,

I'd just forget about the rest of the deal you made with Ashley, and cut them boys loose to go on their own."

Art shook his head. "Can't do that," he said.

"Why not?"

"Because, for one thing, I gave my word to Ashley. And I'm not one to go back on my word. And for another, if I cut 'em loose now, McDill and Caviness will take over."

"The ones who started all this trouble in the first place?" Jeb asked. "Why would they take over?"

"That's just the way of it. And I'd hate to turn them loose on Matthews, Montgomery, and Hoffman."

"That's the other three?"

"Yes, and they're green as grass. Wouldn't take much for McDill and Caviness to prod them into doing about anything they ordered."

"Who's the big fella?" Ed asked.

"That's Herman Hoffman. He's a Hessian."

"He looks like he could take care of hisself pretty good," Ed said.

"I expect he can. Only trouble is, he's a man who believes in authority, and if he figures that McDill or Caviness are giving the orders, he'll follow them."

"You don't plan to trap with those men, do you?" Jeb asked.

Art shook his head. "No. Soon as I make peace with the Indians, I'll go out on my own. Thought I might head up toward Wind River."

"Ought to be some good pickin's up there this winter," Jeb agreed.

"Fight, fight!" someone shouted.

Looking around, Art saw several people running toward the center of the camp area.

"Art, it's Percy McDill!" Matthews said, hurrying to find him.

"Damn, it didn't take him very long to get into trouble,"

Art said, getting up from the fallen tree trunk. By the time he reached the center of the commotion, he saw that the fight was over. McDill was sprawled on his back, and the man he had been fighting with was standing over him.

"You want 'ny more?" the man asked McDill.

"No," McDill replied sullenly. He had his hand on his chin, moving it back and forth as if testing to see if his jaw was broken.

"I reckon that'll teach you to mess with my squaw," the victorious brawler said, brushing his hands together as he turned his back to McDill and started walking away.

The man shouldn't have turned his back because McDill leaped to his feet with his knife in his hand.

"Dog!" Art shouted.

Dog leaped up and clamped his jaws down on the wrist of McDill's knife hand. With a roar of pain and surprise, McDill dropped his knife.

"Get away!" he shouted. "Get away from me!"

"Dog," Art said again, and at this command, Dog let go. McDill stood there, rubbing his wrist.

"What the hell?" McDill said. "What did he do that for?"

"Because I told him to," Art said.

"What's going on here?" McDill's adversary asked, turning around at the commotion.

Realizing that he had lost his advantage now, and not wanting to press the issue any further, McDill waved his hand in irritation.

"Nothing," he growled. "Nothing's going on. Just go on about your business."

"Yeah, I'll do that," the other man said. He pointed at McDill. "So long as you stay away from my squaw."

"He won't be bothering your squaw anymore," Art said. "I can promise you that. Come on, McDill, I expect you better keep yourself out of trouble until we leave here."

"I don't understand you, mister," McDill growled in anger

Eight

A beautiful cabriolet carriage, pulled by a team of matching white horses, stopped on Chestnut Street in front of the House of Flowers. Duane Abernathy, well turned out in a gaberdine suit with silver-buttoned vest, beaver hat, and white gloves, was the lone passenger in the magnificent carriage, as befitting his elevated station in St. Louis.

Constable Billings, mounted, had ridden alongside the carriage, eating its dust. When they stopped, he looked over at Abernathy.

"Are you sure you want to do this, Mr. Abernathy?"

"I'm sure, never surer of anything in my life as a man of business," Abernathy said. "Before he left, Mr. Epson disclosed to me that the occupant of this house was in arrears on her payment. Serve the warrant, Constable. I want her, and all the trollops who work with her, out of the house by noon today. Serve the blessed warrant, my man."

"Perhaps if you would give her an opportunity to pay off the loan in one payment," Billings suggested. He had pleaded with the banker before, when he had first learned of Miss Jennie's financial problem.

"She cannot pay off the loan," Abernathy said. "I have reviewed her bank account. It is nearly depleted. In fact, she recently withdrew an amount of money exactly equal to what she owes my bank. One who was seriously trying to avoid arrears would have used that money to clear the debt. Do your duty, Constable. Serve the warrant, I say again." Abernathy sat back in his comfortable carriage seat and pulled his hat more snugly onto his head. He called to the driver to take him back to the bank.

With a sigh, Constable Billings tied off his horse at one of the several wrought-iron hitching posts in front of the fine white-painted house, then went inside. Jennie met him in the foyer.

"Constable," she said, greeting him with a genuine smile.

Constable Billings removed his hat and rolled it in his hands for a moment before he spoke. He had never been in such an uncomfortable situation in his life. His heart was bleeding.

"Miss Jennie, I hate being the one to do this, but I've been asked to serve a warrant of eviction."

"Eviction?"

"Yes, ma'am," Billings said. By now, several of Jennie's girls had gathered in the foyer as well, to see what was going on. They could see this wasn't good.

"But I don't understand. How can I be evicted from my own house?" Jennie asked. Her dark eyes were wide with question and disbelief.

"Well, ma'am, that's just it," Billings replied. "This isn't your house anymore. According to the loan contract at the bank, it can be foreclosed at any time if a payment is late. And you are late."

Jennie shook her head vigorously. "But that's not true, Constable. I don't even have a loan at the bank anymore. I paid it off—in full."

Billings's eyes opened wide in surprise. "You paid the loan off? When?"

"Why, back in July," Jennie said. "I wrote a bank draft for the full amount to Mr. Epson."

"Miss Jennie, would you come with me?" Billings asked. "Perhaps if we went to the bank, we could get to the bottom of this."

"Yes, I would be glad to come with you," Jennie said.

Constable Billings, Duane Abernathy, and Logan Mc-Murtry, the new chief of tellers, stood in the little fenced-off area that was the office of the chief of tellers. His mahogany desk was covered with correspondence, bank papers, and open ledger books. Several inkwells held inks of black, blue, and red.

"As you can see, Constable Billings," Abernathy said, taking in the papers and open ledgers with a sweep of his hand, "her loan is still outstanding."

"But how can that be?" Jennie asked, incredulous. She was trying not to be intimidated by these men and the situation. "I have paid off the loan."

"By bank draft, you say?" Billings asked.

"Yes, four hundred and seventy-five dollars," Jennie said. "I'm sure if you check the ledger, you will see where I issued an instrument of that precise amount."

"Oh, I agree, you wrote a draft for four hundred and seventy-five dollars," Abernathy said. "For here is the entry, made on July twenty-third, in the year of our Lord, eighteen hundred and twenty-four. But, according to this entry, the funds were given directly to you. You'll see as much right here." He hefted the ledger to show her.

"What? No," Jennie said. "They were to repay the loan."

"Miss Jennie, do you have anything to prove that?" Billings asked. "A receipt, a letter, something to show that the loan was paid?"

Jennie shook her head. She now regretted not asking

Epson for a payment note and the title on the very morning she had paid him. "No, I don't. Mr. Epson said he would take care of it for me, and I assumed that he would. Perhaps it was delayed by his departure to Philadelphia."

"You say you gave the money to Epson?" Billings asked.

"Yes."

"Well, if you gave it to him, but there is no record of it, what do you think happened to the money?"

"I'm sure I don't know," Jennie said. Although inside, she now had deep suspicions, and she was almost sick with fear and regret.

"Oh, I'm sure you do know," Abernathy said. "You kept it for yourself."

"No, I didn't, I can assure you. I gave the money directly to Mr. Epson."

"And yet, clearly, there is no entry to that fact, your assurances notwithstanding," McMurtry said, pointing with an ink-stained finger to the ledger book.

"I wish there was some way we could talk to Mr. Epson. He would be able to clear this up, I'm sure." Jennie looked from McMurtry to Abernathy, but saw no sympathy in either man.

"I did talk to Mr. Epson," Abernathy said. "Before he left, he informed me that if the bank received no more money from you by the next payment date, you would be in arrears."

"Mr. Epson told you that?" Jennie asked in surprise.

"He did."

"But that's not true. He knows that's not true."

"Why, then, would he tell me such a thing?" Abernathy asked.

"I hate to say this but, if he didn't apply the money to my loan as I assumed he would, the only thing that could have happened to it is that he took it."

"You are saying that Theodore Epson stole your money?" Abernathy asked.

"That's the only conclusion I can come to," Jennie replied.

Abernathy let out a long, disgusted sigh, then shook his head. "You know what I think, Constable?" he asked, turning to address Billings. "I think that when this woman learned that Mr. Epson had left our bank to take employment back East, she figured that would be the perfect opportunity to make such a spurious claim. She seeks to defraud the bank at the expense of the reputation of as fine a young man as has ever graced our fair city. I wish there was more we could do to her besides confiscate the house. I wish we could throw her in jail for libel and slander and throw away the key!"

"But I'm telling the truth," Jennie pleaded. "I swear I'm telling the truth! I gave the money to Mr. Epson."

"Do your duty, Constable," Abernathy said. "Evict this woman from my house."

"I'm sorry, Miss Jennie," Billings said, and the tone and expression in his voice gave truth to the fact that he really was carrying out his duty under duress. "I'm afraid I'm going to have to ask you, and your girls, to leave the house."

"But, please, Mr. Abernathy. If you turn us all out, where will my girls go?" For the first time in a very long time, Jennie felt desperate. It reminded her of her days as a slave, when she had absolutely no control over her own destiny, the days before the mountain man had purchased her freedom and given her a chance at a new, independent life.

"Where you and your girls go is none of my concern," Abernathy replied coldly. "However, I would remind you that, while St. Louis has no ordinance prohibiting a bawdy house, we do have a law against street solicitation for immoral purposes. And I intend to see that Constable Billings and his men uphold that law. So, I wouldn't go out on the street if I were any of you."

"I'm sorry, Miss Jennie," Billings said.

Jennie sighed, and with her eyes brimming with tears, reached out to put her hand on Billings's arm. "I know this isn't your fault," she said. "You are just doing your duty."

"Yes, ma'am," Billings agreed. He pulled his arm from her gently, embarrassed at her gesture in front of the bank men. "I'm glad you see it that way." He was caught in a bind, and hated what he now had to do.

Philadelphia, Pennsylvania, Monday, August 16, 1824

Theodore Epson sat across the desk from Joel Fontaine, the president of the Trust Bank of Philadelphia. They were in Fontaine's office, and as a measure of the size of the Trust Bank, Fontaine's office alone was as large as the entire River Bank of St. Louis.

"I've never been to the teeming metropolis of St. Louis," Fontaine said. "But I would dearly like to visit there sometime. How did you find it during your time there?"

Epson shook his head in disgust and disappointment. "I assure you, Mr. Fontaine, you would not like it. St. Louis is a dirty, lawless, and barely civilized town. Its streets are filled with trappers and fur dealers who are little more than wild savages. Prostitutes conduct their business without fear of the law, though I am pleased to say that I put into motion a means whereby the most notorious of all the brothels will, no doubt, be closed very soon."

"Oh? And, how did you do that?" Fontaine asked with genuine curiosity.

"I denied them access to their ill-gotten gains."

"Good for you," Fontaine said. "I'm sure the city of St.

Louis was sorry to see such an upstanding citizen as yourself leave its precincts."

"No doubt," Epson replied. "But I assure you, sir, that feeling was not reciprocated. I can't tell you how happy I was to get your offer so I could leave that Godforsaken place."

Fontaine looked down at a piece of paper that lay on his desk. "And I see that you have just opened your own personal account for nine hundred dollars," he said. "That is an impressive amount of money, so you must've done well by yourself while you were in St. Louis."

"Yes, I, uh, was quite frugal during my stay," Epson said, pulling his heavily starched shirt collar away from his neck. Epson had kept the money given him in confidence by William Ashley, and he had executed the draft given him by Jennie, keeping that money as well. Even after the expense of moving from St. Louis to Philadelphia, he still had over nine hundred dollars left. All in all, a profitable enterprise—albeit with other people's money.

Some might consider what he did as dishonest, but Epson was convinced that he had performed a service for the city of St. Louis. It was clear that a majority of the citizens there wanted the whorehouse to be closed, and this would give them a way to eliminate it. He justified keeping the money from Jennie because it was obviously obtained as a result of her immoral and indecent operation. He also didn't feel guilty about keeping the money given him by William Ashley because he was certain this money came from some businessman. The way he looked at it, everyone benefited from his action except for the two people: the whore, and her mysterious benefactor, who was obviously a hypocritical businessman. And no one would feel sympathy for them.

"Mr. Epson?" Fontaine said.

Epson had drifted away with his self-satisfied thoughts,

and it wasn't until then that he realized that Fontaine was talking to him.

"I'm sorry," Epson said. "You were saying?"

"I was just saying, on behalf of the bank, welcome to Philadelphia," Fontaine said, sticking his hand across the desk.

"Thank you, sir," Epson said, accepting the handshake. He smiled. "I am very glad to be here—in fact, more than you'll ever know."

House of Flowers, St. Louis, Monday, August 16, 1824

There were tears, sobs, and expressions of concern for their immediate future as Jennie called all her girls together. She informed them silently that they were being forced out of the house.

"But why, Miss Jennie? What have we done to anyone?" one of the girls asked.

"We have committed no offense," Jennie replied. "It's just that there are some people who are all proper on the outside, but just plain mean on the inside. I fear we have made enemies of such a person."

"But how can they throw us out of the house? I thought you had paid the bank everything you owed them," Carla said.

"I *have* paid the bank what I owe them," Jennie said. "But it would seem that Mr. Epson was not as honest as he appeared. He ran away with the money."

One by one, the girls came to Jennie, hugged her, then went back to their rooms to pack their few belongings. Jennie lingered in the foyer for a moment longer, allowing her hand to pass over the banister and looking at the crown molding around the room. She realized, with a pang of regret, how beautiful the house was, and how much she was going to miss it.

Slowly, as if by delaying each step she could stave off the inevitable, Jennie climbed the stairs to the second floor and went into the bedroom. This was the same bedroom where, for many years, she had dreamed and fantasized about Art. Recently, as if a fantasy realized, Art had appeared out of nowhere. When she awakened the next morning she saw that it wasn't a dream . . . he was still there. Now, after a glorious reunion, Art had gone back West, returning to the mountains. What if he came back looking for her? Without this house, he might not find her.

Unable to control her tears, Jennie began packing her clothes.

It was more than a loss of livelihood, or even the loss of a roof over her head, that made Jennie cry. The House of Flowers was the closest thing to a real home Jennie had ever had in her life. It had been her plan to make enough money to someday leave the prostitution business. Then the House of Flowers truly would have been a home. Perhaps even a home to which Art might some day come to live.

Deep in her soul, she knew that it was very unlikely that Art would ever settle down in a city, but fantasies of such a future had occupied her thoughts for a long time.

When Jennie came down to the foyer a while later, all five of her girls were gathered in the foyer with all their belongings, waiting for some direction from the woman who had taken care of them for so long.

"What do we do now, Miss Jennie?" Sue Ellen asked.

Jennie shook her head sadly. "I wish I could tell you," she said. "I wish I knew what *I* was going to do."

"I know what I would do if I were a man," Carla said. "If I were a man, I would leave St. Louis."

"Leave St. Louis and go where?" Lisa asked.

"I don't know. West maybe," Carla said. "Yes, I'd go West."

At that moment, the front door opened and a white-haired old black man came into the house.

"Miss Jennie," Ben said, "I got the carriage drawed up out front. You want me to put your luggage in?"

"Yes, I suppose . . ." Jennie said. Then she looked at the other girls and suddenly smiled. "West?" she said to Carla. "You would go West?"

"Yes."

Jennie laughed out loud. "What a great idea!" she said. She grabbed Carla, hugging her as she danced around the foyer.

"Miss Jennie, are you all right?" Millie asked.

"All right? I've never been more all right," Jennie answered, gathering herself and putting on her best face for the girls. "Ben?" she said to her driver.

"Yes, ma'am?" Sam replied, as confused by Jennie's antics as were the girls.

"Do you think you can find someone who would trade us a good, sturdy wagon for the carriage?"

"Miss Jennie, I 'specs you could get two fine wagons for this carriage. This is a fine carriage."

"Even better. Get two wagons, and four mules."

"Mules, Miss Jennie?"

"Yes, mules," Jennie said. She looked again at her girls. "Sue Ellen, Cindy, Lisa, Millie, Carla, we're going West!"

Ponca Village, Upper Missouri, Tuesday, August 31, 1824

The Indians of the Ponca tribe went all out to welcome Artoor and his fellow travelers. The women made Indian fry bread and roasted game, the men performed dances, and Artoor was invited to join them in the inner circle of the council fire. When McDill started to sit in the inner circle as well, without being invited, a couple of warriors stood in his way.

"Art, tell these ignorant savages to stand aside and let me sit down," McDill said.

"You can sit anywhere you want, McDill, except in the front circle," Art said.

"What do you mean I can't sit in the front circle? I'll sit any damn where I please."

Art, who was already seated, turned to look back toward McDill. "You can sit anywhere you want, McDill, except in the front circle."

"You're sitting there."

"I was invited."

"Why wasn't I invited?"

"Perhaps it is because you presumed to sit there before you were invited."

"That makes no sense. If they were going to invite me anyway, why not just let me sit there now?"

"It is the Indian way," Art said without any further explanation. His patience had long since begun to wear thin.

Grumbling, McDill sat further back, joining the other trappers.

Spotted Pony held his arms forward, spread shoulder-width apart, palms up. A shaman placed a lit ceremonial pipe into his hands, parallel with Spotted Pony's shoulders. Gingerly, Spotted Pony lifted the pipe above his head and mouthed a prayer. Bringing the pipe back down, he turned it very carefully, pushing the bowl forward with his right hand, bringing the mouthpiece back with his left. He took a puff on the pipe, then used his right hand to wave some of the escaping smoke back into his face. Afterward, he held the pipe out toward Art, inviting him to smoke as well.

Art smoked the pipe with Spotted Pony, being very careful to follow the same prescribed ritual. Art then passed the pipe around to the others in the inner circle, and only after all had smoked did the conversation begin. He wasn't a regular user of tobacco, but he understood the importance of the pipe to the Indians.

"You are the one called Artoor?" Spotted Pony asked.

"Yes."

"You have killed many Indians, Artoor."

"Yes. I have killed many Indians, and I have killed white men. But I have only killed those who were trying to kill me."

A very old and wrinkled man leaned over to say something to Spotted Pony. This was the shaman, the medicine man who'd lit the pipe and placed it so carefully in Spotted Pony's hands when the ritual began. The shaman spoke in a mixed guttural, singsong voice, nodding his head often as he spoke.

Spotted Pony nodded as well, as the other spoke.

"He Who Sees says that your heart is pure and your words are true, Artoor," Spotted Pony said. "You have killed only those who try to kill you."

He Who Sees spoke again.

"You and another were riding on a big canoe on the water when Arikara attacked you. They killed the one with you, but they did not kill you."

Art nodded, wondering how the old man knew. "They killed my friend, Clyde Barnes."

"You killed many of them." It wasn't a question, it was a statement, and Art saw no reason to reply.

The shaman spoke again.

"But you have made an enemy of Wak Tha Go," Spotted Pony continued.

Art looked confused. "I do not know Wak Tha Go," he said.

"Wak Tha Go is the warrior who killed your friend,"

Spotted Pony explained. "You killed many of his warriors and now, because the tepees of many were empty when he returned to the village, Wak Tha Go is no longer welcome among the Arikara, his own people. He is not welcome by the Ponca, the Mandan, the Sioux, or the Crow. The heart of Wak Tha Go is very hot, and cannot be cooled. He wants only to kill you."

"I hope to make peace with the Arikara, as I hope to make peace with the Ponca, Mandan, Sioux, Crow, and Blackfeet. I would even make peace with Wak Tha Go, if he would cool his heart."

"You have brought gifts for the Ponca?" Spotted Pony asked.

Art smiled, grateful that Mr. Ashley had provided for this moment. "Yes. The fur chief who lives in St. Louis has sent many good gifts to show his appreciation for allowing trappers to take beaver."

"It is good that we should have peace," Spotted Pony said.

From each village, an Indian messenger was sent ahead to the next, telling of the peace mission of the trapper known as Artoor. Because the messengers were sent ahead, every village turned out to welcome Art, and soon he had negotiated peace treaties with nearly all the Indians along the Missouri: the Poncas, Sioux, Cheyennes, Hidatsas, Mandans, and even the Arikara. The Indians all acknowl-edged the rights of the trappers and fur traders to take beaver on their land, and Art promised fair treatment to the Indians on all future trades.

"No more will our people trade bad whiskey for good pelts," Art promised with all sincerity.

For his part, the Arikara chief known as The Peacemaker promised that the Arikara would make no more war, but, he also warned that Wak Tha Go, who had made his own personal war against Artoor, had left the Arikara and now lived with the Blackfeet, and called himself a Blackfoot.

"I think Wak Tha Go and the Blackfeet will not make peace with you," The Peacemaker said.

"I will try to make peace with him," Art replied. "I have lived with the Indian and I consider the Indian to be my brother. I have no wish to kill my brothers."

At the mouth of the Yellowstone, Art sent word to the Blackfeet, Assiniboin, and Crow, inviting them to come talk peace. Only the Crow could be coaxed in, and their chiefs came to the meeting arrayed in their finest blankets and robes.

The meeting, designed to discuss peace, nearly started a war. Art displayed the gifts he intended to give the Indians in exchange for their promise not to make war on the white fur trappers. When one of the chiefs reached for the gifts before he was invited to do so, McDill clubbed him over the head with his pistol butt. Angry, the other chiefs threw off their robes and raised their war clubs, forcing Art and the others to wade into the fray, swinging their muskets. Within a few moments, all five Indians were on the ground and it was obvious to Art that McDill was about to kill one of them.

"No, McDill!" Art shouted.

McDill was on the ground with his knife at an Indian chief's throat. The Indian was staring up at him defiantly, unable to defend himself, but unwilling to show fear.

McDill held the knife there for a long moment, until Art pointed his rifle at McDill.

"I said no. Leave him be," Art said.

"Whose side are you on?" McDill asked. The man or the redskin?"

"I'm on *my* side," Art said. He desperately tried to hold his anger in check. "If you kill him we'll have the entire Crow nation on our backs."

McDill made no effort to release the Indian chief.

"Let him up—now," Art said, cocking his rifle. "If you don't, I will kill you."

The other Indians, who by now had regained their feet, looked on with wide eyes at the drama playing out between the white men. They had never seen such enmity between these fur trappers before.

"You'd kill one of your own?" McDill asked.

"You aren't one of my own, McDill," Art said flatly.

McDill let out a long sigh, then stood up and put his knife away.

"Sure, Art, I was just funnin' with him anyway," he said.

Warily, the chief regained his feet and looked over at Art.

"Help yourself," Art said, pointing to the gifts.

The Indian hesitated.

"Here," Art said. He picked up a fine bone-handled knife and handed it to the chief. "This is for you."

Smiling, the Indian held the knife out and looked at it.

"Here, for you. For all of you," Art said with an inviting swipe of his hand.

"Wait," McDill said. "Not all them gifts is for the Crow. We still got the Assiniboin and the Blackfeet to worry about."

"That's a fact," Art said. He nodded toward the remaining chiefs, who were now gathering up the presents. "But the time may come up here when we need some allies. And these Indians may just be what we need, provided you don't try any more dumb-fool stunts like the one you just pulled."

When the Crow left the encampment an hour or so later, they were laden with every gift Art's little party had remaining. Now, if the trappers encountered the Blackfeet, or any other hostile tribe up here, they might be able to count on the Crow for help. In fact, just before the Crow left, one of them, the one who had nearly been killed by McDill, approached Art.

"You would have killed your own to save me?" he asked, speaking English quite well. Art was surprised because, until this moment, they had communicated only in sign language.

"Yes," he said.

"How are you called?" the Indian asked.

"I am called Artoor."

The Indian nodded. "I have heard of you, Artoor. I am Red Tail." Red Tail put his right hand on Art's left shoulder, and Art did the same to him.

"And I have heard of you," Art said.

"It is good that you would kill one of your own to save the life of a Crow. Because you would do that, we will throw out all that has passed behind us. The Crow will be the friend of Artoor."

"And you will not make war with the trappers and fur traders?"

"We will make no war," Red Tail said. Abruptly he turned and joined the others. Mounting, they rode away quickly, yipping and howling as they proudly displayed their gifts.

Nine

On the Missouri River, North of the Yellowstone

Perched high on the end of a bluff that protruded over the water, stood a fort constructed of palisade logs. There were two projecting blockhouses on corners opposite each other from which the guards would not only have a view of the river approach and surrounding countryside, but could also cover, by rifle fire, the outside walls of the fort itself. The American flag fluttered from a wooden pole atop the nearest blockhouse.

Although the structure had all the appearances of a U.S. Army fort, it was actually the trading post Ashley had told Art about. It had been established by the American Fur Company, and was ably commanded by Joe Walker, the head of the trading garrison.

The front gate to the fort was closed tight when Art and his entourage arrived. Art looked toward the blockhouse that had a view of the gate; it appeared to be empty.

"Maybe there's nobody here," McDill suggested.

"Someone is here," Art said. "The gate has to be closed from the inside."

"Is not good military sense to leave blockhouse empty," Hoffman said.

Dog barked, and a face appeared over the balustrade of the blockhouse.

Art laughed. "Dog had the right idea," he said. "All we had to do is knock."

The man in the blockhouse pointed a rifle down toward them, more than a bit unsteadily.

"Who are you, and what do you want?" he called.

"The name is Art, and we've got a letter for Joe Walker," Art said, holding up the letter. "From Mr. William Ashley in St. Louis."

The man in the blockhouse stared at them for a long, silent moment. His face was screwed up, as if he had been eating lemons.

"For God's sake, man, do we look like Indians to you?" McDill called up to him.

The guard called down to the inside of the fort. "Open the gate."

A moment later the gate creaked open and Art and his group rode inside. Just inside the gate in the middle of the open area, which resembled a small parade ground, sat a cannon. A dog came running toward them, his fangs bared. Dog hunkered down toward the ground and growled. The canine who had approached stopped, barked a quick, ribbony yap at Dog, then turned and ran away. A man came up to meet them.

"You the one the Indians called Artoor?" he asked.

"Yes," Art replied.

"We heard you were coming. Come on in, Mr. Walker is waiting for you."

"How did you hear we were coming?"

"Word spreads upriver faster than people do," the man said.

Joe Walker was only two inches over five feet tall, and nearly as big around. He had a bald head and a full brown beard, and he scratched at his bushy whiskers as he read the letter Art presented to him.

"How are things back in St. Louie?" he asked.

"Noisy," Art replied.

Walker laughed. "Noisy indeed," he said. "Yes, I would say the city is noisy, all right. I miss it, though, all the people—and especially women . . . not many women out here, except the Indian gals, who are nice but don't palaver the American language much."

Art said, "Some people talk too much as it is."

"You and your men must join me for dinner. I am anxious to hear more about your trip."

Art's party actually cleaned themselves up a little before they sat down with Joe Walker in his quarters for a sumptuous meal.

"How goes your peacemaking mission?" Walker asked over the meal of fried trout and baked potatoes.

"How did you know of our mission?" Art asked.

"Word has come from the friendly tribes downriver," Walker explained.

"So far it has gone well. We have made peace with the Arikara and they were on the warpath last year."

"But you have not made peace with the Blackfeet."

"No."

"Nor will you," Walker said. "The Blackfeet are why we built this fort. Such savages are they that even their own kind will have little to do with them. However, I wish you good luck in your effort. Were peace to be made with them, it would make our task much easier."

"Well, we sure want to make your life easier," McDill said. The Hessian, Hoffman, shot him a hard look. But McDill was unaware of his own stupidity. "What did I say?" he asked when there was only silence after his remark.

Walker went on. "We are here to improve the business

prospects of the American Fur Company, and we appreciate the efforts you gentlemen have exerted to ensure our success."

"Glad to be of service," McDill muttered under his breath so that only Caviness could hear him.

After the meal, Art and Walker talked on long into the night about the goings-on in the territory, swapping information. Art was determined to know as much as he could about what lay ahead for him and his men.

In the Blackfoot Village

Wak Tha Go got up with the sun and walked through the quiet village. The fire of last night's council had been reduced to a pile of white ash that gave off only a tiny amount of smoke.

The Blackfeet were aware that Artoor was making peace with all the other nations, and they held council to decide whether or not they would accept his peace offer. There were some who counseled peace. Chief among the peacemakers was a man named Running Elk, who was the oldest and wisest shaman of the village.

Wak Tha Go was very much against making peace. And though Wak Tha Go was a recent émigré to the Blackfoot Nation, he had been totally accepted as one of them. This was in part because of his reputation as a fierce warrior, and in part because he was a member of the Bear Society, one of the most honored of the war societies. Wak Tha Go proposed that, instead of making peace with Artoor, they send out a war party to find him and kill him. Wak Tha Go even offered himself as leader of the war party.

The discussion was heated on each side of the issue, but by the end of the evening no real decision had been made. As far as Wak Tha Go was concerned, "no decision" was just as effective as a decision in favor of war. That was because it effectively kept the current policy in place. And the current policy of the Blackfeet was belligerence with the white trappers and hunters.

Still thinking about the council of the night before, Wak Tha Go left the tepees and the smoldering campfires, then climbed to the top of the one-hundred-foot promontory that jutted out over the Yellowstone River. From there he could see the sun, now a glowing orange ball poised just over the distant horizon. As the sun rose higher in the sky, it began to spread pools of brilliantly shining gold and silver across the surface of the water. Then, when it became so bright that it started to hurt his eyes, Wak Tha Go turned to look back at the village he had just left.

Here and there wisps of smoke curled up from holes in the tops of the tepees, evidence that the people of the village were just beginning to rise. Then, quite unexpectedly, the rising hackles on the back of his neck told Wak Tha Go that he was not alone. He spun around quickly and was shocked to see Running Elk behind him.

Wak Tha Go had not heard Running Elk approach, indeed would not have thought him capable of even climbing the hill, and yet there the old man was, sitting cross-legged on the ground, looking at Wak Tha Go with a gaze that seemed to penetrate to his very soul.

"How did you get here?" Wak Tha Go asked.

No answer.

"What are you doing here?"

When Running Elk still didn't answer, Wak Tha Go went on, speaking to cover the awkwardness of the moment.

"If you have come to speak again of making peace with the white man, you may as well shout your words into the wind, for my ears are closed," Wak Tha Go said.

Running Elk remained silent.

"Why do you not speak?"

The old man stared with eyes that were so penetrating as to be almost frightening. Wak Tha Go had never seen such intensity in anyone's eyes before.

Running Elk was wearing a red shirt, trimmed in yellow. This was not the kind of clothes one wore on ordinary occasions, and Wak Tha Go wondered about that. He also noticed that Running Elk's knife, bow and quiver of arrows, his war club, and his pipe all lay on the ground beside him.

"How did you get by me?" Wak Tha Go asked. "And why are you wearing your finest clothes and carrying your most prized possessions?"

Wak Tha Go was very uncomfortable now, and the more he tried to cover his embarrassment, the more obvious his embarrassment became. "Are you making a journey?"

"Yes," Running Elk replied, speaking for the first time. "I am making a journey."

"Where are you going?"

"Where I go is not important," Running Elk said. "I have come to tell you of things to come."

"You will tell me of things to come?" Wak Tha Go scoffed. "Are you one who can see into the future?"

"I am a man of knowledge," Running Elk said.

"So, you are a man of knowledge, are you? Then tell me of my future."

"You have two futures."

Wak Tha Go laughed. "How can one man have two futures?"

"You have two futures, but can only choose one. One is the future of peace. One is the future of war."

"I will not ask you which future I should choose, for I know what you will say. You would have me choose the future of peace."

"I cannot choose for you."

"Then I choose the future of war."

"You choose war so you can have revenge against one white man."

"Yes."

"You are a brave and ferocious warrior. But you have not chosen wisely. Many of my people will be killed."

"I don't care how many are killed as long as I kill the one called Artoor."

Running Elk shook his head. "Artoor will not be killed."

"He will be killed, and I will kill him," Wak Tha Go insisted.

Running Elk held up his hand to silence Wak Tha Go. "I do not have much time," he said. "Hear my words so that you know what I speak is true."

"I will listen," Wak Tha Go said.

"The time will come when the one called Artoor will visit our village, and while he is here his tongue will speak without ceasing from sun to sun. The people will not understand his words, but they will feel his power and the one called Artoor will be given a new name."

"One cannot be given a new name unless one does a great deed," Wak Tha Go said. "What great deed will Artoor do, that he will be given a new name?"

"He will do not one great deed, but many great deeds. He will live long and become a man of the past and the future," Running Elk explained. "Among the Indians of all nations, songs of Artoor's deeds will be sung in councils and around campfires. White men will tell stories of him in the places where they gather, and they will write of him in their books. He will be remembered by the grandchildren of the grandchildren of their grandchildren."

"And what is this new name to be?"

"He will be called Preacher."

Wak Tha Go laughed. "Preacher? Preacher is what white men call the teachers of their religion. It is not the name of a great warrior."

"He will make it the name of a great warrior."

"How is it that you know all these things, Running Elk? Do you have the gift of seeing into the future?"

"I do not see the future, I am the future," Running Elk said.

"You speak in riddles, old man," Wak Tha Go said. He turned away from Running Elk and looked back out over the village. The pearlgray of early morning was sharpening in tone and tint, and the tepees took on definition from the bright light of day. He saw three women in mourning dress approaching one of the tepees. "And if I kill Artoor, what will happen to the future you see?"

Running Elk did not answer, but Wak Tha Go didn't repeat the question. He was too interested in what was going on in the village below. He saw that one of the three women was carrying a deerskin. She stopped just outside the tepee, laid the skin down, unrolled it, then took out a red and yellow shirt, a knife, a bow and quiver of arrows, a pipe, and a war club. It wasn't until then that he realized what was going on. The three women were part of a funeral.

"Look, someone has died," Wak Tha Go said. He pointed. "The women of his family have come to prepare the body." Wak Tha Go looked more closely at the women. "Wait, I do not understand what I see. Those are the women of your family," he said. "Your wife, your daughter, and the wife of your son. Running Elk, what are they doing?" Wak Tha Go turned around to ask his question, but Running Elk was gone.

"Running Elk?" Wak Tha Go called. Running Elk was nowhere around. Wak Tha Go wondered where the old Indian had gone, and how he had gotten away without being seen.

Wak Tha Go turned back toward the village and saw that the women had gone into the tepee. Suddenly he felt a strange, tingling sensation, and his body convulsed as if he had had a chill.

"No!" he shouted. "No, this cannot be!" He hurried down the side of the hill, running so hard that he was panting for breath when he reached the tepee. Pushing open the flap, he went inside. The oldest of the three women looked around at him, and Wak Tha Go saw that her eyes were filled with tears.

"What has happened?" Wak Tha Go asked.

"My husband has died," she said.

Looking beyond the women, he saw the body of Running Elk, lying on a bed of furs.

"When . . . when did he die?" Wak Tha Go asked in a strained voice.

"Last night, after the council," the woman answered.

"But no, this can't be," Wak Tha Go said.

The women misunderstood his reaction.

"It is good to see that you are saddened," said Running Elk's daughter. "You spoke against him in council. I am glad he is not your enemy."

Wak Tha Go realized then that he would have to accept a fundamental truth. The person who had come to speak with him this morning was not Running Elk, but Running Elk's spirit. He turned and walked away from the tepee, thinking about the things Running Elk had told him. Wak Tha Go felt privileged to have been visited by Running Elk's spirit, for only those warriors with great medicine were given such visions. But he couldn't tell anyone about it, because Running Elk had come to him to advise the path of peace, when he wanted to . . . suddenly Wak Tha Go had an idea.

He would tell everyone of the visit of Running Elk's spirit. And when they would ask him why Running Elk came to him, he would tell them it was because Running Elk had changed his mind and now wished to say that the Blackfeet should make war against the trapper named Artoor.

* * *

Outside St. Louis, Missouri

Jennie and Carla rode in the wagon bed as old Ben, Jennie's longtime driver, handled the reins and gently slapped the horses forward. They were heading West. Four other girls rode in the second wagon, and they would share the driving duties, following Ben's lead. The only problem was, they weren't sure exactly where they were going, other than West. There was precious little in the way of civilization out there beyond St. Louis, and all of them were more than a bit scared at the prospect of leaving behind the place and the people who were so familiar to them. But they sympathized with Jennie's plight and wanted to support her—and they trusted her to take care of them.

Her mind, though, was occupied with thoughts of Art and where he might be, and whether she would ever see him again. . . .

She remembered when they met, how Art had been such a boy, and how he had tried to be her friend. He didn't know how the world worked then. He didn't know about slavery and the evil things that men do to each other. He'd found out quickly enough—those were dark days when Jennie had been owned as property, and used as property by her masters and other men. Lucas Younger had been one such owner. Art had joined up with the Younger party one time, and he and Jennie had become friends.

One day they talked as she sat in the back of the moving wagon. Art was riding close behind to be with her and try to comfort her.

"Why do you call your pa Mr. Younger?" he had said. He didn't know any better.

Jennie looked at Art, surprised, shocked even at his naïveté. She said: "He ain't my pa."

"Oh, I see. He's your step-pa then? He married your ma, is that it?"

At that, Jennie shook her head. "Mrs. Younger ain't my ma."

"They ain't your ma and pa?"

"No. They're my owners."

"Owners? What do you mean, owners?"

"I'm their slave girl. I thought you knowed that."

"No, I didn't know that," Art said. "Fact is, I don't know as I've ever knowed a white slave girl."

"I ain't exactly white," Jennie said quietly.

"You're not?"

"I'm a Creole. My grandma was black."

"But how can you be their slave? You don't do no work for 'em," Art said. "I mean . . . no offense meant, but I ain't never seen you do nothin' like get water or firewood, or help out Mrs. Younger with the cookin'."

"No," Jennie said quietly. "But gathering firewood, or helping in the kitchen, ain't the only way of workin'. There's other ways . . . ways that"—she stopped talking for a moment—"ways that I won't trouble you with."

"You mean, like what you was doin' with all them men last night?"

At that moment, Jennie cut a quick glance toward him. The expression on her face was one of total mortification. "You . . . you seen what I was doin'?"

"No, I didn't really see nothin' more'n a bunch of men linin' up at the back of the wagon. Even when I went to bed, I couldn't see what was goin' on on the other side of the tarp."

"Do you . . . do you know what I was doing in there?"

Art shook his head. "Not really," he said. "I got me an idea that you was doin' what painted ladies do. Only thing is, I don't rightly know what that is."

Jennie looked at him in surprise for a moment; then her face changed and she laughed.

"What is it? What's so funny?" Art asked.

"You are," she said. "You are still just a boy after all."

"I ain't no boy," Art said resolutely. "I done killed me a man. I reckon that's made me man enough."

The smile left Jennie's face, and she put her hand on his shoulder. "I reckon it does at that," she said.

"You don't like doin' what Younger is makin' you do, do you?"

"No. I hate it," Jennie said resolutely. "It's—it's the worst thing you can imagine."

"Then why don't you leave?"

"I can't. I belong to 'em. Besides, if'n I left, where would I go? What would I do? I'd starve to death if I didn't have someone lookin' out for me."

"I don't know," Art said. "But seems to me like anything would be better than this."

"What about you? Are you going to stay with the Youngers?"

"Only as long as it takes to get to St. Louis," Art replied. "Then I'll go out on my own."

"Have you ever been to St. Louis?" Jennie asked.

"No, have you?"

Jennie shook her head. "No, I haven't. Mr. Younger says it's a big and fearsome place, though."

"I'll bet you could find a way to get on there," Art said. "I'll bet you could find work. The kind of work that wouldn't make you have to paint yourself up and be with men."

"I'd be afraid. If I try to get away, Mr. Younger will send the slave catchers after me."

"Slave catchers? What are slave catchers?"

"They are fearsome men who hunt down runaway slaves. They are paid to find the runaways, and bring 'em back to their masters. They say that the slave hunters always find who they are lookin' for. And most of the time they give 'em a whippin' before they bring 'em back. I ain't never been whipped."

"I can see where a colored runaway might be easy to find. But you don't look colored. How would they find you? Don't be afraid. I'll help you get away."

"How would you do that?"

"Easy," Art said with more confidence than he really felt. "I aim to leave the Youngers soon's we get to St. Louis. When I go, I'll just take you with me, that's all. You bein' white and all, you could pass for my sister. No one's goin' to take you for a runaway. Why, I'll bet you could fine a job real easy."

"Maybe I could get on with someone looking after their children," Jennie suggested. "I'm real good at looking after children. You really will help me?"

"Yes," Art replied. He spat in the palm of his hand, then held it out toward Jennie.

"What . . . what is that?" Jennie asked, recoiling from his proffered hand.

"It's a spit promise," Art said. "That's about the most solemn promise there is."

Smiling, Jennie spat in her own hand as well, then reached out to take Art's hand in hers. They shook on the deal.

Now Jennie was on the move again. She had achieved her dream of living in St. Louis, but had seen the dream shattered by evil men and women who hated her for her race and her profession. Had the world changed at all since that day she and Art had made their spit promise? How she wished she could see him here by the side of this wagon as she headed West again.

How many times had she been bought and sold since

she was a young girl—the girl Art saw when they first met? Both of them had been sold as slaves after that, but he had escaped and fled into the mountains, become a man whom other men respected. Well, in the last decade she had become a successful businesswoman. No one had owned her. Respect was harder to come by, though, for a beautiful Creole woman who lived by her wits and her body.

Yet she knew one thing. She would never be a slave again. She would die first. That much was certain.

Ten

Art's party of trappers rode west along the upper reaches of the wide and wild Missouri. All were alert to the danger that they knew lurked behind every stand of trees and every hill. They kept to the lowest point everywhere they went, and on the third day out from the fort Art led them onto an old Indian trail that looked well traveled. It took them up to a shallow tributary of the Missouri River and into a wide ravine that gave them shelter and hid them from view throughout most of the day's travel.

The floor of the ravine was wide, and most of it was the streambed, nearly two hundred yards across, sandy and rocky. Along each side of the river were low bluffs, almost black in color from the dark earth and the shadows when the sun did not strike them directly. As the ravine opened to the high plain ahead, there was a small island, only about fifty yards long and thirty yards wide. It was dense with willow, alder, and a few tall cottonwoods standing proudly. It took Art's men the remainder of the day to reach the little island.

"We'll camp there tonight," Art said, pointing to the island. He turned his horse into the cold stream. Dog followed, then ran ahead, leaping from the water that wasn't even chest-high to him onto the dry, brushy shore of the island. He immediately went to explore its length and breadth.

"Yes, sir," Herman Hoffman said unthinkingly, the first words he had spoken for the entire day. He was dependable, though Art wondered what kind of trapper he would make. Still, it was none of his concern.

McDill and Caviness grumbled something about Art's decision, but they were wise enough not to share it with the rest of the party. The cousins, Montgomery and Matthews, willingly led their pack animals across the wide, shallow stream onto the island, without a word of protest. Green they might be, but they knew enough to follow their leader's orders for their own safety.

They all ate a light, cold supper. Art and Hoffman, along with Dog, took the first watch after dark, followed by McDill and Caviness. The youngsters took the final watch, which would last until breakfast time.

They kept the horses together in a tight circle at the center of the island, tethered to the strong cottonwood trees. Art had insisted on this, even though McDill had laughed at such seemingly needless precautions.

Wak Tha Go had formed a party of twelve men, including himself, from the Blackfoot village. He had hoped for more, since he had announced Running Elk's "prophecy" that the white trappers would be annihilated by the Blackfeet. But he thought he would have more than enough strength, outnumbering the whites two-to-one—in country familiar to the Indians and strange to the trappers.

He was dressed in full war costume, wearing buckskin leggings and moccasins elaborately trimmed with beads and feathers, with a single eagle feather fastened in his scalp lock. He wore a white buffalo robe, which was very rare, tanned and soft, over his otherwise-naked torso. And his face was painted in lines of red and black, which gave him a fierce, menacing appearance to anyone who might meet him in battle.

The others were similarly dressed. Each warrior carried a rifle or musket, as well as arrows and a hand ax for close-up, hand-to-hand fighting and scalping. The war party rode out from the village before dawn, heading southwest to where their scouts had said the white men were camped on an island in the river.

As their leader, Wak Tha Go rode about two horse lengths ahead of his men, so they could admire his courage and fierce appearance. The enemy, too, would be cowed by his warrior's paint and regalia, he knew.

He had told the braves his strategy the night before, when one of the scouts had returned with word that the whites were making camp. "We will ride up to their camp in the early morning and attack before they leave, while they are unprepared." He planned to approach from the east, with the rising sun at their backs. It was a simple attack plan that should work easily.

Nothing would give him greater satisfaction than wiping out the white trappers and counting coup on their property. They could use the horses and rifles too. It was going to be a good day to have a fight.

Art rose before sunup and folded his bedroll neatly and began packing his horse. He did not light a fire. Something told him that they should not this morning. He didn't know why, but he had learned to follow his instincts on such things.

Dog was patrolling the island, sniffing and snooping around in the underbrush. He also kept an eye on the horses, which whickered nervously whenever he was close by. He seemed to enjoy making them nervous, Art thought.

"Come here, boy," he said, tearing a piece of jerky in half and tossing it toward Dog. He chewed on the other half himself. He was hungry, but he had learned to live with hunger as a fact of life in the wilderness. Dog too, being half wolf, instinctively knew to eat when it was available because he could not know the next time there might be an opportunity.

The other men began to get up to face the new day on the trail. Art watched them. There had been plenty of time for him to form judgments of these men. And there was no question that, other than McDill and Caviness, he liked them; in fact, he respected all of them, even the two hostile ones, for their trail sense and ability to adapt to new, sometimes dangerous conditions away from the city. He only wished there was more of a chance for peace with the Indian tribes—then all of his party would have better prospects for survival and profit from pelts, as would Mr. Ashley himself.

But Art couldn't take on the whole world by himself. He had to have friends and allies to change the ways of the frontier. It was a daunting task. How could you change men? Take McDill, a born bully and a bad man. Still, in a fight he would be a valuable man to have on your side. The Hessian, Hoffman, was another case: a good heart and fiercely loyal to his leader. The others too were fighters with whom Art could trust his life. If it ever came to that . . .

Just then he heard the war shrieks coming from the other side of the riverbed, from atop the bluffs there to the northeast of the camp. He jumped upright and snatched up his rifle, checked the load.

"Everybody up! We've got trouble!" he called to the men.

From a slow, deliberate waking, they all leaped to their feet, guns in hand.

"What the hell?" McDill sputtered.

Again the war whoops arose, high-pitched and threatening.

"We're being attacked," Art said simply. "And we better be prepared to defend ourselves. They're coming in from over there," he said, pointing across the flat, shallow river. The rising sun lit the black bluff from behind, and skylined atop the ridge there were several Indians on horseback, brandishing their war spears.

They knew better than to stay there. After a minute to show themselves and, they hoped, to scare the white men on the island, they rode down to the other side—all but one. That one, a tall man with a single feather on his head and his face painted, remained visible and defiant, as if he were challenging them to take a shot at him.

Art was tempted to do just that, but until he knew how many of them there were and where they were coming from, he held off shooting anybody.

He turned to the others. "McDill and Hoffman, you two take the rear and see if any of them are attacking from the other side of the river. I doubt it, but we just don't know for sure." Those two turned and went to their positions.

To the others, he said, "Caviness and Montgomery, take the left—over there by those trees—and Matthews and I will take the right. If the Indians split up their party to attack from two ways, we'll be covered. If we see them coming from just one direction, we'll regroup to face them there. Okay?"

"Yes, Boss," Montgomery said, and saluted smartly.

Caviness grumbled something about how they were likely to die today, all because of Art—or something like that.

Art paid no attention to the grumbling. He and Matthews turned, moved over to some tall scrub to their right, and hunkered down there, rifles at the ready, powder and shot close at hand for reloading.

He had divided up the men to put one quick loader with

one slower man. He was the quicker between Matthews and himself. McDill was quicker than the Hessian, and Montgomery was lightning-fast on the reload, while Caviness was slow as molasses. Art could only hope for the best, hope that each man and each pair would hold position. The trouble was, how many Indians were about to attack?

The men could only wait. Then the attack came. From atop the bluff the tall Indian, who certainly was the leader of the raid, rode straight down the side of the bluff, his horse kicking up black dirt and rocks as he came. He gave out a high-pitched war cry that was answered by the others.

To the left, from where Art's men were, a column of attackers came around the bluff, brandishing guns and spears.

"McDill, any sign back there?" Art called out loudly, trying to be heard above the sound of the attackers' war whoops.

"Nobody—not yet!" came the reply. "I don't think they're coming from here!"

Art had to make a quick judgment. He had no way of knowing whether the Indians had ten or a hundred men in their war party, or some number in between. He would have to go with his gut instinct on this. His own men's lives were in his hands now—just like his own.

"All right, move up, cover Caviness and Montgomery, but don't bunch up too tight. We've got to present a wide front."

He had learned some about military tactics during his brief time with Jackson's army and in talking with old soldiers over the years at Rendezvous. But he was mainly following common sense in the situation at hand. His ears were splitting from the Indians' whooping and shouting, but he tried not to let that scare him or distract him. He had to stay in control and get these men through this situation.

Matthews said, "What should we do?"

Art said, "Stay put for just a second. Look, they're

listening to the chief. I count a total of twelve. That's not a lot, but twice as many as us. At least that's how many we can see right now."

It looked pretty bad for Art's men. He counted again: twelve, including the chief. "They look like Blackfeet," Art surmised aloud.

"Yeah," Matthews said. "All painted up for war." He tried not to sound as scared as he felt.

Earlier, Wak Tha Go had risen before dawn and said his prayers to the Spirit to guide him in his holy purpose, to wipe out these evil intruders on the sacred land of the red people.

His purpose was simple: to kill them all. He would achieve this by a swift surprise attack at dawn. He outnumbered them two-to-one, and each of his braves had the fighting heart of five men! It would be a simple task to wipe them out long before the sun reached its zenith in the sky.

He urged his followers to keep their horses quiet as they first approached the bluff that overlooked the enemy's camp. They rode closely together and arrived at their destination in good time. In near-silence they all rode up to the top of the bluff, Wak Tha Go in the lead. He indicated that they should line up so they would be visible to the men below against the pink and red morning sky.

When all were in place, Wak Tha Go let loose a long, loud war yell: "Yee-yee-iii-haa! Yee-yee-ii-haa!"

The other warriors followed with their own shrieking cries that were meant to terrorize the enemy, who was presumably still in his bedroll. They smiled and laughed to each other. A good day for a raid! Too bad there were so few white trappers; they would have to fight each other for their scalps.

"Go now," Wak Tha Go ordered them, according to his plan of attack.

He remained alone on the very top of the bluff, looking down into the camp of the enemy. He could see the forms of the men as they scrambled from their bedrolls. One in particular moved slowly, was not in a panic. It was hard to tell from this distance, but he appeared to be a young white man, tall, and there was a dog near him. This man looked up at Wak Tha Go. Did their eyes meet? Wak Tha Go was not sure, but he did know that he had sent a message of fear into this man's heart—and into the hearts of the others as well.

Wak Tha Go smiled to himself. Then he unleashed another powerful yell, which was the signal to his braves to move down the slope and around to the riverbed. He pulled his own horse around and reluctantly moved away from the ridge top, where he had been skylined to those below. He would meet them face-to-face now, not from above. . . .

He was proud of these men who had stepped forward to go on this raid. They were the bravest of the brave from among the Blackfoot village where he had found refuge and purpose. He would proudly lead them into battle this day.

When he got to the bottom of the bluff, he wheeled his pony around and went to the head of the column of warriors, then rode with them onto the sandy shoreline of the river. Again, he looked across to take the measure of the men who would die today, his enemy. They did not look like much. They were armed, seemingly ready to meet the attackers. The dog was still there, pacing back and forth, prowling like a wolf, not barking.

The fierce Indian leader raised his own spear and lifted his voice in a shout. The others followed suit, raising a huge, eerie war cry. Wak Tha Go kneed his mount into action and plunged into the river. His men did likewise, their horses kicking up the shallow water.

As he charged, Wak Tha Go threw his spear toward the man he thought was the leader of the whites. It missed. The Indian took up a rifle that had been loaded and primed and lay across the horse's neck. He held it high, to keep it dry, and pushed his mount forward into the gunfire from the men on the island.

Art shouted to his men to hold their fire until the attackers came closer. He watched the tall, fierce warrior who led the party. The man's spear came whistling toward him, and he ducked beneath the rock and scrub for cover. The spear missed. He lifted his rifle and took aim. When the charging leader was within about ten yards, he fired. He missed.

The Indian whooped and the other defenders started to fire their guns. Art quickly reloaded and primed his weapon and lifted it again.

In the first fusillade, one of the Indians was shot from his pony and fell into the shallow river. They kept yelling and kept coming. They released their spears, which flew just over the defenders' heads.

"Keep shooting!" McDill shouted from his position, the sound of panic in his voice.

The young mountain man, Art, didn't feel panic or fear. He knew what had to be done. He didn't shout, just carefully aimed his rifle at another of the Indian riders and slowly squeezed the trigger. The weapon kicked him back and black smoke exploded from the barrel. The attacker, about the sixth along the line, fell from his horse. There were two down.

Now the Indian leader wheeled his horse to the right, and just missed getting shot by Montgomery, who had been trying to get a bead on him. Montgomery's gun roared and the ball shot past Wak Tha Go's shoulder. The big Indian turned and smiled, as if to say, "You can't hurt me!" He pulled his horse to the rear of the attacking party, then turned to charge again.

The Indians kept coming, and now they had their own rifles and bows at the ready. Arrows thunked into the earth by Caviness, Matthews, and Hoffman. McDill frantically reloaded and lifted his gun, just in time for a ball from one of the Indians to whiz past his head, missing him by just a few inches.

In a huge explosion of gunpowder and shot, the island defenders fired almost simultaneously, causing the Indians' horses to rear and wheel madly, splashing and snorting. Another man fell. The trappers were cutting down the odds with each passing minute.

The braves circled and fell in behind their leader and charged again. The arrows flew and buzzed. One arrow struck Hoffman in his right arm, just below the shoulder. It passed through his flesh and left a bloody pulp. But he barely flinched as he reloaded his rifle, ramming a ball into the barrel.

Art saw the blood streaming down the German's arm, but couldn't stop to respond. He fired again at the attackers, missing his target as the Indian weaved out of harm's way.

In the melee, a couple of the Blackfeet had managed to pull the bodies of the fallen braves from the river and put them on the riverbank, so they wouldn't be trampled by the repeated charge against the island. All the whites could see was the splashing and the oncoming arrows as the Indians kept up the attack, even in the face of strong gunfire.

It was a miracle that Art had not lost a single man yet. He looked around and saw that his men were fiercely concentrated on doing their best to fire, reload, fire, and reload—again and again, almost like machines. He was proud of them, but there was no time for sentiment. He focused on his own job, and was able to get off another shot. This time he hit one of the horses, which went down in a violent, trumpeting death. The rider leaped off in time, and ran back to the other side of the river.

Wak Tha Go was unhappy at this turn of events. He had expected to wipe out the whites with the surprise attack, but instead he had lost three men and the whites none. He called to his men to take the three fallen braves away, back to the far side of the bluff where they had come from in the morning. He cursed the white men who had killed the Blackfoot warriors.

Secretly, he wondered if he had done something to offend the Great Spirit of Breath who protected his people. What had he done wrong? The bullets of the whites had cut down three brave Blackfeet. This was not the way it should be.

He left two men to watch the defenders so that they would not escape. Then he led the others, with the bodies of the fallen braves, to a camp about a quarter mile away, in a tree-sheltered area where they could regroup and plan the next attack.

One of his men came to Wak Tha Go and said, "Why have we lost these warriors, my chief? Were we not supposed to kill the evil white ones? Instead, they have killed our men."

"This I know, my brother, and I will pray for an answer to your question. I do not know what is in the mind of the Spirit who guides and gives life to all His creation."

The brave rode ahead with his head down, leading a horse with one of the corpses draped over it. There would be sadness back in the village when they returned with the dead.

Wak Tha Go knew that his grandiose promises must be fulfilled. He must wipe out these men on the island, or else he would lose face with the village, and with his own men. Hatred and vengeance flared up inside his soul like a roaring campfire. He must go and pray and think about what to do.

He rode off away from the other men after instructing them to make camp and prepare the bodies of the dead for eventual burial by their families and the other people of the village.

He was gone for several hours. At dusk he returned. The warriors awaited him. They had kept up their watch on the island. The whites were hunkered down in their defensive positions, expecting another attack. But the warriors couldn't move without Wak Tha Go to lead them, so they had stayed in camp and mourned their dead. They all jumped up and greeted him when they saw him riding in.

When he had dismounted, he said to them: "Tomorrow we will attack again. The Spirit has told me that victory is ours. We will avenge our dead brothers with the scalps of the evil men."

Clouds covered the moon. Art was grateful for this as he sneaked out of the island camp at the far end of the island from where the Indian sentries watched through the night. He had blackened his face with charcoal and dirt to take off the pale shine that could be seen by a sharp-eyed watcher.

He carried only his knife and had pulled his hat low over his eyes. He half-crabbed, half-swam to a stand of cottonwoods on the bank about a hundred yards upstream from the scene of the day's fighting. He moved slowly but steadily so that he would not create any unusual movement in the water and so that he could blend into the night shadows.

Dog watched him with one eye, seeming to understand that he had to go out alone.

He had not told the others what he was going to do. They did not even know he had sneaked away. Caviness and Hoffman were standing watch, and he had successfully eluded even them. That idea didn't make him very happy, but he put it aside and kept moving, stealthily, until he came to a point where he could cross over the river and step onto the rocky bank.

Once on dry land, he darted toward a sheltering rock and then circled around in a wide arc through some trees to the other side of the black bluff, careful that he didn't make a sound as he moved through grass and underbrush. His moccasins trod over the earth like feathers and carried him to within about fifty yards of the Indians' encampment.

There he waited. The moon eventually fell lower in the sky, below the treetops that ringed the quiet camp. The horses were tethered nearby, and Art avoided them, staying downwind as much as he could.

He knew what he had to do, but it would be the most difficult thing he had ever done in his life. He must kill the Indians' war chief and end their siege of the island. The cool night wind blew over his still-wet body, and he clenched his teeth so that they would not chatter in the surprising cold. He was reminded how winter could come down fast and hard in this high country, even in August or early September. He had even known it to snow at this time of year.

He waited. He was armed only with his knife, which never left his side. The steel blade was clean, extremely sharp, ready to do its killing work. He measured his breathing so that it was smooth and soundless. He waited some more.

After he had been in place for more than two hours, the young mountain man moved. Very slowly he crabbed forward until he was within fifty feet of the camp. He surveyed the sleeping forms of the enemy to determine which was the leader—the one farthest from the three bodies of the dead Blackfeet, separated a few feet from the others. It was a calculated risk, but he would take it. He trusted his own instinct on this.

Keeping his breathing as shallow as a snake's, he got on his belly and crawled forward. Now there was no moon, no light, just the wind. He remained downwind from the camp, knowing that the slightest scent or movement would betray him and that would be the end of his life.

The smell of the dry summer grass filled his nostrils. It was like being in a dream, and suddenly he remembered the same smell from when he was a boy. He had always spent his time outdoors, away from his family's home, exploring and hunting and sleeping out under the stars. He had always felt comfortable in the grass, or propped up against a tree. Those days were long past, and he was no longer a boy. Now he was a man on a killing mission.

He was forty feet from his target. He stopped. Waited. Then he moved again, pulling himself forward with powerful arms, his belly sliding against the cold dry earth.

When he got within twenty feet of Wak Tha Go, he removed his knife from the sheath at his belt. He held it in his right hand. The handle, wood covered with leather, warmed in his hand. Sweat beaded his palms.

He crawled closer. Art almost stopped breathing now. Any sound would betray him. He was within fifteen feet. With agonizing slowness, he got within about ten feet. He pushed himself. Sweat covered his brow and his entire body, making him nearly as wet as he had been after coming out of the river. He stopped blinking his eyes as he got even closer.

Then there was a sound! He held himself completely, utterly still. What was it? It wasn't the wind or any animal movement—it sounded human. Then he realized what it was: the war chief's sleep-breathing! He was close enough now that he could almost feel the breeze of the man's breath.

Art's hat formed a tent at the top of his vision. It was completely dark now, and as if by magic he had been transported to this spot, within five feet—almost striking distance—of Wak Tha Go. He did not know the man other than as an enemy.

Wak Tha Go expelled a long, loud breath. Then he turned slightly in his sleep. Art froze. He waited nearly ten minutes, then crept closer, using his toes now to propel him forward. Five feet. Four feet. Three feet. Truly, he felt like a snake slithering toward its prey. Eyes unblinking.

Now he made a bold move. He brought himself parallel to the sleeping man's body. He rolled himself over one time until he was nearly face-to-face with the enemy. With a swift movement he clamped his left hand down over Wak Tha Go's nose and mouth.

The shock startled the Indian awake. His eyes opened wide and he saw Art for an instant. Art felt him start to struggle, to fight off his attacker. But it was too late.

With a blindingly powerful swing, Art brought his knife up, then down, plunging it directly into the Indian's heart. He had to push Wak Tha Go's head down, stifle his cry. It took every ounce of strength the young man had to hold the powerful Indian's mouth and nose and push the long steel blade as far as possible into the chest. Then he withdrew the knife.

Blood bubbled up out of the deep, deadly wound in the chest cavity. Art smelled it, felt it on his hands and arms. It was warm and wet. Still trying to be absolutely silent, he wiped his hands in the grass and started to turn to make his way out of the camp without being detected by the others.

He stopped himself. If he wanted to end the siege of the island, he must send an unmistakable signal to the Indians. They had lost three men in the battle, now their chief to a killer in the night. But how would they know who had done it?

Art removed his hat. He hated to lose it, for a hat was a part of a man on the trail, as necessary as a gun, though for vastly different reasons. He placed the hat on Wak Tha Go's upper chest. Then he reached around and found Wak Tha Go's own knife. In the brief struggle before his life had ended, the Indian had groped for the knife and his dead hand was close by.

The mountain man took the knife and plunged it through the brim of the hat, pinning it to the dead warrior's chest.

What would they say to that? he wondered. He hoped it would spook them enough to call off another attack. Pushing himself away, he crawled for several yards before he got to his feet and ran quietly away into the night.

The next day came and the Indians did not attack. None of the men on the island knew why—except Art himself. As they packed and prepared to leave, he told them.

Eleven

The party was somber, glad to have survived the siege of the little unnamed island, grateful that Art had put a knife in their enemy's chest. Even McDill and Caviness were quiet for the first two or three days out, after such a close call. Dog held back, but followed the party off the island.

The man who would one day be called Preacher, leader of this column, rode out one morning to scout the forward area west of the Missouri River, which rolled wide and shallow around boulders and over rocks up in this north country. He rode about five miles out, ahead of the other trappers.

From the day he had left his family in Ohio, Art had been a fiercely independent man. He remembered to this day the letter, just a brief note really, that he had left behind. It said, simply:

Ma and Pa
 Don't look for me for I have went away. I am near a man now and I want to be on my own. Love, your son, Arthur.

He was on his own, all right, and had been for more than twelve years as he grew into manhood among the Indians and mountain men of the West. He had known more adventures than he could have ever dreamed up back in Ohio. . . . As he breathed in the Missouri badlands air untainted by man, he said a silent prayer of thanksgiving to the only God he knew, the Creator of this land of savage beauty. He was not much given to introspection, and had never been a churchgoing man, but sometimes he just felt that he had to look up and say thanks.

He was almost unaware of the men he had left behind. Ahead lay a thicket that stretched out like a green island on the brown land. He kneed his mount in that direction. Maybe this was a place where his party and their horses could rest for a while at midday, out of the sun that was already beginning to beat down hard on them. There hadn't been rain here for at least two weeks, and the ground was sere and hard-packed, stony even away from the river.

Art dismounted when he was about twenty yards outside the thicket, leading his horse forward, alert to sounds and smells out of the ordinary that would signal danger. He cradled his trusted rifle after he had loaded and primed it, then hobbled the horse when he got to the edge of the thicket.

Moving through the underbrush, he peered into the shadowy area beneath the trees, measuring each step with as much silence and stealth as he could manage. He entered an opening that must have been about ten yards by twenty yards, enough space for a house and garden, he thought—though it was unlikely that any white settler would ever come to this remote part of the world to build such a house. Dog, who had followed him, yowled.

Then, with a suddenness that nearly took his breath away, he saw it: a grizzly bear with its long black-brown back turned to him. The animal became still, then sensed Art's presence, then turned toward him and stood at its full height. As the bear turned, he could see three smaller animals—cubs. This was a mother, a grizzly sow, who was tending her young. She was as dangerous as ten men. He knew this when he heard her roar, an earsplitting howl of anger and defiance.

The huge, dark bear stood nearly ten feet tall on her hind feet. Her giant clawed paws slashed at the air as the cubs, not knowing what was happening, scurried over each other to stand behind their aroused mother.

Her black eyes locked on Art, who stood stock-still at the edge of the opening beneath the trees. He took one step forward, toward the grizzly that was ready to attack. This was unexpected, and the bear cocked her head, then opened her mouth again, baring yellow teeth and fangs. The sow trumpeted a warning to the approaching man and to the wolf-dog.

Art had never seen anything like it: this monster with black eyes towering over him. Deliberately, he raised his rifle and aimed, held steady. With almost lightning speed, the grizzly attacked.

The mountain man fired his rifle, sending a ball directly into the chest of the advancing bear. She shuddered as she took the impact of the lead in the center of her huge body. But it did not stop her. The grizzly came on, flailing her razor-claws, roaring in pain. With immense speed and power the wounded sow pounced, her arms extended.

Art reacted just as quickly, ducking first as the bear-talons swept the air where his head had been. He felt the wind of her violent swipe. He dropped his rifle, useless now, and ran toward a nearby tree. He scrambled to get a foothold in a low branch, and had to jump up to reach for a higher branch. He slipped, jumped again, and took hold this time.

The bear spun almost a full circle with the momentum of her attack. Her back was to the man. The ball in her chest was the source of incredible pain, and blood leaked from the entry wound. She turned, spotted Art as he tried to clamber up the tree.

She shook her gigantic head, mouth open, and saliva sprayed all around her. In two steps she was at the tree where Art hung, trying to gain a footing. As she grabbed for him, he swung out of her reach and pulled himself up higher into the tree.

He thought if he could hold out and not let the grizzly get him for just another minute, she would die from the wound he had inflicted. But she showed no sign of dying. The cubs watched from the side of the clearing as their mother attacked yet again.

This time she stood at her full height and reached for Art, clawing him across the back with one paw, pummeling him with the other. Art felt the deep cuts in his back and the blow to his left shoulder, shaking him from his precarious perch in the tree. He wanted to howl in pain himself, but did not. He had to hold on, had to try. . . .

The great grizzly sow seized her prey then, holding both of Art's legs and pulling him off the tree. Dog yapped at the bear's legs, but she ignored him.

He tumbled to the earth, falling with a hard thud and wincing at the pain. His back was in shreds and he felt the warm blood from the razor wounds there. He rolled away from the attacking bear, but was not quick enough.

With an ear-shattering roar, the grizzly went after him again. She reached down and swiped, this time slicing into his arm with her claws. He wanted to scream, but did not. His only thought was escape—but there was nowhere to go. He struggled unsteadily to his knees. He pulled free his hunting knife from its sheath at his belt. With his good arm he pushed the knife toward the mad animal, found his target.

As he stabbed the blade into the wounded grizzly's chest, he felt it scrape against the giant's ribs. The foamy spittle at the gaping mouth became pink, then red. The bear's black eyes locked on Art, who could barely breathe as he was caught in a savage tent made by the huge animal's body.

Then it closed in on him and fell on top of him. Art was crushed beneath the thousand-pound weight of the grizzly sow.

It was only an hour, but it seemed like days to Art, who drifted in and out of consciousness. His men found him lying beneath the carcass of the bear he had killed. It took all five of them another hour to figure out how to lever the dead body off the man. The bear's blood mingled with Art's, leaving him a bloody, pulpy mess. He fought through the pain to remain alert.

"She-bear . . ." he gasped. His eyes sought the three cubs who had sniffed around their mother before Art's party arrived.

McDill looked around, cursed, and shot at the nearby cubs, who scattered out of sight. There was little hope for them now. They would soon join their mother in death.

Hoffman, ignoring his own injury, and the others knelt beside their leader. He lay on his back more dead than alive. He bled from claw wounds in his face, chest, back, shoulder, and thighs. One leg and several ribs were broken. His face was a red mask of blood, and he had to spit to keep it out of his mouth as he breathed.

"He's tore damn near to pieces," Don Montgomery said. Matthews turned away and got sick. "Aw, Joe, come back here and help him."

"He should be dead," McDill muttered, standing over Art.

"Maybe we should put him out of his misery," Caviness suggested.

"By God!" Hoffman, the big German, leapt to his feet and pushed his face against Caviness's. "You will not kill our captain as you say! You will die if you try to hurt him, because I will kill you!"

It was the longest speech any of them had ever heard the Hessian give. His face was red from heat and anger. Caviness took one step backward.

"I was just saying maybe it would be the merciful thing to do, that's all." Caviness looked around at the others, but no one came to his defense. He had not won any friends on this journey, and even McDill looked away.

"All right, all right, I'm sorry," he said finally.

"It is good," Hoffman said, then went back to tend to Art.

All of them had thought it, but only Caviness had said it. As they looked at the tall young mountain man lying in a pool of red-black blood, none of them thought he could survive the day. But carefully they cared for him, washed his wounds, and bandaged him. McDill tended to his horse, then fetched his bedroll, which they laid out in a semi-sheltered spot by a tree. Hoffman went to the stream close by and filled Art's canteen with fresh water.

He brought it back and propped it up next to his wounded friend. "Here is water for you," he said.

"He's a regular orator," McDill commented to Caviness as they built a cook fire.

No point in riding farther today. They would camp here for the night and start out in the morning. As the others ate, Art listened to their palaver, drifting in and out of consciousness.

"We should rig up a travois," Matthews said. "Maybe we could get him back to the fort for medical help." He looked at the others, sitting around the fire. "We can't leave him here."

"He's gonna die," McDill spat.

"We don't know that," Matthews said angrily. "He's our leader. We've got to stay with him."

"He can't lead us nowhere now." McDill was relentless, couldn't let go of his hatred for Art and his need to take over the expedition and prove himself.

Montgomery and the German knelt by the severely injured man, and helped him drink some water from a canteen. For all they knew the water, like his blood, would leak out of puncture holes in his body. But they had to do something. Art couldn't eat anything in his condition, and he was barely conscious enough to move his lips to drink. The two men looked at each other in despair.

"Damn," Montgomery said simply. He was not a man of words.

Hoffman too was sad and angry at the grizzly sow who had nearly killed his friend—and angry at the disloyalty shown by McDill and Caviness. "We must keep an eye on those men," he told Montgomery in a low voice. "I do not trust them."

"Hell, no," Montgomery hissed. "They's a pair of snakes if there ever was, damn their souls to hell."

That night the members of the party slept fitfully. All were exhausted but full of uncertainty about their mission. Without their designated leader there was nothing to hold them together. They stood watch in three shifts through the night, but there was no sound, no threat from man or beast. The dawn came suddenly.

Art drifted between sleep and unconsciousness, his injuries stabbing him with pain in nearly every part of his body. At sunup, when the camp began to stir, he was aware of the activity, heard the men's voices and smelled the morning cook fire, but his eyes remained closed.

The wound in his throat was especially painful, and he could feel the copious dried blood on the bandage there. He was more than half-certain that he was going to die.

"So I'm in charge now," McDill announced to the others as the men drank their morning coffee.

"The hell you are," Matthews said, glaring at McDill and Caviness.

"Maybe it's hell for you," Caviness said, "but McDill here is the only one with the experience to do it. So you just shut up and listen to him. He'll get us out of here in one piece, like Art there can't do just now."

"Besides," said McDill, "those Blackfeet are liable to attack again. You want us to sit here and wait for them to gather their forces and come wipe us out?" McDill tossed his coffee dregs onto the ground and glared at Matthews and the other men.

For a minute no one said anything, then the Hessian, Hoffman, said to McDill, "You will leave Art here to die?"

"You want to stay here and die with him?"

"He might live if we can care for him."

"Look at it this way. Do you think he would endanger the whole group if you were injured and going to die?"

Again, the men were silent. It was hard to stand up to McDill when he was like this, at his bullying worst. He stood there like a big mule, his fists clenched, scowling at them all.

"Well—what do you say? You want to be women and stay here and watch him die and likely get killed yourselves?"

Caviness added, "And probably a lot worse than poor old Art here—scalped and gutted like a deer by them Blackfeet."

"It ain't right to just leave him," Montgomery muttered.

"What's that? Speak up," McDill demanded.

Hoffman said, "He means we got to do something. We cannot just leave the man here to die."

"All right, you want to do something, you can leave him some food and water. Maybe he'll want to eat something— if he can. I'm not saying we shouldn't do anything for the poor soul." His words were sympathetic, but McDill turned and gave a wink to Caviness that the others couldn't see.

That seemed to satisfy Art's friends. They settled in for a quick breakfast, saying nothing among themselves and watching McDill and Caviness with suspicion.

The men changed that bloody neck bandage after they had eaten. Matthews cleaned and loaded Art's rifle, and the others put a full canteen and a supply of food beside the wounded man. Caviness stood to one side and watched. But McDill helped, brought Art's horse around after he had watered it, and ground-tethered it nearby.

All the while, Dog, the young mountain man's faithful sentry, walked around Art's still form, occasionally licking at his wounds, eyeing the other members of the party who approached. He growled at McDill, who kept a safe distance at all times, spitting and cursing at the animal. Dog didn't interfere with the others who were trying to help Art.

"C'mon, let's get movin'," McDill said finally. He swung into the saddle alongside Caviness, who was already mounted.

"Good-bye, friend," the Hessian said as he stood stiffly above the unmoving injury-racked body.

Matthews and Montgomery put a blanket over the long-legged mountain man, who lay with his eyes closed, breathing raggedly. They looked over at Dog, who sat at the alert just a few yards away. "Take care of him," Matthews muttered beneath his breath so that McDill couldn't hear him.

"I said time to move out!" the new leader of the group barked. "It'll be noon before we know it and you women won't be too happy then, believe me." He reined his horse around and started off.

The others mounted and rode away without looking back at their gravely wounded leader.

* * *

Percy McDill had worked out a plan with his pal Ben Caviness. When the party had ridden about three miles he suddenly pulled up and halted their advance.

"Damn it all!" he cursed. "I left my spare canteen back at the campsite."

"Since when did you carry a spare canteen?" Matthews piped up. He was very observant and hadn't noticed that McDill was so extra-prepared.

"Since none of your damn business," McDill said. "But I'm not going to leave it there to rust when we may need it on the trip."

"Art could use it," Matthews suggested.

"He's got a canteen full of water. He don't need no extra. I do. Ben, you'll be in charge of this outfit until I get back. I'll push hard and catch up with you in a couple of hours. I won't hold anybody up." McDill wheeled his horse around and started off at a brisk pace.

Caviness said, "All right, you heard him. Let's ride."

McDill pushed his horse pretty hard, and made it back to the campsite in a short time. He had never carried a second canteen, never even thought of it until he and Caviness hatched this scheme for him to return and finish off Art once and for all.

Nothing was different: The young man lay there like a corpse, except that his chest moved up and down in shallow breaths. And Dog was not there!

Good, McDill thought. That damn wolf-dog won't stop me from doing what I have to do. First he took Art's canteen and food cache from beside him and put everything in a saddlebag. The rifle he concealed as best he could in a makeshift saddle holster that he had rigged the previous night so the others wouldn't see that he had stolen the soon-to-be-dead man's gun. Then he went back to the injured man. He moved as swiftly as he could, to get the job done and get back to his companions.

The others had cleaned Art's deadly knife and left it in his belt holster. McDill bent to retrieve the knife. He'd then slit the younger man's throat and be off. . . .

A low, intense growl shattered McDill's concentration and made him stiffen and stand up straight.

There stood Dog, fangs bared, eyes black with anger and hatred for Art's enemy. It seemed that the animal knew exactly what McDill was up to. But Dog wasn't going to let it happen. He'd kill the man first, before he touched the knife. The canine growled again, threateningly, an evil sound from deep within its gut.

McDill froze. His eyes grew wide as saucers and he took a tentative half step back from Art. Dog's growls increased in volume with each move McDill made. The man had to think quickly. He looked over and saw Art's horse just a couple of yards to his right. Dog was still about eight or nine yards away. Almost without thinking, McDill took two quick steps until he had put the horse between himself and the wolf-dog.

Then he whistled quietly, and his own horse ambled over toward him. Using the second horse as a shield, he was able to mount his own and, holding the reins of Art's horse, start moving back from Art's body. He wanted to take out his rifle and shoot the vicious guard dog to death, but he couldn't and still keep a hand on the reins of each horse. Slowly, he backed both horses away from the campsite. Art had not moved or given any indication that he knew what was going on.

Dog was frustrated. He walked closer to the badly injured man, growling all the while but powerless to attack McDill.

The man smiled, showing yellow teeth. "So, you think you're tough, you dad-blasted devil," he said aloud. "I've outsmarted you this time. He's gonna be dead by the end of the day anyhow."

Dog barked, as if in response.

"Shut yer trap, you damned wolfhound. I hope you get ate by a bear. More'n you deserve." As he talked he kept moving, then when he had enough space between himself and Dog, deliberately turned the horses.

"Hee-yah!" he shouted suddenly, kneeing his own horse and yanking at the reins of the other. In a cloud of dust, he galloped off, leaving the yowling wolf-dog to tend to his master.

McDill rode hard for a mile, then slowed to a more even pace. It took him a few hours more to catch up finally with the trappers. But it gave him time to get his story straight.

"Well, boys, our friend Art is dead. Sorry to be the bearer of bad news and all."

"He wasn't no friend of your'n," Matthews said. He didn't like the sound of Percy McDill's voice, the barely concealed satisfaction when he told them of Art's passing. "He was a damn fine fellow, worth more'n ten of you and Caviness put together."

"Now no need to get bitter," McDill said in response. "We all did the best we could to help the man recover, but nobody could survive with those wounds—and you all know it."

The Hessian, Herman Hoffman, eyed McDill skeptically, watched him giving some secret hand signals to Caviness, his partner in crime. He suspected that something was not quite right about all this, but he could not afford to ride back to the campsite to see for himself what had happened. He had to take McDill's word that his friend was dead. It made him sad, and even angrier at McDill for his pompous stupidity.

They rode on till sunset, covering almost thirty miles. McDill was glad to put as much distance between himself and that damned Dog as humanly possible.

* * *

When the sun had gone down, Art's eyes opened. Dog was there, breathing in his face and occasionally licking it with his scratchy tongue.

A fever had gripped him, and he shivered as if it were wintertime and sweated as if he were lying under the desert sun. Because it was getting dark and the stars hadn't come out yet, he could not even see Dog, only a black shadow where the animal's head should be.

Where am I? he wondered. It took a while for him to recall what had happened to him. His fevered brain was weak, and drifted away to strange places. He knew he was thirsty, realized after a while that he was suffering from a fever, and felt incredibly intense pain in nearly every part of his body. After a while he lifted one hand and touched his neck. He felt the bandage there, covered with dried blood. He felt his face, a stubbly growth of beard there, and winced when he ran his hands over the still-open wounds from the giant bear's claws. He tried to sit up, but could not. His head spun and he fell unconscious again. . . .

He dreamed about Jennie . . . the beautiful Creole woman he had last seen in St. Louis. Their lives were intertwined in ways he did not understand. He couldn't have a regular woman in his life, not the life he had chosen that kept him away from people and from civilization for months, even years at a time. It was no life for a refined woman like Jennie. It would kill her. And he loved her too much for that. Or did he? What was love anyway? What did it mean to say, "I love you"? He had never said that to any other person, even Jennie.

He saw her in his dream. She was dressed in a fancy white dress that showed off her caramel-color skin.

She was calling to him, but he didn't know what she was saying, couldn't hear her because there was a roaring in his head like a great wind. She beckoned with her arms open, as if she wanted to take him in an embrace, to be with him

as a woman is with a man . . . but he couldn't get any
nearer to her, no matter how hard he tried. The pounding
pain in his head was so great that he thought it would ex-
plode. Still, he strove with all his might to reach her.

All the memories of his first wanderings and his own captivity came rushing back at him when he saw Jennie's face
in his dream. Then the dream changed and he was the young
mountain man on his first journey in the country of the
upper Missouri, when the river became his woman and he
followed her to his destiny. He had been alone then. . . .

He had shot a turkey with his Hawken, and had built
himself an oven to cook the bird when suddenly a voice
startled him from his task. It was a man in soiled buckskin
and homespun who called out to him.

"Hello the camp!" The man was tall, gaunt, bearded.
"You campin' all by yourself, are you, young feller?"

Art thought for a moment about lying to the stranger,
telling him that he wasn't alone, but he realized that the
man had probably already scouted the area and would
know that he was lying. And if Art lied, it would be a sign
of weakness and fear, a sign that he was afraid to admit
that he was alone.

In his fevered dream it was as real as if it were happening for the first time.

"I am alone," Art said.

The man stuck out his hand, calloused and gray. "Bodie
is the name. How are you called?"

Bodie . . . he had driven a mule named Rhoda and traded
her to Art for the horse the youth had stolen in his escape
from Lucas Younger, who'd held him in slavery. He remembered how Younger had been about to shoot him
when Art jerked at the chain that bound him and caused
Younger to shoot himself—dead. Bodie then traded him
the mule, a more surefooted animal for where Art was
going. He also told Art about the Rendezvous, because Art

was so green he had never even heard of such a thing. And most importantly, Bodie, the crusty old mountain man, had told Art to look up some friends of his.

Art heard Bodie's voice now, loud and clear in his mind:

"Listen, when you get up into the mountains, if you run into a couple o' ugly varmints—one is named Clyde, the other calls himself Pierre—why, you tell 'em that ol' Bodie says hello, will you?"

"Yes, sir. I'll do that," Art said. Then Bodie said some things that Art had never forgotten, even to this day.

"This be your first time in the mountains, boy?"

"Yes, sir."

"I thought so. Well, watch yourself up there. Winter comes early to the high country. Before too much longer you're goin' to be needin' to go to shelter. You any good with that there Hawken?"

"Tolerable," Art replied.

"Then I advise you to get you some meat shot, couple o' deer, an elk, maybe a bear. A bear would be nice 'cause you'd also have its skin to help you through the cold."

"Thanks for the advice."

A bear . . .

Now the image of the huge grizzly sow that had nearly killed him came back to Art in a feverish nightmare that took his breath away and left him sweating and panting for thirst. He was running . . . running . . . running . . . away from Jennie, away from the bear, away from McDill, away from Bodie, away from Clyde and Pierre, away from his family—away from everybody he had ever known in his life. His whole body ached from the running, yet he could feel the bear's hot breath on his neck, as if she was going to leap on him and devour him in that gaping pink maw of a mouth. Her razor-talons swiped at him, and he could feel their sharpness slicing into his skin. He was naked, alone, running—running for his life from the giant she-bear, and there was no way to escape, no way to fight, no way . . . no way . . . "You campin' all by yourself, are you, young feller?" Alone . . . alone . . . alone . . .

Dog's breath in his face suddenly shocked him awake. He sensed it was nearly sunup. His body felt limp and damp from the night sweats. He wasn't even sure if he was alive or dead. Had he been dreaming all those things? He slowly moved his hands over his body under the blanket that Montgomery and Matthews had carefully placed over him. The morning air was cool and he gulped it in like water. His hands felt the bruises, bandages, and broken bones that he had become.

I'm in one hell of a mess, he thought, wincing with every slight move he made. But he felt that the fever had passed, and weak as he was, maybe there was a chance he could survive.

Dog stood there, slowly wagging his matted tail. It was the most beautiful sight Art had ever seen. He was still alive. He struggled for an hour until he could finally sit up. He looked around. No canteen, no food, no rifle, no horse.

"They really left us with nothin'," he said out loud to Dog. But he had his knife. He could feel its cool blade against his leg. That was something.

"Thanks for your help, Dog," he said. "Now, let's get something to eat. You know any fancy restaurant around here?"

Twelve

For the first four days, unable to walk, Art crawled. He stayed by the river so he could be close to a source of water. It was already September, he calculated, and winter would come sooner than any man liked in this high country. Just as Bodie had told him so many years ago. He crawled, not knowing where he was going. He had to keep moving, somehow to get back to the fort or to find some other human being—anyone.

He had heard some of the remarkable survival stories of other men who had been lost in the wilderness with no weapon, no food, no one else. He had been a man of the mountains himself for a dozen years, through every season, every condition of nature. He was determined that he too would survive.

He ate berries and nuts that he found close to the water's edge, and he crawled on, sleeping at night, moving during the daylight hours. Luckily, he still had his clothes and his knife. And Dog. So he felt he wasn't totally alone.

His fever lingered for several days, but slowly receded, lessening with each slow, agonizing mile and each troubled night of sleep. The nights were getting cold.

One day he rested on a flat, open table away from the river, during the afternoon, with the sun warming his face. He dozed off for a few minutes, then awoke with a start. He noticed that Dog was silent, staring at something.

Looking about five yards ahead, in the direction that he was moving, Art saw a rattlesnake coiled, sunning itself. He could have sworn the snake was looking at him too.

When he moved slightly to sit up, the snake's tail rose and rattled. It was on the alert and preparing to strike. Art moved his hand imperceptibly, feeling the dry grass, groping for something he could use as a weapon. He found a rock about the size of his own fist.

The rock felt hot from sitting in the sun. Art's hand closed around it. The snake rattled, raised and lowered its head. Art gripped the rock.

He tried to measure the distance and figure out how much time he would have when the snake moved to strike. Best to try when the snake was still coiled, which made a better target.

Holding his breath, he squeezed the rock and in a quick blur of motion flung it at the rattlesnake. He hit it, and the rock smashed the snake's head into the earth. Art forced himself halfway upright and half-crawled, half-walked over to the snake. It was still moving. He took his knife and quickly sliced the reptile's head off, then cut the body in half.

He was so starved that he started chewing on the snake, biting off a piece, chewing the innards and spitting out the skin. Then he bit off another piece and ate it. He didn't even think of the foul taste and the idea of eating a raw, bloody snake. He was so hungry he would have eaten anything that wouldn't poison him.

From that point he could walk, though slowly and with great pain. He cut a tall stick to use as a sort of crutch. He continued, day after day, to keep to the river, and he found edible roots that he could dig with the knife and stones. The water of the river brought new life into him, and even though he was incredibly sore from his injuries, he bathed in its cold current and washed away blood and ache and trail dirt. He lay out naked in the sun to dry and drink in the healing warmth and rays of the sun.

Dog stuck with him each painful step of the way. Day in and day out, the faithful beast was there. Dog was able to capture a stray rabbit or squirrel for himself, and sometimes ate the food that Art dug from the earth.

Art tried to keep track of the days, repeating the count to himself each morning and night: six days, ten days, fifteen days. . . . He headed toward the east and south as the great river wound its way through the badlands.

"Well, Dog," he said aloud one day, "where do you think we are? Any hope we'll find the fort or any human being soon?"

The animal looked up at the young mountain man, cocking its head and growling with impatience.

"All right, boy, if that's the way you feel about it. I was just asking a question. Don't bite my head off, now."

Art laughed. He couldn't remember the last time he had laughed. He lifted his head and felt the sun strike his face full on, and he breathed in the high plains air and swung his arms around. He realized that he wasn't in constant pain anymore. Oh, sure, there were pains and aches and bones still mending, and he depended a lot on his walking stick-crutch. But for a few minutes he felt better, felt that he might survive after all.

He thought about his men. Wondered where they were and what they were doing. McDill, no doubt, had taken over the leadership of the party—which he had felt was his all along. He vaguely remembered when McDill had returned to the camp to check on him. He felt then that he was going to die, but Dog had warned the man off, probably saved Art's life. McDill had taken Art's horse and rifle and canteen. He had left him there to die.

Art wasn't angry at McDill, but he knew that he would

probably have to kill him when they next met—if they ever met.

Three weeks into his arduous trek, the mountain man awoke one morning to the sound of something moving on the earth. He felt it first, then heard it: far away but getting closer. What the hell? Then he knew—it was a herd of buffalo moving across the land, probably approaching the river to ford.

The herd must be late in leaving the high plains for the lusher, taller grasses south of the Upper Missouri and the warmer hills and valleys of the lower country. Art looked around for Dog, didn't see him. The wolf-dog had heard the same thing he had and gone in search of the herd.

It took him two hours to walk about a mile through a densely treed area above the river and into an open hilly stretch. Clouds streamed across the sky, sometimes blotting out the sun and taking away the shadows from the land. He climbed a low hill, and when he got to the top he could see for several miles, and there, like a sea, was the wandering herd of buffalo.

He saw Dog, who stood like the wolf he was, salivating at the sight of enough meat for a thousand lifetimes.

If only he had his favorite Hawken, he could take down one of the huge beasts and have real food for the first time in weeks, and a buffalo-skin blanket for the increasingly cold nights! His body was still mending, and he could walk better and better each day, but he certainly couldn't run—yet. So there was no way he could hunt on foot.

The vast herd was moving south, rumbling over the brown-green grass of the low rolling hills. He couldn't even imagine how many there were. He followed Dog, who trotted closer to the moving mass of brown and black animals.

Dog's hunting instincts took over. Art watched with fascination as the wolf-dog got closer and closer to the western edge of the herd and watched, inspected the passing animals for potential targets. Dog would pause, run alongside the herd for about a hundred yards, circle back and look, then run again. The larger animals ignored the comparatively small beast who yipped and howled at them.

In the middle distance, about a half mile away, Art could see a pack of wolves out in the open, circling, trying to identify a likely victim, just as Dog was. Then Dog saw them too, some of his own kind.

He ran in their direction, barking and howling. The pack ignored the newcomer, sticking together tightly. Dog retreated, ran back toward Art, even wagged his tail, which was unusual for the mongrel.

"All right, boy," Art said. "We'll stay clear of them and they'll stay out of our way." He began hiking to the north, the direction from where the herd was coming. He kept the same wide distance between the wolf pack and himself, not wanting them to sniff him out as a potential meal himself.

Dog went about his business, plunging back into the fringes of the advancing herd of bison. It didn't take him long to cut out a youngster and turn him around and separate him from the rest of the herd. The calf was confused, scared, and it started to run away from Dog, to the west. Art moved after it. He knew Dog could take the calf down, but he didn't want to lose it to the wolf pack, who hadn't yet culled a calf or an injured adult for themselves.

The calf ran in crazy circles, and Dog pushed it farther away from the herd, over a low hill into a narrow ravine. Soon it could not see the herd at all, and bellowed like a wounded pig. Dog closed in. Art watched the whole thing happen. He drew his knife as he walked closer to the buffalo.

Even though it was a calf, the animal must have weighed more than four or five hundred pounds. It was unsteady on its legs in unfamiliar territory. It was scared of Dog and frightened to be apart from its family for the first time ever. It would be the last time too.

Dog attacked, leaping at the hapless calf's legs. It tripped and fell, breaking a spindly leg. It bleated in pain. Dog attacked again, this time going for the animal's throat. He tore into it viciously, immediately drawing blood. The buffalo calf tried to fight off the wolf-dog, but the harder it fought the worse it got—Dog held onto his prey, digging his teeth deeper into the poor calf's flesh.

Art hobbled closer, approaching with his knife drawn. He waited for his chance as the two animals struggled, then fell onto the calf and plunged the knife into its heart. He rolled off the big body as blood leaked out, soaking the earth.

Art heard the wolves approach from behind him. He swung around, holding his walking stick and knife. "Yah, yah, yah!" he challenged. Dog turned too and growled, his mouth dripping with blood and saliva.

The wolves—there were seven or eight of them—looked at these two creatures protecting their kill. Certainly they outnumbered the man and his dog, and might be able to fight them, but something about the threatening noises and movements of the two made them pause and back away. Then the pack leader turned and trotted off toward the buffalo herd, and the others followed.

"That's the way to do it, Dog," Art said.

Dog growled in agreement, then turned back to the kill. The young buffalo lay there like a small mountain, and Art set to work immediately dressing out the carcass as best he could by himself with a single knife. Dog patrolled the immediate area to make sure that none of the wolves came back to try again to claim the kill.

He wasn't finished by nightfall, so he and Dog slept right there at the site. The next morning he rigged a very primitive travois to carry away some meat and skin to a camp by the river. There he made a fire for the first time in weeks and cooked some of the meat for himself. Dog ate his supper raw, burped, and lay down for a nap.

Art ate his fill, then scraped the hide and washed it in the river and set it out, pegging it to the ground to dry. He felt better than he had since his encounter with the grizzly, finally healing and regaining some strength.

For the next few days he traveled with the travois, dragging it behind him, eating the meat each night for supper. He worked on the buffalo skin to soften it in order to make a blanket. The nights were fast getting colder, and he did not know how far he was from any human contact or civilization.

As the days passed, he resolved that he was going to catch up to his men—one way or another—to reclaim leadership of the expedition. He would have quite a story to tell Mr. Ashley—and Jennie—when they all returned to St. Louis.

The Blackfoot village had mourned their dead from the ill-fated attack led by Wak Tha Go against Art's exploratory party. Now, nearly two moons later, the people were restless for revenge. They had lost sons and brothers, and they had trusted the hotheaded war chief to bring them victory and count many coups against the white invaders. It had not happened.

Those who had returned alive had advocated another attack on the whites, with more men from the village. They were bitterly angry that Artoor had slain their leader, Wak Tha Go. They knew he had done it because he had left his hat pinned to the great warrior's chest in a gesture of defiance, like counting coup on the dead man. But he had not scalped the war chief, which surprised them.

They had also lost their great elder, Running Elk, who

had died before the war party went out to fight the trappers led by Artoor.

The men sat around the council fire and smoked, talking about their village's misfortune and what could be done about it.

"We must bring war to the whites again," said Brown Owl, one of the younger men who had ridden with Wak Tha Go. He had lost a brother in the battle.

An elder named Buffalo Standing in the River, who was a respected nephew of Running Elk, said, "We cannot afford to lose any more of our young men. It is not our task alone, but for all red brothers to take up their war clubs against Artoor's men."

"But he has made peace with some of the others, like the Arikira," Brown Owl reminded the council.

"White man's peace." Buffalo Standing spat onto the earth in front of himself. "The word of such men is worthless. They know only war and destruction."

"It is true, Grandfather," another of the younger men said. "This is why our people will not make peace. But we must not sit here and moan like women. We must make another war party and seek out these white killes."

Others murmured agreement, and some spoke in favor of forming another war party. Brown Owl, though he was young, had earned the respect of the other men of his village. He joined the debate, speaking with confidence.

"I saw Artoor and the others with my own eyes. I shot arrows at them and I believe I wounded one of them. Even though we lost one battle, we must fight another. Then another after that, if necessary."

"Young men fight. Old men talk," Buffalo Standing said, nodding in agreement with what Brown Owl said, puffing on the long-stemmed pipe.

"Then let us prepare to fight," Brown Owl declared. He counted about ten warriors among the men around the council fire. "We will hold a war council tomorrow and make our plans."

"It is good," another of the elders said.

The men of the council whooped and cheered at Brown Owl's words. They looked at this very young man with new eyes, with new respect. He would make a good war chief for their people.

But Brown Owl was frustrated after the council ended, and instead of going to his own lodge and the arms of his wife, he walked alone outside the village. He climbed the tall, one-hundred-foot bluff above the Yellowstone River from where he could look down on the village of his birth. It was past sundown and the moon, a shimmering crescent, had risen in the blue-black sky.

The land stretched out beneath him, the vast country that lay between the Missouri and Yellowstone Rivers, where his people had lived and hunted for generations. And they had fought wars there too, against many enemies, to defend what was to them sacred ground.

The young warrior thought back on the events of the past two months, beginning with a similar council discussion when Wak Tha Go urged them to go to war against Artoor. Then the death of Running Elk, who took with him some of the soul of his people and left an emptiness in the village with his passing. Then the war party itself, the attack on the island where the trappers fought back against Wak Tha Go's men, Brown Owl among them.

Wak Tha Go had been stunned, unhappy at the turn of events, and must have thought that the Great Spirit had abandoned him. In fact, Wak Tha Go himself did not survive that night. He had been killed and humiliated that very night. It was tragic that the war chief had not died in battle, but in his sleep. Stories would be told for many generations in the future of the defeat of Wak Tha Go.

Perhaps it was time for a new war chief to lead the people's best fighters against the whites. . . .

As he was thinking these thoughts, Brown Owl felt the presence of another, which was surprising because no one had walked with him to this place—nor had he seen anyone following him. He could see everything from this vantage point. He turned and saw, in the white-silver moonlight, an old man.

He had not heard the man approach, and wondered how he could have climbed the hill. He also wondered who this man was, for it was not a man of his village. Or was it?

The old man sat cross-legged on the ground, wearing a red shirt, trimmed in yellow. This was a ceremonial shirt, not the kind of clothing a man wore ordinarily. Also, the man's knife, bow and quiver of arrows, war club, and pipe all lay on the earth beside him.

"Who are you? How did you get here?" Brown Owl asked.

The old man said nothing.

"You are not of my village. Where did you come from?"

Again no answer.

"Why do you say nothing? Why do you follow me?"

The old man remained silent, but more than silent, eerily still, as if dead. But he wasn't dead, or else how could he have gotten here?

"Speak to me, Grandfather," the younger man insisted.

The elder man's eyes were wide open and staring, black discs that were the opposite of the bright moon.

"And why are you wearing such good clothes and carrying your weapons and your pipe?" Brown Owl asked.

"I was dressed this way by the women," the old man said finally, breaking his silence. "The women of the village."

"What village?"

The strange old man turned and pointed over the side of the tall bluff toward Brown Owl's own village.

"How can this be?"

"What is past cannot be changed. What is future can be chosen, until there is no more future. Until death."

Brown Owl was confused and scared, and angry that this man should disturb his prayers with his nonsense. It was the way of old people, sometimes. Their minds wandered to many places and they did not make sense. He would have to help this man climb back down the side of the rise. But who was he?

"You speak of the future and of death."

"What else is there to speak of?"

"I have seen death."

"So have I, Brown Owl."

"You know my name."

"I know many names."

"Do you know the name of Wak Tha Go?"

"Yes, it is right you should ask about this man. I spoke to him before he led you into battle against the man named Artoor."

"He did not tell me of this conversation."

"He kept many things in his heart. He chose the way of war, the way of revenge against one man—a white man."

"Artoor killed him," Brown Owl said.

"I told him that Artoor would not be killed."

"How could you know this?"

"I know many things. I know things that are true. This I tell you: The one called Artoor will one day come to our village."

"How can this be? And why do you say 'our' village?"

The old man remained sitting, but his voice became stronger and more animated as he spoke. "I was born in this village and ended my life in this place. The women of the village took care of me. I married a girl of the village."

"But who are you then?"

"You know my name well, but I cannot speak it, for it is no longer my name," the man said mysteriously.

Brown Owl might have seen something of battle, but he was still young and naïve, and he could not figure out what the old man was trying to tell him.

"Speak to me, Grandfather, of what you said to Wak Tha Go."

"Yes, it is good that I should tell you. Know this—Artoor will not be killed. The people may capture him, but he will gain his freedom through his tongue, which will speak without ceasing from sun to sun."

"This sounds crazy. Why can we not kill Artoor?"

"Because he is a great man, and the Spirit who creates all men does not want Artoor to die. He has another name for Artoor."

"What is this name?"

"It is a name that white men and Indians alike will call him. It is the name Preacher."

"That is very strange," Brown Owl said.

"Not as strange as other things that will happen to the people. You are young and will live long to see many things change, many things pass from the earth. You will speak to Artoor with your own tongue and listen to him with your own ears."

"I intend to kill Artoor, to avenge what he has done to my people."

"This white man seeks the way of peace. But his people and our people will not know peace."

"What are these riddles that you speak, Grandfather? I do not understand."

"You will seek the white trapper, Artoor, and you will find him. Then you will know why I speak of these things."

Brown Owl turned to gaze down upon the sleeping village below. Many fires had burned out, and there was darkness in all but a very few tepees. It was time for the people to rest. Suddenly he felt tired, ready to go to his wife and sleep in his own bedroll.

"Grandfather, I—" He turned to speak to the old man again, but he was gone. There was no one sitting there, no war club or arrows or pipe. Where had he gone?

The young warrior ran down the side of the hill and ran toward his lodge. When he hurried past the tepee that had been Running Elk's, he realized who the old man was. A chill of fear and elation ran up his spine. He would tell no one of this vision that he had received.

It rained, hard and cold, for three days straight. Art sought shelter in a stand of trees near a sheltering bluff. He used the young buffalo skin as a makeshift tent to stay at least partially dry.

He had no more meat from the kill, but continued to subsist on roots and small game that Dog shared with him. It was a way to survive, but he didn't know how much longer he could exist in this way.

It was good to stay in one place for a few days. His arm and ribs had nearly healed. His beard was long and scraggly from lack of a razor, and his hair was long enough to have to pull back and tie with a thong made from the buffalo hide. He kept his knife sharpened and clean, free of rust or any blemish.

On the first day after the rain had stopped, about six weeks after his ugly confrontation with the grizzly, Art awoke to Dog's growling, snarling alarm. He got to his feet as quickly as he could, pulled down the buffalo skin lean-to, and erased traces of his campsite as best he could. Then he hid among the trees and waited.

Within a few minutes he saw a group of Indians approaching, armed and on horseback.

He counted ten, and he was sure they were Blackfeet.

Although he couldn't be sure, he thought that some of them had been in the war party that had attacked his men on the island in the river.

Dog was nowhere in sight. He had run off to scout the oncoming party, and he was probably behind them by now, sniffing them out and trying to determine their intention. Art knew from looking at them what their intention was: to find and kill any white man, himself included. Especially him.

He held in his breathing in order to keep perfectly still, but there was little chance that the Indians would not spot his camp, if they were a serious search-and-fight party, as he suspected.

The leader was a young man, of average height but broad in the shoulders, bare-chested, the customary eagle feather in his scalp lock. He signaled for two of his men to scout the immediate area. He must have sensed the presence of someone by the way he looked around, his own nostrils flaring, his eyes sharp and penetrating.

The young war chief spoke in quiet tones to his men. Two more split off and rode to the rear, another two forward to the bank of the river. Now it was clear. They weren't going anywhere until they found what they were looking for—Art.

He had to decide what to do—hunker down in hiding or show himself and face the consequences. He hated the idea of them flushing him out like a timid rabbit, so he decided to come out and face them like a man.

He knew a smattering of several Indian languages, including Blackfoot, so he called out. "I am here," he said in their tongue. "I am here. I come out."

The Indians, especially the leader, stopped and looked.

From the thicket of trees and underbrush, Art walked forward, carrying the folded-up buffalo-calf skin. He kept his gaze locked on the leader of the party, who sat his horse proudly. He was sure this had been one of the attackers of the trappers' party.

"I am here," Art repeated. He stood in the clearing and threw the buffalo skin down on the ground.

"Yes, you are here," Brown Owl said. He called out to the others, the scouts who had split off from the main party. He stared at the mountain man, who looked haggard and worn with the scraggly beard and long, unkempt hair. Something had happened to this man, he realized.

Then he said, "You are Artoor."

Art nodded. "Yes, I am Art."

In his own language, the Indian said, "I am Brown Owl of the people you call Blackfoot. You are our prisoner now."

Art understood some of what the man said, figured he had given his own name as Brown Owl and confirmed that he was a Blackfoot. Then he tried something, using sign language as well as speech. He said, "You and I have met before—in battle."

"Yes, I was with Wak Tha Go when we fought you. You killed Wak Tha Go."

So that was the name of the war chief whom he had killed. There would be no peace until these men had avenged their leader, and Art's chances of surviving that were nonexistent. He knew that. He wondered where Dog had gone, but figured that the animal was watching from a safe spot. No reason to show himself and get killed. Dog was one smart wolf-dog.

Speaking quickly, Brown Owl ordered one of his men to tie Art's hands behind his back.

"You will be our prisoner. We are not far from my village, and we will take you there to face the judgment of my people for what you have done."

Art was pretty sure he understood what the man was saying. He said, "I have done nothing. I want peace with your people."

"Yes, you talk of peace. You even make peace with some of the Indian tribes. But one day you will break the peace. It is the way of the white man who speaks like a god-spirit, then acts like a devil."

The mountain man knew he could not argue with the Indian, and he knew that the man was right in some respects. He thought of McDill and others like him who only wanted to give the Indians drink and addle their minds and kill them off. Art, on the other hand, truly believed that they could live together in the mountain country, that trappers could coexist with hunters and Indians of all tribes.

But too many promises and treaties had been broken over the years for Indians such as Brown Owl to believe a white man.

After a while, they began the ride back to their village. Art was neck-tethered to one of the horses, and had to trot to keep up with the pace. After only a mile or so he was exhausted, ready to drop. His injuries began to ache again, and he grew incredibly thirsty. Once in a while the leader would look back at him to see if he was keeping up with the war party. At one point Art stumbled and nearly fell. The leader, Brown Owl, ordered them to slow down slightly. He could tell that Art had been injured somehow, and felt some pity for the white man.

They were only a few miles from the village, so they made it there by about noon.

A couple of scouts had ridden ahead to alert the people that a prisoner was coming. So, the entire village turned out to see Art, the famous "Artoor" they had heard so much about. They jeered at him and threw stones. Dogs in the village barked at him and bit him in the legs.

He could barely breathe, and he was dizzy from thirst and hunger. He was nearly crippled from the run, and wondered whether he had re-broken any bones. His ribs burned with pain. As he ran along the dusty path through the middle of the village, he gagged and nearly retched his guts out.

Finally, the party stopped in the center of the village, near the place where the council fire was held. Brown Owl dismounted and came around to Art, took the tether from the rider, and did not remove it from the white man's neck. Art's hands were still tied securely behind his back.

"Artoor, you will not be ill treated before you are judged by the council of the people. Come, you will go to my lodge and my wife will feed you. You will rest before tonight when the council fire is lit."

Art said nothing, but followed Brown Owl to his tepee. There a woman, the war chief's wife, fed him a stew and gave him water. He had never tasted anything so good in his entire life, though he didn't even know what it was— and didn't want to know for fear it might be dog meat.

He tried to say thank you to Brown Owl and his wife, but they ignored him. She had prepared a resting place for him and, after he had drunk some more water, Art collapsed onto the skins and fell asleep immediately.

Brown Owl tied the neck-tether to a lodge pole. He said to his wife, "This is the man who killed Wak Tha Go. Now he will meet the judgment of the people and lose his own life."

"It is good, my husband," the woman said. "I am proud of you for having captured this man."

Brown Owl wanted to tell her about the dream-vision of Running Elk, how he had seen and spoken to the dead man the night before. But he held his tongue. She would not understand, or perhaps she would not believe him. It was something a man should keep in his own heart and not share with a woman.

Instead, he said, "Today I have become a war chief of my people. I have led the warriors and we have captured a

Thirteen

Along the Southern Platte River

Jennie's party of women from the House of Flowers in St. Louis had found their way overland to Westport, then turned northwest and followed the Missouri River trail until it forked off along the Platte River. About a hundred miles west of the junction, where a trading town for trappers and explorers was located, lay a tiny, isolated settlement. The settlement consisted of a sutler and general store, a blacksmith, a three-room "hotel," and a small cluster of tent dwellings—about ten people in total, including Jennie's girls.

Ben, her faithful driver—and the only black man for five hundred miles in any direction, as far as she knew—rigged a place for himself in the back of his wagon. There he could attend to the horses and guard Jennie's valuable possessions: some cooking pots and a few dresses.

Clara, the young woman who had been caught up in the commotion surrounding the House of Flowers, stayed by Jennie's side as often as she could. Jennie and the few other girls did not try to talk her into becoming a prostitute to earn her keep, so she did some cooking and sewing and started a ledger book that recorded any money transactions—few as they were—that took place between Jennie and some "gentlemen customers."

The days were long and dry, hot during sunlight, and cool at night. The little village saw boatmen and trappers and a few Indians coming and going periodically. Most of the time, the men sat around in the front room of the hotel, which was a makeshift saloon with planks set over barrels and a few kegs of increasingly stale liquor that were rarely replenished. They played cards and gossiped like women—about the women in their midst.

Certainly, they didn't turn Jennie away when she came. They were glad to see women—any women—let alone women as pretty as she and as nice as her girls. They became occasional customers too, though they had little cash to pay. Jennie came up with a barter system, so that she and her girls could obtain food and supplies in return for their services. Within about a month, they had the system down, and it seemed to work well for them.

One day it rained, and the men gathered for a card game in the stale-smelling saloon.

"How did we get so lucky?" Bartholomew Wills, the owner and only resident of the Platte Hotel, said. He had come here from St. Louis, like Jennie, on the run from the law. He was a natural-born gambler, but unfortunately not very good at it. His debts had caught up with him, forcing him to flee as far west as he could. There was nothing beyond this little settlement, as far as he knew.

The others were men of similarly questionable backgrounds. They didn't probe into each other's pasts and didn't reveal anything about their own.

"I mean, to have Miss Jennie of the famous House of Flowers in St. Louie right here amongst us. Must have done something right at some time in our lives." He laughed. He was holding a winning hand.

The others were silent, concentrating on their cards. Compared to the rest, Wills was a chatterbox. He liked to boast of his business prowess and successes back in St.

Louis. No one believed him, and he didn't even believe himself. But it passed the time in this dreary, lonely place.

Thunder rumbled and crashed outside. The men smoked cigars and bet on their hands.

Just then Jennie came into the saloon-hotel lobby. She held a blanket over her head against the downpour, but it hadn't helped much. She didn't wear a hat, so her black hair was damp and hung down over her lovely face. The men stopped and gaped at her as she stood there and shook her head. Drops of water flew everywhere, even over the card table, but the men did not protest.

"Well, Miss Jennie," Bartholomew Wills said. "Welcome to our humble establishment. You light up the place like a lantern, like the sun, which we so sorely miss today."

"Thanks, Mr. Wills. One of my girls is sick and I need some medicine."

There was no doctor in these parts, unsurprisingly, so Wills kept some medicines and chemicals behind the bar. Mostly powders and potions that were months, if not years, old. He had won them in a card game with a traveling medicine salesman who had accidentally wandered far from civilized society. Word had it that the man had lost his scalp somewhere out on the plains after he had left the little village with no name.

"Hope it's nothing serious, ma'am," Wills volunteered as he rattled around among the bottles behind the bar.

Jennie said nothing. She thought she knew what was the matter with the girl: She was pregnant. It was probably the worst thing that could happen to the young woman. And it would be another mouth to feed for Jennie and the others. But her heart went out to the girl, who was desperately sick this morning.

"Thank you," she said finally when Wills handed her a bottle of powdered stomach medicine.

"You're quite welcome. Are you—er—that is, are the

girls going to be around tonight?" he asked, somewhat sheepishly.

Jennie smiled, even though she didn't feel like it, and she said, in her best professional voice, "Yes, Mr. Wills. I would love it if you were to call on us this evening at any time. You're always welcome, as I hope you well know." She lifted a wet strand of hair from her eyes and put it behind her ear.

"Thanks, Miss Jennie," Wills said like a schoolkid.

The other men looked down in amusement and embarrassment. They would all probably come calling at some point that night.

Jennie took the medicine, put the blanket over her head again, and stepped into the rain. It was pouring hard, in sheets, and she stepped through mud puddles on her way back to the tent where the sick girl lay. She administered the medicine and helped the girl get comfortable, then went to her own tent. There, Carla was expertly sewing a torn undergarment for one of the other girls.

"Is Marie doing better?" Carla asked.

Jennie said, "Yes, but I'm afraid she's in for a long haul."

"What do you mean?"

"I mean she's probably expecting a baby."

"Oh, my!" Carla exclaimed innocently. "How can that be?"

"It probably happened in the usual way," Jennie replied.

"What way is that?"

"I hope one day you marry a nice young man and have lots of children, Carla. Then you'll find out."

"Oh . . ."

Jennie wished she were as naïve and trusting as Carla—then again, she certainly had been trusting with Mr. Epson, the damnable thief who had stolen not only her money, but her house and her livelihood, her chance at a normal life one day.

She felt almost like a slave again, trapped in a place from which there was little chance of escape. But at least she was her own mistress, she did not have someone telling her what to do every minute of the day. She vowed she would never go back to that life—not ever. She would die first.

"Do you think I'll ever get married, Miss Jennie?"

She was startled from her dark thoughts by Carla's voice. "Surely you will—one day," she lied to the girl.

Jennie went to the tent flap, opened it, and looked out on the rain. It reminded her of the old Bible story that she had heard as a girl, the story of Noah and the great flood that had covered the whole world. Maybe this rain would wash away her own cares and troubles. Maybe it would wash the whole world clean. Maybe, somehow, it would bring Art back to her—one day. . . .

In the Blackfoot Village

On his second night in the Indian village, Art was brought before the council fire. He had eaten and slept and regained some strength, and he knew he would need it for whatever ordeal lay ahead.

They had taken his knife and his buffalo robe when they had captured him. They'd left him only his clothes, which were ragged and dirty, and his moccasins, which were worn but still good. So he stood before them, the Blackfoot elders and warriors, with no weapon or means of defense except his own hands.

He had heard how they might make him run the gauntlet, which meant taking blows and taunts from every man, woman, and child of the village. And after that—he didn't know. But he assumed they would put him to death. How? Again, he had no idea, but he had heard stories of men being tortured or burned to death by various plains tribes.

If he were a praying man, now was the time! But Art had never been particularly religious or churchgoing . . . though he did remember that preacher in St. Louis who had preached nonstop for hours and hours along the waterfront, and he had been spellbound by the man's gift for words and his faith.

The men began speaking among themselves around the council fire and passing the pipe from hand to hand. Each man took a few leisurely puffs of the smoke when his turn came. They seemingly ignored Art, who stood in their midst. He listened, but could only make out part of what they were saying.

"He must be put to death. Tomorrow."

"First we must hear his story. How did he kill Wak Tha Go?"

"What happened to him after the battle with our warriors? Why was he lost?"

"His own men turned against him and left him for dead."

"We do not know what happened. He must tell his story."

When the pipe had been completely around the circle, Brown Owl stood. He had gained stature among the people for his capture of this much-feared white trapper, Artoor. The men listened with respect to what he had to say.

"I agree with those who say we will hear his story. There are too many things unknown to us, too many questions."

The elder, Buffalo Standing in the River, agreed with the younger man. "Yes, let the white one talk. Even if he lies to us, we will learn more than we know already."

"I think he will not lie," Brown Owl said. "I think he is a man who speaks truth, even if we do not like what he says."

With sign and speech then, Brown Owl said to Art, the mountain man: "Artoor, you will tell us your story, what happened in the battle with Wak Tha Go and the others, then what happened to you that you were separated from your men."

Since it was his first chance to ask directly, he said to the warrior, "Were you there at the battle on the island in the river with Wak Tha Go?"

"Yes, I was one of the warriors."

"Were you the one who wounded my man Hoffman, the tall man with the yellow hair?"

Brown Owl smiled for the first time in a very long time. "Yes, my arrow struck his arm and drew much blood."

"Yes, it did. But Hoffman is a strong man. He was not badly injured."

"Then you will tell me, how did you kill Wak Tha Go?"

"It was not easy, but I sneaked into your camp. I stabbed him in his heart as he slept. I left my hat as a sign. I hoped your men would then go away. Which they did."

Brown Owl was unhappy to hear Artoor tell this part of his story. But he had to grant that it took much heart for him to have done this deed. He could have been killed by a sentry or by Wak Tha Go himself, if he had awakened.

"We retreated but vowed to fight again," Brown Owl said. "We will find your men and kill them one day."

"Well, I guess you might do just that," Art admitted. "Are you going to kill me?"

Brown Owl did not answer immediately. He spoke a few words to the other men in council. They grunted, nodded, and some raised their fists in a defiant gesture. None of it boded well for the trapper who was their prisoner.

"I guess that answers my question," Art said. He was resigned to his own death now, as he had not been after the mauling by the grizzly, after surviving in the wilderness for more than forty days. In fact, there had been many close calls in his life. Looking back, he was surprised that he had survived this long.

But this didn't mean he was going to give up without a fight. He had plenty of fight left in him. The only question was, how and who was he going to fight? He couldn't take on the whole village—or could he?

The man called Brown Owl was speaking to him: "Tell the men of my people how you came to be here. What happened to you? Why were you alone when we captured you?"

Art figured this would buy him some time, so he told the story of what had happened to him after the battle on the island. He told them of his encounter with the bear sow that nearly killed him, then about how his own men had left him behind—especially McDill, who probably would have killed him if it hadn't been for Dog's vigilance. He told them of his weeks of wandering and healing, of his killing the buffalo calf and eating its meat, crudely tanning the skin to make the robe that had sheltered him.

"My Great Spirit was looking out for me, I guess," he said in words and signs.

The men around the council fire could barely believe what he was saying. How could one man, a white man, do this—fight off a grizzly attack and survive for two moons without food or shelter? It was almost beyond comprehension. They nodded in admiration of this man.

"Truly, he is touched by the Great Spirit," one of the Indians said, echoing the thoughts of all the men around the council fire.

Brown Owl too felt a great respect for Art after hearing his story. But he knew that the trapper must die, could not be allowed to live since he was an enemy of the Blackfoot people. So Brown Owl put it before the council, for their judgment. "Now that we know the power of our enemy, who among you would want him to live to fight us in another battle and kill our warriors?"

"But must such a man be killed?" the elder Buffalo Standing asked, looking around at the others.

"Yes," Brown Owl said. "It saddens my heart in a way to say it, but this is the only answer: He must die."

Again, Art followed the discussion as best he could, but he knew immediately what was happening. It was his death sentence.

His mind went blank, free of fear or anticipation of what might happen next. The Indians kept talking, debating how and when he should be killed. They came to an agreement that he would be kept under double guard through the night, then killed the next day at noon. He could hear their voices, but what they said did not penetrate his consciousness.

Brown Owl was speaking: "This man has killed a great bear and survived for a long time with wounds that would have ended any other man's life. He has been alone in the dangerous country and killed a buffalo calf with just a knife. We must treat him carefully and with respect. He is a great warrior."

The others nodded and grunted in agreement with the plan to put two men on watch over the white man who had performed these great deeds of strength and survival.

He would not escape the judgment of the people, against whom he had fought so valiantly.

One by one the Blackfeet rose and filed away from the council fire, leaving Art there with Brown Owl and two men who were assigned to take the first watch. Art's hands were still bound with strips of buffalo hide, and they took him away to a tree near the council tepee and bound him to the trunk.

He stood there calmly, observing everything, watching Brown Owl who supervised the other men. Then the young Indian war chief spoke to him.

"You, Artoor, will die tomorrow. It will be a swift and

honorable death for a warrior." He spoke in words and signs so that the trapper would understand.

Art just stared at Brown Owl. He did not defend himself or beg for mercy. That would not achieve anything but loss of respect from these men. The two guards stood on either side of the tree and watched him.

As Brown Owl walked away, Art thought back to his visit to St. Louis and Jennie. He thought of Mr. Ashley and their business arrangement, how he liked and respected the man for his seeming honesty. He remembered the great General Lafayette, who had visited the city to a warm greeting by the citizens and the town fathers.

Then he remembered the itinerate preacher who had been moving among the crowd down at the waterfront. The man had worn a long, black coat and a black stovepipe hat that had seen better days. He was skinny, probably hadn't eaten in days, with a narrow, hooked nose and pointy chin that almost touched each other, like a puppet that he had seen once.

The preacher's thin, bony finger had stabbed at the air, and his equally thin body had rocked and moved, as he spoke in a singsong voice, spouting Scripture and calling down God's wrath on the people of "sin and debauchery," on St. Louis itself, a "den of iniquity."

Art almost smiled as he remembered the scene and how the preacher had held him riveted, listening to his sermon, wondering if the man were crazy or just on fire with the word of the Lord. Crazy . . . the word of the Lord . . .

An idea formed in his head as the young mountain man stood there, a prisoner of the Blackfeet in their village, with no chance of help or escape.

Luckily, Brown Owl had made sure Art was comparatively well treated, and that he had drunk some water after eating a few bites of supper earlier, before the council meeting.

Art swallowed once and began to speak, to preach in the same tone of voice as the man he had heard on the wharf in St. Louis. "Hallelujah, hallelujah! Sweet Baby Jesus, come to me, Lord," he proclaimed like a born-again, water-baptized, true believer in the Lord Almighty.

"Come to the aid of your servant who has wandered in the wilderness for forty days in search of your righteous blessing upon him. Deliver me, O Lord, from the hands of my enemies, from the clutches of the devil himself who has blasphemed your name. Release me from bondage as you did your people, freeing them from the Pharaoh. Release me from the lion's den as you did your prophet Daniel, against the king who would have him devoured by the lions. Open the doors of your heavenly city and let the sinner enter the gates of salvation!"

The two guards were startled by their prisoner's words, which were incomprehensible to them. But they were also mesmerized by them, by the outpouring of the rhythmic, chantlike prayers and proclamations.

"Lord, you sent hellfire and brimstone upon the evil cities of Sodom and Gomorrah who had raised up the devil to worship instead of the Almighty, and their evil deeds made a stink that could be smelled all over the world. You sent the plagues upon the Pharaoh, who would not let your people go, the water turned to blood, the frogs, the locusts and mosquitoes, the death of Egypt's cattle, the boils on man and beast, the hail that fell from the sky, the darkness that fell over the earth, and finally the death of the firstborn of Pharaoh. You have the power to make right what is wrong and to set free the unjustly imprisoned.

"You stayed Abraham's hand when he went to the rock to sacrifice his only son Isaac in obedience to you. You lifted up the suffering Job when he did not despair of your love. You made David a king when he was a simple shepherd and singer of praises to you, and gave him the power to slay the giant who made war on your people. Give this servant the strength to slay your enemies and to lift up your people in righteousness. Hallelujah, hallelujah! Even though I be spat upon and persecuted for your sake, you shall lift me up to glory if I am faithful to you O Lord. . . ."

In the morning, Art was still preaching. He had not ceased all night long. He was amazed that the words and stories from his youth came back to him, that he had the strength to stand and to preach throughout the entire night. Throughout the village the people were talking about this amazing man.

Everyone knew the story of the grizzly bear and Art's trek across miles and miles of the badlands even though he was nearly dead. Over time it would become a legend among the Blackfeet, but now it was still a freshly told story, and the man who had accomplished these feats was still among them, a prisoner tied to a tree near the council lodge.

Like most of the village, Brown Owl got very little sleep through the night. He made sure the guards were replaced, and each time he came to the tree where the prisoner was bound, he heard his ceaseless preaching. He had never heard a white missionary preacher before, though he had heard about them from others.

Over the years black-robed priests and black-coated preachers had come among various tribes to try to convert them to their strange religion. They were called Christians, and they taught that the Indians were bad for not believing the same things that *they* did.

Brown Owl respected the stories of others and cherished the stories of his own people. Why was one wrong and the other right? That he did not understand. And it made him angry that anyone would try to force their stories on someone who already had his own.

Before the sun rose, the young Blackfoot war chief stood with some of the other people of the village and listened to Artoor's strange and magical words.

"The Lord shall show portents in the sky and on the earth, and blood and fire and columns of smoke will be seen by all the people. The sun will be turned into darkness and the moon into blood before the day comes, that great and terrible day. And all who call on the name of the Lord will be saved, for on Mount Zion will be those who have escaped the fires and plagues and the wrath of the one true God."

Whatever he was saying, it sounded frightening and powerful to all who heard him.

Art stood as straight and tall after several hours of preaching as he had when he had first been brought to the tree and bound there. His eyes were dark and glittery, as if he were under a spell. In fact, he was possessed by a powerful spirit.

He almost didn't realize what he was saying, but he kept talking, kept preaching, letting his voice roll out in the singsong cadence with the words that tumbled back into his mind from the times when he was a child and his parents dragged him to church services and traveling preachers' revivals.

"Proclaim this among all the nations. Prepare ye for war! Rouse the champions of the people, who will defend them in my name. Armies, prepare to advance. Hammer your plowshares into swords, your hooks into spears. Even the weaklings will be given strength in the Lord's name. Let the nations arouse themselves and assemble in the Valley of Jehoshaphat and be led by the champions of war!

"The sun and the moon will grow dark, and the stars will lose their brilliance. For the Lord God roars from Zion, He thunders from Jerusalem, and the heavens and the earth tremble at the sound of His mighty voice!"

For the rest of the morning, Art preached without stopping or faltering. The people of the village, men, women, and children, all came to the tree and stood and listened to him. All of them heard him, though they did not understand the strange white man's language.

The elders of the village huddled in an impromptu council nearby and whispered among themselves. They were amazed and concerned about this man, wondering whether he was a white devil who had come among them to destroy them.

As the sun rose in the sky, the mountain man preached on:

"When that day comes, the mountains will run with new wine and the hills will flow with milk, and all the streambeds of the country will run with water. A fountain will spring forth in the temple in the great city. Egypt will become a desolation and the land of the enemy a desert waste on account of the violence done to the Lord's people, the innocent children whose blood they shed in their country.

"But the land will be inhabited forever, and Jerusalem from generation to generation! 'I shall avenge their blood and let none go unpunished,' saith the Lord, and he shall dwell in Zion with the righteous ones."

Throughout the night the people of the village had heard him preaching without stopping. Very few had gotten any sleep that night. Throughout the morning women and children gathered around the tree where the man was bound and listened to his strange words. They talked among themselves, saying they thought he was crazy—that is, touched by the Great Spirit who created and protected all things.

Buffalo Standing in the River met with the other elders in the impromptu council. They watched and listened to Artoor, shaking their heads. They decided to call a full-fledged council meeting.

Buffalo Standing went to Brown Owl's tepee. There the

younger man sat with his wife, who had been among the women listening to the prisoner preach throughout the morning. It was nearly noon, nearly time for the prisoner to be killed.

"Owl, my young friend, the men of our village must meet to discuss what we are going to do."

"The decision has been made. He is to be killed today. He is an enemy of our people."

"Yet he spoke of peace to many before Wak Tha Go came and told us we must fight him. And now we hear him speak and we think he is crazy. If this is true, he is under the protection of the Father and Creator of all."

Buffalo Standing led the young war chief to the council tepee where the others awaited. A pipe was lit and passed from man to man. Each one spoke his heart about this situation. All agreed that the prisoner should not be killed, that he should be released because he was clearly crazy.

When Brown Owl's turn came, he took the pipe and was silent for a moment. In the silence, from outside Art's words penetrated the council lodge:

"Listen, my people, to the words of the Lord. 'It was I who destroyed your enemies. It was I who brought you up from Egypt and for forty years led you through the desert to take possession of the Promised Land. I raised up your sons as prophets and warriors.

"'But because you have turned away from the Lord, I will crush you where you stand. Flight will be cut off for the swift, and the strong will have no chance to exert his strength, nor will the warrior be able to save his life. The archer will not stand his round, the swift of foot will not escape, nor will the horseman be able to rescue the fallen warriors. Even the bravest of men will throw down his weapons and run away on that day!'"

Finally, Brown Owl spoke. "The words of my brothers and fathers are correct. Although I have seen this man Artoor in battle and know that he is a skilled fighter, I see also that he is touched by the Great Spirit and we must honor the Spirit by letting him go."

All of the men nodded and grunted in agreement. Then, one by one, they rose and filed out of the tepee. Outside, the elders and warriors gathered by the white prisoner. Brown Owl ordered the guards to untie him.

Art stopped speaking for the first time in nearly eighteen hours. His mouth was parched and sore, and he staggered, had to steady himself by holding onto the tree. His vision was blurred, and he blinked to gain clear sight of all those who were gathered around him. At first he did not understand what was happening.

Brown Owl signed to him that he was free. Others stepped forward and gave Art a blanket, his own hunting knife, and a parfleche of food.

"You are free to leave us, for you have the protection of the Great Spirit. Do not come back to make war with our people, or else we will fight you, and this time we will kill you," the warrior told him.

Art took the gifts that were offered. Without a word, he walked away toward the east, away from the village. His head swam with words. His heart was full of strange emotions, but he was glad to be free. Now he would find his men, come hell or high water.

He wondered if Dog was out there somewhere waiting for him.

Fourteen

Junction of Platte and Missouri Rivers

Percy McDill had kept the trappers' party together, but through curses and threats rather than true leadership as Art had done. Along with Caviness, he bullied and cajoled the men, Matthews, Montgomery, and Hoffman, to stay with him when they threatened to split up and go their separate ways.

He practically had to kill Hoffman early on to keep him from going back to check on Art. The Hessian was certain that McDill had done something underhanded, and the others were too, though they didn't talk about it among themselves.

"You're taking orders from me now," McDill had told Hoffman with a sneer. "I say jump, and you jump. I say stay, and you stay. Got it?"

"Yes, sir." Hoffman had swallowed his pride and hatred and said the words that he was born and bred to say.

"That goes for all of you men. *Men*," McDill spat. "More like a bunch of women, if you ask me. I don't want no more trouble out of any of you—or else Caviness and me will deal with you."

That had been about eight weeks ago. Now, McDill led the men back to the temporary tent-town where they had been in August, the settlement that was maintained for fur traders and trappers, where the mountain men stopped to resupply and get drunk and spend a few hours with some women.

The tents, some sod huts, and a few hastily erected log structures were the same. There may have been one or two more of each. And there were whites and a few Indians and mixed-breed children living there. There was a smoky, greasy pall over the whole encampment, a sense of impermanence and death.

McDill led the party into the settlement, coming from the opposite direction, the west, and met the stares and quizzical looks of the mountain men who happened to be there.

The big man didn't want to admit to anyone—including himself—that his leadership had been a complete failure. But he did what he did best: bluffed and blustered his way from one fiasco to another. His party had precious few pelts to trade, too few to bring back to St. Louis. This was because he was not an expert trapper, because he had not been able to stay in the mountains through the winter season when the furs were at their best. And because he wouldn't make alliances with any of the Indian tribes they had encountered on their journey after they left Art to die.

And his henchman Caviness was not very good either. The others were too green to know the ways of the wilderness well enough to salvage the mission. They knew that McDill was a lousy peacemaker—unlike Art—but they said nothing. They had decided to stick together rather than split up for the winter, and they went along with McDill's decision to return to St. Louis before the weather got too cold.

So, as they rode through this ramshackle excuse for a town, they were a pretty bedraggled, dispirited bunch. They had lost their original leader and had not recovered from that. Despite McDill's bluster, they all knew it.

He led them to a trading tent, where they offered their paltry supply of pelts—very few, and not very good—for sale to finance their trip back to St. Louis. He tried to demand the best price, but had to settle for much less. He kept all the money.

"I'm boss of this outfit and I'll take care of the money," he said, brooking no challenge to his decision. Behind the others' backs he looked at Caviness and winked. He'd take care of his friend, and the others could go to hell, as far as he was concerned.

"We're only gonna stay for a day or two here, rest up and buy some supplies for our ride back to St. Louie. Let's find a place to camp for tonight."

They walked their horses and gear over to a small clearing on the edge of the makeshift town. There was another two-man camp nearby with a campfire burning, the men sitting on a fallen tree trunk and tending the fire. There was a pot of coffee cooking in the fire.

McDill ordered his men to set up their camp and build their own fire, ignoring his neighbors.

After a while one of the men came over to the larger group and said, "You all are welcome to some coffee if you want."

"Maybe later," McDill said curtly.

"Sure we would," Montgomery piped up, poking Matthews in the ribs, and Matthews said he would too.

"Now look, you men—" McDill sputtered. "I told you we need to stick together here. We'll fix our own supper."

"Just tryin' to be neighborly, friend," the man said.

Then Hoffman said, "We met you before. You're a friend of our captain, Art."

"Yeah, I'm Jeb Law. We met before. And this here is Ed," he added, pointing to the other mountain man with whom he was sharing the camp.

McDill cut in. "Art used to be our captain. He's dead now. I'm the leader here."

"That so?" Jeb said, and left it at that. He returned to his own campfire. He called over to them, "You're welcome to some coffee and grub—any time."

A little while later, Matthews and Montgomery drifted over to Jeb Law's campfire and sat down to drink a cup of coffee, the first they had drunk in many weeks. Then the Hessian, Hoffman, came over, and finally even McDill and Caviness gave in and came over, bringing their own drinking cups.

Jeb Law said, "Well, we heard you men ran into some trouble out there on the Upper Missouri."

"We're doin' fine," McDill said. "We did lose poor old Art. He got mauled by a big old grizz. It was painful to see him all beat up like that," he said with phony sadness, as if he had been a good friend of the young mountain man instead of a bitter and resentful enemy.

But Jeb Law wasn't fooled. He smiled. He had an ace up his sleeve. "That so? He was dead when you left him?"

"Yeah," Caviness lied. "We was on the run from some Indians, fought 'em off pretty good, but we had to keep moving fast."

Matthews shifted uneasily where he was sitting. He cleared his throat and started to say something, but McDill glared at him as if to tell him to keep his mouth shut.

The German couldn't help himself. He hated McDill and Caviness. He blurted out, "No he wasn't dead. He was hurt badly. We left him with his rifle and food. We don't know what happened to him."

"Really?" Jeb said. "Well, now, I wonder if he's the one the Injuns are all palaverin' about for the past month or so."

"What do you mean?" McDill spat.

"There's a man they're callin' Preacher. The Blackfeet captured him—seems he was wanderin' the country after he had been attacked by a bear. He had nothin' except his knife and a buffalo robe that he made hisself—I guess he kilt a buffalo to get it. Anyhow, the story is the Injuns caught him and brought him back to their village to kill him. But he started acting crazy-like, started preaching like from the Bible. Didn't stop talking for almost a whole day. Well, mister, seems like the Blackfeet couldn't bring themselves to kill him. They let him go and started calling him Preacher. Sounds an awful lot like my old friend Art."

McDill looked at Caviness. It was just about sundown and the shadows were long and dark. But McDill's face was white, like the moon. He and Caviness got up and left the campfire.

The others stayed and drank more coffee, and even ate some supper with Jeb and Ed. They pumped Jeb for all the information he had heard about Art. They were happy to learn that their old boss was alive and well. But the question in all their minds was: Where is he?

On the Missouri River, North of the Yellowstone

Art made his way back to the American Fur Company trading post on the river, commanded by Joe Walker. Along the way he had bartered for a horse from a friendly Indian, so he was able to save valuable time by riding the last fifty miles or so. Already it was past the middle of October and the days were getting shorter, the nights much colder.

He had been reunited with Dog after his captivity by the Blackfeet. The wolf-dog had remained outside the village, aware that his human companion was in trouble. He'd kept to the woods and brush throughout the day and night, and when Art had emerged a free man, he'd followed him for about a mile before showing himself. The young mountain man was glad to see his canine friend, but he wasn't surprised. Dog had proven himself many times over as reliable and faithful.

As he traveled, Art looked back on the events of the past few months. The primary mission was mostly a failure, though there had been some successful peacemaking along the way. Still, Art wouldn't have much to report to William Ashley besides his own adventures—which he could barely believe himself.

Approaching the fortlike structure he saw that, like before, the front gate was closed. The blockhouse that overlooked the gate was still empty. He almost smiled at the thought that he had been here before, that it was like being in a play and repeating the same scene over and over again. Then Dog barked, just as he had the time before, which only confirmed the feeling that Art had.

"Who goes there?" came the voice from the blockhouse.

"I'm here to see Joe Walker. My name is Art."

"You again?" the voice said.

Minutes later Art was in Walker's lamp-lit, windowless quarters, talking to the bald-headed, bearded commander of the trading garrison.

"You don't look too healthy," Walker said. He was smoking a pipe, and the smoke filled the cramped space. Papers and maps were strewn over the top of his desk.

"Well, I've had some tough days recently."

"So I hear—Preacher."

Art looked at Walker with surprise. "What did you say?"

"I called you Preacher. That's what the Indians are saying. I just did some business with an Arikara scout who told me all about it—all about your captivity by the Blackfeet. I told you they were savages."

"They actually treated me pretty good, all things considered." Art scratched his beard. He wanted to shave and to clean himself up. He couldn't believe that Walker had already heard of his experience with the Blackfeet. "What else are they saying about me?"

"Well," Walker said, "there is something about a fight with a grizzly bear. Seems you won but came out the worse for wear."

"Pretty near killed me," Art admitted. "She was a big mother bear with a bunch of cubs. I didn't mean to bother her."

"She couldn't have known that, I suppose. So your men left you behind, wounded?"

"They did what they had to do. I would have done the same if it was one of them."

"And where are you going now?"

"I'm looking for my party. You remember them from when we came here in August. They been throug here?"

"Haven't seen them, but word is they're headed back to St. Louis. They don't have much by way of pelts."

"What?"

"Don't know why, but they were seen moving east just a few days ago. Probably they'll head down toward the Platte for resupply, maybe do a little trading, then head on down the Missouri to St. Louis. I've dispatched a message to Mr. Ashley to tell him to expect them. Didn't know about you, though. I'll write him a letter to tell him I have met with you." Walker puffed on his cigar. "And that you have a new name," he added.

Art said, "I will tell him myself what happened to me and to our expedition. Not sure what he will think about all this."

"Well, I hear Mr. Ashley is a reasonable man."

"I like him and respect him."

"I wish you good luck, sincerely. And I know you'll be back out here. You've never been a city man. You belong out in the mountains and the high plains, with men like me. That's who you are now, son."

"Well, I've got to keep moving. I'm going to try to catch up with my men. If I move fast I can do it."

"I have no doubt you will, Preacher. No doubt at all."

Jennie had made a decision. She was going to go back. Maybe not all the way to St. Louis, but she was going to take her girls out of this primitive place and back into something that resembled civilization. The settlement on the Kansas and Missouri Rivers, called Westport or Kansas City, just beyond Independence, might be a place to settle. But it was hopeless out here, even though she had come to like the few bedraggled men who were trying to make a go of the little settlement.

It was getting close on to winter, so it was time to move. She told Ben and Carla Thomas and the other girls about her decision.

"I want you to pack up all your belongings and be ready to leave first thing in the morning," she said.

Then she told the men of the settlement. They couldn't believe their ears. They were sad because they had come to like her and her girls. It was beyond their wildest dreams that Jennie and the girls from the House of Flowers had come to their little village in the first place. What would they do without her when she was gone?

"You'll be fine," she assured them. "I'll miss you too."

But she wasted no time in gathering her girls, reloading the wagon, and ordering Ben to drive—east this time. First she would return to the trading settlement at the junction of the Missouri and Platte Rivers, and from there decide which direction to head next.

It took two days of hard overland travel to get there.

They rolled in near the end of the second day, the sun low in the sky. Jennie sat up front in the driver's seat with her old friend Ben, the freed black man. He had stuck with her through the worst of times and hundreds of difficult miles. He did not question her decision to turn back east—in fact, he was glad she was doing it. It would be safer for her and the girls.

"Look, Ben, this is a bustling community. There are even some women here. Most of them Indian girls as far as I can see. And a lot of trappers. Hmmm, I'll bet there's some money to be made here for a person of business."

"It's also pretty rough, Miss Jennie." Ben rarely ventured an opinion of his own.

The encampment was nothing pretty to look at—tents and crude sod and log buildings. The men hanging around stopped as the girls passed, and waved and whistled. No doubt, they were glad to see this train pull in to their humble way station.

"Look, there are some boats," Jennie said, pointing at some keelboats along the river's shore. "We could take a boat as far as Westport, maybe settle there for a while and see if we like it."

"Yes, Miss Jennie," the faithful black driver said simply. He knew by now that whatever Miss Jennie decided on was what they would do, no arguments from him.

They drove to one of the more substantial buildings, which was a fur dealer's headquarters, and Jennie went inside to get the lay of the land. She found out that they could camp anywhere they pleased, that there were no authorities in this place other than the gun and the fist, and that the trappers and traders and other men in the vicinity would be mighty glad to see them.

McDill got drunk during the second day in the sprawling tent-town. He spent a sizable chunk of the money that he had collected for the entire party's pelts. That left him with next to nothing to buy supplies, but he was too far gone by noon to care much.

He wandered the sprawling encampment looking for a woman. Any woman would do. He had almost forgotten about the time he'd been here before and the trouble he had caused by making a play for another man's squaw. But he hadn't forgotten how Art had sicced his wolf-dog on him, how Dog had bitten his knife hand and humiliated him.

"Shoulda shot that damn dog-monster when I had a chance," he muttered to himself drunkenly. He staggered through the makeshift "streets" of the town, glassy-eyed and angry. This time nobody was going to prevent him from getting what he wanted.

He headed toward the center of the settlement, where the Eastern fur traders had set up their frontier offices. A better class of people was living there, he had convinced himself. Maybe that meant a better class of woman.

Putting his hands in his pockets, he realized that he had very little money left. He'd given Caviness ten dollars off the top of their meager take, just to keep his friend off his back. The others were going to be mad when they found out he had spent all his money on liquor—and maybe a whore.

"Damn them to hell anyway," he breathed. "They got out of this thing with their lives, which is more than that young Indian-lover woulda done for 'em." Despite Art's skills and easy way with people, McDill wasn't about to give him credit for anything. "Like to get us scalped with his Injun-palaver. If I hadn't been there on the island, I don't know what woulda happened. Saved all of our damned lives . . ."

Percy McDill looked up and couldn't believe what he was seeing. There, directly in front of him, were the girls from the House of Flowers in St. Louis. At first he thought he was dreaming or maybe somehow imagining this sight. He had never gone into the famous house of prostitution—

the likes of him couldn't afford the fancy prices for fancy women. But he had hung out nearby enough to recognize a few of the faces and figures of these girls.

What were they doing way out here in this Godforsaken place? A jumble of thoughts clogged up his brain and he couldn't think straight, couldn't figure out what was going on. All he knew was that he wanted a woman and here were some women. How lucky could a man get?

He smiled evilly and staggered forward.

Art wasn't sure why, but something propelled him forward. He rode without stopping to sleep, only to rest and water his horse. Turned out it was a good bargain, this horse: very sturdy and reliable and didn't seem to mind Dog tagging along for the ride. From Joe Walker, Art had obtained a rifle, shot and powder, a new canteen, a new saddlebag for food and supplies. He was all set now, and with each mile he felt stronger and more determined to find the men he had once commanded.

He hoped Hoffman, Montgomery, and Matthews were all right. He hoped McDill and Caviness were healthy too, so he could beat the hell out of them. He had no doubt that McDill had bullied the others and lied to them to make them do whatever he wanted. That was his way.

He remembered the first time he had encountered Percy McDill, in the tavern in St. Louis. The big man had been full of it then, a coward at heart, selfish, with nothing good to say about another human being. McDill had been so cocksure that the job of leading the expedition for Mr. Ashley would be his. And he'd been so angry when the assignment went to Art . . . and a thorn in Art's side ever since.

Late in the afternoon of the third day out of Walker's fort, Art rode into the tent city at the junction of the Missouri and the Platte. There was something familiar about

the look and feel of the place, the men who populated it—
for they were his kind of people, men of the mountains. As
he rode through, he got more than a few hellos and
howdies.

They looked at him differently, however. That dad-
blasted preacher story must have gotten to them too, he
mused. He looked around for someone he knew well.

He found what he was looking for. There was Jeb Law,
his old friend. Art rode over to Jeb's campsite. The old man
looked up from his fire, broke out into a big grin. "Well, if
it ain't my oldest and dearest friend and—" He looked
down at the lean and hungry Dog. "And his pal Dog."

Art dismounted and shook Jeb's rough hand. Jeb looked
him over, from head to foot.

"You be needin' a good meal, son. Let me fix you up
some beans. Got coffee cookin' on the fire. Take a load
off'n your feet."

"Thanks, Jeb. Good to see you too."

The two men sat. Jeb Law looked directly into the
younger mountain man's eyes and said, "You came to the
right place if'n you're lookin' for your explorin' party.
They're right here."

"McDill and the others?" Art wasn't surprised except
that it had taken him a lot less time than he had thought.
He calculated that they'd be well on their way to St. Louis
by now. McDill didn't like to linger in places like this, especially since he'd gotten in trouble over a woman last time
through.

"They're all alive," Jeb said.

"I'll be damned. Well, that's a good thing. Guess they
didn't need me after all."

"Ha! You should see the long hound-dog looks on those
men. They sure missed you. They thought you was dead."

"McDill. He told them that, didn't he."

Jeb nodded. "Sure thing. The others didn't like it one bit

when they found out he had lied to them. Other than that one that's joined to him at the hip—what's his name?"

"Caviness."

"Yep. He and Caviness are a pair of evil children if'n I ever laid eyes on any in my whole miserable life." Jeb smiled. "And you are a sight for sore eyes, boy. Here, have some of old Jeb's coffee. Best brew west of Nowhere."

Dog sidled up next to Art, sat alertly right beside his leg. The coffee slid hotly into Art's belly, and he felt the effects of no food in three days.

"I told them all about you bein' called Preacher and all that. They were sure surprised."

"Now, where did you hear about that?"

"I hear things. Don't take long for stories to get passed around out here. You know that. And it was a pretty good yarn, about how you killed a bear and wandered around wounded and got yerself captured by Injuns. I said to myself, 'That sounds just like the Art I know.'" He grinned, showing the few yellow teeth he had left. "Sure 'nuff, it were you!"

"Where are my men?"

"Why, they're campin' right next door there." Jeb pointed. "They must be out galavantin' around. McDill got himself drunk early on today. He's either passed out or dead somewheres round about." He cackled like a woman. "That one's got death marked on him. It ain't gonna be long for him, I'll wager."

Art stayed and ate some of Jeb's beans cooked with a fistful of pork fat. He hadn't tasted anything so good since the last time he and Jennie had eaten together in St. Louis. His belly settled down and his mind became more focused on what he had to do: find his men and reclaim his leadership.

It wasn't going to be easy or pleasant, he knew. Not with McDill and Caviness fighting him every step of the way.

The sun had begun to fall below the distant hilltops. He had better get moving before it got fully dark. "Thanks, Jeb," he said. "I'll be back."

"I'll wager," Jeb said again.

He didn't know where to start, so Art just walked into the center of the tent town. He ran into some other acquaintances along the way and stopped briefly to say hello. All of them seemed to know about his adventures, and some of them even called him "Preacher."

Dog tagged along with Art, never leaving his side. He avoided other dogs, faded into the background if any barked or challenged him. Like his master, he didn't want any trouble or distraction at this time.

The mountain man came to one of the fur dealers' buildings, a squat log structure chinked with mud and sod. He went in. There were a couple of men there stacking pelts and going over their books. He asked about his men.

"Oh, yeah, they're here. Their captain, McDougal I think his name is, was around here earlier. Drunk as a skunk."

"Sold us a few pelts yesterday, not very good quality," the other man said.

Art thanked them and went out. He was close. Maybe he should just go back to the campsite and turn in and let them come to him.

Fifteen

In the darkness, illuminated only by a single candle, Jennie faced a terrifying apparition. Percy McDill had burst into her tent, and now moved toward her, his face twisted by lust and anger into a grotesque mask. The candle's reflection in his dark eyes gave Jennie the illusion of staring into the very fires of hell. She stepped backward, but found little room to maneuver in the confines of the tent.

Jennie screamed.

Outside, Art heard a woman's scream. It came from a nearby tent. It startled him—not because of the cry itself, but because he thought he recognized the voice of the woman who screamed. But it couldn't be . . . it couldn't be who he thought it was. Could it?

Running in the direction of the commotion, Art wondered what Jennie would be doing out here. It couldn't be her, could it? She was in St. Louis. And yet, something about the scream touched his very soul. He hurried toward the tent.

McDill lunged, clamping his dirty hand over her mouth. Jennie bit his hand and he ripped it away, howling like a wounded animal. She screamed again. Outside the tent she could hear people moving around, and she hoped someone would come to help her. She fought back, pummeling his chest and face with her hands, but he was so big and strong that it had no effect.

"You bitch!" he sneered, cradling his wounded hand. "I was gonna pay you, whore that you are, but now I'm not— I'm gonna take it for free."

"Stay away," she warned. "For your own good, mister. I don't want to hurt you."

"Ha! You don't want to hurt me?" he said with a lopsided, drunken grin. "Tell me, bitch, how you plannin' on hurtin' me?"

She couldn't stand the smell of him, and his ugly leer. Yet she realized that she had to be careful, that she couldn't rile him even more—or else he was liable to kill her. She had known men like him for her entire life.

She gathered what composure she could, and brushed a fall of hair back from her face. She forced herself to smile at him.

"Look, you're right, whoring is my business. But I was just getting ready for bed and I must look a mess. Why don't you go away now, give me a chance to get ready, then you can come back later," she said.

"No way, little lady, I'm here and here I am. You'll get to like me when you know me better. I promise."

Jennie doubted that she would ever be able to bear the sight of this man, let alone like him. He was grotesque, and it didn't matter that he was drunk. She had met this kind before, and he reminded her of her old master, among others.

"But you'll like me better if you give me a chance to get ready for you," Jennie said, making one last attempt to get through to him.

"I like you fine just the way you are," he said, starting toward her again.

Jennie felt the world closing in on her and smelled blood in the air; she could only hope it wasn't her own. Again she screamed for help.

At that moment the tent flaps opened, and it was as if God himself had heard her plea. The one man in the world whom she truly loved stepped inside. It was Art, the man she had known as a boy, the man who was a part of her life even when they were not together. She had heard the stories of him over the last several weeks, how he had beaten off a bear attack, then wandered through the wilderness, surviving on berries, roots, and whatever he could kill with just a knife. She had also heard of his escape from the Indians, and of the new name the Indians had given him.

"Art!" she cried.

McDill turned to see the man he hated most in the world—the man he had thought was dead—moving at him swiftly and angrily. He ducked to avoid Art's first swing, and came up with a hard punch of his own, taking Art off guard, smashing into his chin. He laughed as the younger man staggered backward.

"Well, now, if it ain't my ole' pal Art," McDill said. "Only I hear tell the Indians call you Preacher now. Is that right? Are you goin' to preach to me, Preacher? Are you going to save my soul?" He laughed.

Art got to one knee, and shook his head, trying to clear away the cobwebs of the hammerlike blow. He stared up at McDill, and at the hideous leering grin on his face.

McDill held his hand out and curled his fingers, tauntingly inviting Art toward him.

"Well, come on, Preacher," he said. "You don't have a pistol under the table now, do you? Oh, wait, I forgot. It was a fork, wasn't it?" The leering grin left his face, to be replaced by an angry scowl. "Come on, you son of a bitch. I'm going to beat you to a pulp."

His head cleared, Art leaped up again and charged at McDill. He buried his head in McDill's midsection, and both men went crashing to the ground.

Art scrambled to his feet and grabbed McDill by the collar, then dragged him outside. He wanted to take this confrontation away from Jennie. By now a crowd, drawn by the screams and the commotion, had gathered just outside. They surrounded the two men, who were locked in a deadly confrontation.

Among the people there were Matthews, Montgomery, and Hoffman, the big Hessian. They couldn't believe what they were seeing. Here was their leader, returned as if from the dead. They were overjoyed to see him, but not in these circumstances. He was locked in mortal combat with the larger, loathsome McDill.

The crowd cheered for Art and jeered McDill. Art, still exhausted from his long ride, and not yet fully recovered from all his injuries, stood still to catch his breath. That allowed McDill to get to his feet, and the big man charged like a bull. Art stepped out of the way, and McDill went hurtling into the crowd.

Laughing at his awkwardness, the men in the crowd caught McDill and pushed him back into the circle of combat. The two men faced each other again, and Art punched him as hard as he could. McDill doubled over. Art landed a strong right to McDill's jaw, straightening him out and sending him back on his heels. Art massaged the hand that had struck the blow.

Caviness was watching with the others in the crowd. He wanted to go to the aid of his friend, but he dared not, for fear of retribution from the others. McDill was on his own now. Caviness melted away into the growing darkness. Even as the fight was going on behind him, he saddled his horse. If Art won, he might come after Caviness. If McDill won, he would want to know why Caviness didn't help him. Under the circumstances, Caviness knew that this was no place for him to be.

"Art," Jennie said, coming out of her tent then.

Art turned toward Jennie, then held his hand out, as if telling her to stay away. "Jennie, stay back, keep out of the way!" he cautioned.

As Art looked away from McDill for just that quick second, McDill pulled his long-bladed hunting knife from its sheath and lunged at Art, the knife pointed at his guts. Now, enraged and humiliated by the beating he was taking from this younger and smaller man, McDill was more animal than human.

Jennie saw McDill and called out to Art: "Look out! He has a knife!"

Art turned just in time to see the blade flash in the flickering light of the nearby fires. He reared back to avoid the killing knife, then circled his enemy barehanded. Someone from the crowd tossed him a stick. Art used it as a defensive weapon, swinging it at McDill to keep him at bay. With one swing, McDill's knife chopped the stick in half.

"What are you goin' to do now, Preacher?" McDill taunted, holding the knife out in front of him, moving the point back and forth slightly, like the head of a coiled snake. "You think that little stick is going to stop me? I'll whittle it down to a toothpick, then I'll carve you up."

Then Art realized he had no choice, he must fight this madman on his terms—no rules, any weapon at hand, and to the death. He drew his own knife, the same knife that had seen him through the past two months from the killing of Wak Tha Go, to the killing of the grizzly she-bear, and through his wandering and captivity. The same knife that had been returned to him by the Indians, when they granted him his freedom.

Art held the knife up, showing it to Percy McDill, saying without a word that he intended to kill the man who had threatened Jennie, who had left him for dead, who had lied and cheated his way through a worthless life. Well, that life was about to end.

Suddenly it seemed as if McDill had sobered up. The taunting, leering grin left his face and he became deadly serious and focused. With a steady hand he held his own knife up, challenging his opponent, his face now a mask of calm determination.

"I should've killed you when I had the chance. You'd better start preachin' your own funeral, Preacher," McDill said. "It's time for you to die."

Now, for the first time, Art grinned. It was neither taunting nor leering. Instead, it was confident, and it completely unnerved McDill. "I don't think so, McDill," Art said easily. "I think you are the one who is going to die."

"I'm going to kill you, and that damned mutt of yours," McDill said with false bravado, trying now to bolster his own courage.

Out of the corner of his eye, Art could see Dog, standing near Hoffman on the edge of the watching crowd. If it hadn't been for the wolf-dog, McDill probably would have slit his throat and left him for dead some two months earlier.

The young mountain man put aside all thoughts other than one: McDill must die for his crimes. Trying to hurt Jennie was the last evil thing this son of a bitch would ever do.

The two men circled each other like gladiators in a Roman arena. The crowd became silent. Even Jennie, who watched in horror, could neither speak nor cry out. Dog stood at alert. He could've attacked McDill, but somehow seemed to sense that this was something Art needed to do by himself.

McDill moved first. He swung his blade at Art, missing his face by only a few inches. Art felt the wind of the swift knife blade and jerked his head back. In almost the same movement, he swung his own knife low and hard, aiming for McDill's belly. He missed.

The big man then punched Art on the side of his head.

Art was stunned, and for a second couldn't see anything. He backed away quickly to avoid the oncoming McDill, then stepped to one side. As McDill shot past him, Art stabbed with his knife blade and felt it slip into McDill's midsection.

He pushed the knife in as far as it could go, then held it there. The two men stood together, absolutely motionless, for a long moment. Art felt McDill's warm blood spilling over his knife and onto his hand.

Howling like a stuck pig, McDill pulled himself off the knife. He stepped back several feet, then came back toward Art. But before he could even lift his own knife, he gasped, dropped his knife, and put his hand to his wound. Blood filled his cupped palms, then began oozing from his mouth as well. His eyes turned up in their sockets, showing the bloodshot whites.

From her position by the front of her tent, Jennie looked at McDill's eyes. They had caught the reflection of the campfires and, once more, she had the illusion of staring into the pit of hell. She shuddered, and wrapped her arms around herself as she realized that, within minutes, McDill would be there.

"Damn . . . you . . ." McDill managed to gurgle through the blood and spit that filled his mouth. "Damn . . ."

Art took one step toward the dying man, then stopped. McDill's big body shuddered, then collapsed in a heap on the ground. Beneath him the blood pooled darkly from his leaking wound.

Jennie ran up, threw her arms around Art, and kissed

him. He stood there unmoving, unable to take his eyes off the crumpled heap that had once been a man.

His own men now came forward: Montgomery, Matthews, and Hoffman. Dog followed warily, his nostrils filled with the blood scent from the dead man.

"Well, Boss, good to see you again," Matthews said. The others clapped him on the back. There were tears in their eyes.

Jennie said, "Yes, so good. You're alive. You saved my life. If you hadn't been here—I don't know what might have happened."

Still, Art said nothing. His body and mind were spent. He didn't feel good about killing McDill, even though the man was a bastard and nothing but trouble for everyone around him. He had never enjoyed killing for the sake of killing, but only killed as a last resort. In this case, it had been a necessary last resort—no question.

Finally, he spoke: "I'm glad that you're all alive and well. Where did Caviness go?"

"I think we will never see him again," Hoffman said with his heavy German accent. "I saw him sneak away like a dog."

"Careful when you say that," Art said, nodding toward Dog, who cocked his head at the big Hessian.

They all laughed. Dog even wagged his tail, sensing that they were talking about him.

"Let's clean up this mess and bury it," Art said.

"I tell you, Art, that's more than he would have done for you," Montgomery observed.

"Call me Preacher," Art said.

"Preacher? Yeah, I heard you'd picked up a new moniker. That's what you want to be called, huh?"

"Yeah," Preacher said. "That's what I want to be called."

Later that night Jennie washed off the blood and trail dust that clung to the man who would now, and forever more, be called Preacher. She coaxed him to eat some supper, then to sleep off the aches and pains of his long ordeal. She lay beside him until he fell asleep.

The next morning Preacher set out early, before Jennie awoke. Dog followed him to the edge of the settlement. Preacher rode toward the ford. He would cross the Missouri and ride back to St. Louis to report to William Ashley as he had promised to do. It seemed a long time ago since that last trip to St. Louis. A lot had happened, and he felt like a different man now. It was good that he had a new name to go with this new man. Maybe he had grown up. He was still young, but he had been through more in the last few months than most men would go through in a lifetime.

"Dog," he said, "I want you stay here with Miss Jennie. She needs you. I don't. I'm on my own now."

The wolf-dog stopped. Preacher stopped too, turned his horse, and faced his faithful companion. "You understand what I'm saying, don't you?"

The animal cocked his head and wagged his tail again. At this moment he looked more like a dog than a wolf, though you couldn't separate the two canine natures. Dog seemed to speak; he barked twice, looked at Preacher, then slowly walked back toward the settlement.

Now the lone rider, a man of the mountains who had left the only home he had ever known more than a dozen years ago, reined his mount around and headed toward the river.

The man called Preacher would start a new chapter in his life—and he would be alone, as the men of the mountains always were.

For a sneak preview of
PREACHER'S JUSTICE—
coming from Pinnacle Books in
January 2004,
just turn the page. . . .

One

A lone rider, tall and rawhide lean, sat his saddle easily as the horse picked its way down from the high country. Preacher was riding one horse and leading two more. The pack animals were carrying five hundred plews each, beaver pelts perfectly skinned, dried, and stretched so as to be the finest quality.

The trail followed alongside a meandering brook where cool, sweet water broke white over rocks as it rushed down-hill. At the end of the trail there would be a rendezvous, a gathering of mountain men and traders, trappers and fur dealers, Indians, whiskey drummers, Bible salesmen, and whores, friends and strangers.

Many a mountain man spent his entire winter thinking ahead of the next rendezvous, using it as an incentive to help him through the long period of isolation. Preacher wasn't one of them. The man who had been given the Christian name of Art at his birth but was now and forever more known as Preacher, reveled in his isolation, and enjoyed being alone in the vastness of the Rocky Mountains. There were times, during the winter, when he would see in the distance another trapper. Some would go out of their way to close that distance, to visit and palaver.

Preacher would not. In fact, he often changed trails to avoid these occasional meetings. For him, rendezvous was a necessary part of doing business. It was not two weeks of drinking, gambling, and whoring.

Those who knew Preacher best understood that about him, and accepted it. He wasn't exactly a misanthrope; he was friendly enough when he was with others, and no one could want a better friend than Preacher. He had also been known to have more than a few drinks on occasion, would bet on an honest game of cards or a shooting match, and was not without experience with women. But for the most part he was sober, upright, honest, and hard-working. These were attributes that all admired, but few could emulate.

Preacher could smell the rendezvous first, the aroma of coffee and cooking meat, the smell of wood and tobacco smoke, and the more unpleasant odor of scores of bodies, unwashed for months, gathered in one place.

Next, he could hear it. The sounds of people began to intrude upon the sounds of nature until soon, the babbling brook was completely overpowered by loud, boisterous talk, raucous laughter, and the high, skirling sound of a fiddle.

Finally, he rode into a clearing and saw it. Men and women moving around, clad in buckskin and feathers, homespun and store-bought suits, bits of color and flashes of beads, silver, and gold. Dozens of tents and temporary shelters had been erected, many of them little more than canvas flaps that protruded from the wagons that had brought the traders, dealers, and goods here from Back East.

In front of him, and slightly to the right, Preacher suddenly saw a flash of light and a puff of smoke, at almost the same time he heard the shot and the sound of a ball, whistling past his ear.

Looking over in surprise, he saw Henri Girardeau toss his rifle aside, then start clawing for the pistol he had sticking down in his trousers.

Preacher leaped from his horse, not away from Girardeau as Girardeau might have suspected, but directly toward him. Girardeau was caught off guard by Preacher's unexpected reaction and, rather than pulling his pistol cleanly, he dropped it as he jerked it from his trousers. Preacher shoved him hard, and Girardeau staggered back, a tree breaking his fall.

Girardeau pulled his knife and held it in front of him, palm up, the knife moving back and forth slowly, like the head of a coiled snake.

"That's all right," Girardeau said. "I'd rather gut you than shoot you anyway. Shootin' kills too fast."

Preacher held a hand out in front of him, as if warding Girardeau off. He pointed at Girardeau.

"Girardeau, there's no need for all this," he said.

"The hell there ain't no need," Girardeau said. He nodded toward the pack horses Preacher had brought in. "By rights, them should be my plews. You pulled my traps out of the water and set your own."

"My traps were there first," Preacher said. "You pulled them out and replaced them with yours. I was only returning the favor."

"Who give you title to Snake Creek anyway?" Girardeau asked.

"Nobody has title to any land up here," Preacher replied. "It's first come, first served, same as it's always been. And I was first there."

"You wouldn't even have know'd about it, if'n you hadn't heard me talkin' about it last year."

"I've trapped that same creek for nearly ten winters now," Preacher said. "You can ask anyone here."

"That's right, Girardeau. I know he was there five years ago, 'cause he took me in for the winter when I got stoved up," one of the trappers said. He, like several others, had been drawn to the point of commotion. From other parts of the camp, people were moving quickly, to see what was going on.

"Yeah, well, he ain't goin' to be trappin' it no more, 'cause I aim to split him open from his gullet to his pecker."

Girardeau lunged forward and made a swipe with his knife. The move was unexpectedly quick, and Preacher barely managed to dance back out of the way.

"Girardeau, I don't want to fight you," he said. "If you've got a dispute with me, we can take it up with the trappers' court."

Trappers' court wasn't an official court, it was just a group of trappers who would hear arguments from both sides of a dispute, then suggest a settlement. Their suggestions had no power of law, only the power of public opinion, but for most mountain men, that was binding enough.

"Nah," Girardeau said, his evil grin spreading. "I think I'll just kill the son of a bitch, then there won't be nothing to settle." He lunged forward again, but this time Preacher was ready for him, and he easily slipped the knife thrust, then countered with a hard blow to Girardeau's ear.

Girardeau jumped back, then put his hand to his ear.

That gave Preacher the opening he needed, and he reached for his knife, only to discover that it wasn't on his belt. He looked back toward his horse and saw that his knife was in a scabbard on a belt that was hanging around the saddle pommel. His rifle was in the rifle boot, and his pistol was in the saddle bag. He was barehanded against Girardeau.

"Well now," Girardeau said, when he noticed Preacher's predicament. "Ain't this somethin'? You've come to a knife fight, without a knife."

Girardeau crouched over and held the knife in front of him, still moving it back and forth. The smile that spread across his face wasn't one of mirth, but rather one of smug satisfaction. Girardeau, who was from New Orleans, had grown up with the knife. Even in a fair fight, he might have had an advantage. But, as Preacher was unarmed, there was nothing fair about this fight.

Suddenly a knife whizzed by in front of Preacher and stuck in the tree beside him.

Preacher had no idea where it came from, and didn't know who to thank. But, at this point, he had no time to consider such things. He pulled the knife from the tree, then faced Girardeau. The easy, confident smile left Girardeau's face, but the determination did not.

"Good," Girardeau said. "This'll make it fun."

Armed now, Preacher was no longer at a disadvantage. His posture mirrored that of Girardeau. He came up on the balls of his feet, crouched slightly, and held the knife firmly, but not too tightly, palm up in his right hand. The two men began moving around each other warily, now entirely circled by people who had come from all over the rendezvous, drawn to the spectacle of a fight to the death.

Girardeau moved in, raised his left hand as if to shield what he was going to do, then raised his knife hand to come in behind that shield. Preacher raised his left hand to block. Seeing the smile of triumph on Girardeau's face, Preacher realized, almost too late, that he had been suckered, that he had reacted exactly as Girardeau wanted him to react.

Girardeau moved his knife hand back down swiftly, as quickly as a striking snake, and he thrust toward Preacher. Preacher managed to twist away, barely avoiding the killing thrust, but not escaping entirely. He felt the knife burn as it sliced a cut in his side.

Even as Preacher was avoiding Girardeau's deadly stab, he responded with a quick counter-thrust. Girardeau, thinking he had won, wasn't prepared for the instantaneous response, and was wide open to Preacher's attack. Preacher's knife went just under Girardeau's ribs, slipping in cleanly, easily, all the way to the hilt. Girardeau let out a grunt, as if he had had the breath knocked out of him. The two men stood together for a second, then Preacher felt Girardeau falling, his body tearing itself off the knife, ripping open an even larger wound.

Girardeau fell on his side, then rolled over onto his back. He looked up at Preacher.

"I'll be dammed," he said. "I come here to kill you. Instead, you kilt me. Ain't that a hell of thing now?"

Girardeau wheezed a few times, then the ragged breathing stopped and his eyes, still open, glazed over.

"Whose knife?" he asked, holding up the knife he had used to kill Girardeau.

When nobody spoke up, Preacher looked over toward the tree where he had gotten the knife. Grasping the point of the blade with his thumb and forefinger, he threw the knife at the tree, sticking it in the trunk in almost the same place from which he had pulled it.

"You done what you had to do," one of the trappers said, and several others agreed.

"Girardeau was a pain in the ass," another insisted. "If there was ever any son of a bitch needed killin', it was him."

Preacher had killed before, and no doubt would have to kill again. But it wasn't something that ever set well with him, even when acting in self-defense. One or two men started toward him, probably bent on offering their congratulations, but the expression on Preacher's face let them know that he wasn't in a celebratory mood, so they backed away.

Walking over to his horse, Preacher took off his shirt and laid it across the saddle while he examined the wound in his side. Fortunately the cut wasn't very deep, and it had already stopped bleeding. He was just putting his shirt back on, when someone came up to him. Preacher could tell by the way the man was dressed that this was one of the traders from Back East.

The trader looked over the pack animals. "Looks like you had a good season," he said.

"Tolerable," Preacher replied.

The trader looked at the pelts more closely, folding them back to examine several of them.

"More than tolerable, I'd say. These are some of the best I've seen brought in since I been here."

"Thanks."

"You the one they call Preacher?" the man asked.

"I am," Preacher said.

"I work for Mr. Ashley. William Ashley? I believe you know him."

"Yes, I know him," Art said.

William Ashley was the biggest fur dealer in St. Louis, and one of the biggest fur dealers in the nation. He treated the trappers fairly, and Preacher had done business with him many times before. In fact, Preacher had once negotiated a peace with the Indians for Ashley and his traders. In this world of few contacts, and even fewer friends, William Ashley was a man that Preacher would count as a friend.

"Mr. Ashley said to treat you fair."

"He always has. That's his way," Preacher replied.

"Oh, and I almost forgot. He told me to give this to you," the trader added, handing an envelope to Preacher.

"Thanks," Preacher said.

As the trader continued to look through the pelts, Preacher opened the envelope and pulled out the letter.

Dear Preacher,
   It is with great sadness that I must inform you of the death of our mutual friend Jenny.

"Oh, shit," Preacher said, pinching the bridge of his nose.

"Somethin' wrong?" the trader asked.

"You don't know what's in the letter?"

The trader shook his head. "Wasn't my letter, wasn't my place to read it," he said. "Do you mind if I take these pelts on over to my wagon so I can count and grade them?"

"No, go ahead. I don't mind," Preacher replied.

Preacher was a loner, a man of the mountains. There was no place in his life for a woman, for few women could handle the isolation, or stand up to the brutal winter blizzards, or face the perils of Preacher's regular existence. But if there had been a woman in his life, it would have been Jenny. He had known her since he was fifteen. She was the last connection with his youth, and his first connection to manhood.

He went back to the letter.

> I wish I could tell you that she died peacefully, but I cannot. She was murdered, Preacher, in a way so vile as to defy any attempt to describe by written words. I can only say that the person who did it must be the spawn of Satan himself.
>
> At this point, nobody knows who her murderer is and in truth, what with Jenny being a whore and all, I'm afraid there will be no justice.
>
> I'm sorry to have to be the one to tell you such sad news, but I knew you would want to know.
>
> > Your friend,
> > William Ashley.

Folding the letter, Preacher stuck it down into his saddlebag, then walked over to sit on a log. He glanced over toward where the fight had taken place, and saw that a couple of men were already digging a grave for Girardeau.

How odd the sensation was. Moments earlier, he had been locked in a life-and-death struggle, a struggle that he had barely survived. Yet now it seemed so remote to him that it could have happened to someone else. His thoughts were only of Jenny.

He wondered where Jenny was buried, and if anyone had showed up to say a few words over her.

When did it happen? The letter didn't say. He had thought of Jenny many times over the past winter. Was she already dead, even when he was thinking about her?

Preacher felt an overwhelming sense of sorrow at her loss. But as he considered the fact that she was murdered, the sorrow gave way to anger.

Then, anger gave way to resolve. Preacher didn't know who killed Jenny, but he would find out. William Ashley was wrong. There would be justice, all right. It would be Preacher's Justice.

Western Adventures
From Pinnacle